Allan Pinkerton

The Spiritualists and the Detectives

Allan Pinkerton

The Spiritualists and the Detectives

ISBN/EAN: 9783337332570

Printed in Europe, USA, Canada, Australia, Japan

Cover: Foto ©Andreas Hilbeck / pixelio.de

More available books at **www.hansebooks.com**

THE

SPIRITUALISTS

AND

THE DETECTIVES.

BY

ALLAN PINKERTON,

AUTHOR OF

"THE EXPRESSMAN AND THE DETECTIVE," "CLAUDE MELNOTTE AS
A DETECTIVE," "THE SOMNAMBULIST AND THE DETECTIVE,"
"THE MODEL TOWN AND THE DETECTIVES," ETC.

NEW YORK:

G. W. Dillingham, Publisher,

SUCCESSOR TO G. W. CARLETON & CO.

LONDON: S. LOW, SON & CO.

MDCCCLXXXIX.

TROW'S
PRINTING AND BOOKBINDING CO.,
PRINTERS AND STEREOTYPERS,
205-213 East 12th St.,
NEW YORK.

CONTENTS.

CHAPTER XIII.

CHAPTER XIV.

CHAPTER XV.

CHAPTER XVI.

CHAPTER XVII.

CHAPTER XVIII.

CHAPTER XIX.

CHAPTER XX.

CHAPTER XXI.

PREFACE.

I WISH to anticipate any adverse criticism that may be made upon the following pages, by being as frank with the public as I trust the critics will be fair with me.

Therefore I must say at the beginning that I expect many well-meaning people to differ with me as to the propriety of giving this book to the public; but I am exceedingly hopeful that that difference will not amount to a serious condemnation. Nor can I think it will when I earnestly assert that I have caused its publication out of as honest a motive as I ever possessed; and I am sure that whatever the American people have come to think of me in other respects, they are pretty certain of my honesty.

The incidents related are true, though, out of a proper regard for my patrons and many who do not sustain that relation, but who unavoidably become identified in numberless ways with my operations in ferreting out crime and criminals, I have deemed it best to locate the story in a city several hundred miles from the place where the occurrences really transpired, and, for the same reason, have given the characters fictitious names; but the inci dents are exact parallels of the original facts, and in many cases are literal transcripts of, while in every instance they agree with, the records of the case as minutely reported during its progress.

By way of further explanation, I desire to remind my readers how very difficult it is for those not familiar with the detective business to realize the masses of iniquity we are often obliged to unearth, unpalatable as the work may be and is. But while, from the nature of my business, my records are necessarily so exhaustive, and have been made so thoroughly minute, as to contain simply every-thing, good or bad, regarding an operation, and are, therefore, as records, reliable and true—though they thus become repositories of much that is vile—I have striven in every instance, while relating the truth and nothing but the truth, to speak of unpleasant things in as delicate a manner as possible, and in a way which, while plain enough to convey with proper force and directness the moral lessons that these developments cannot fail to im-press upon the minds of all readers, might still leave no unclean thought behind them; and the only sense in which a charge that my " Detective Stories " were in any respect untrue might be sustained, would be in the fact that I have in numberless instances, for the very good reason mentioned, told immeasurably less, and never more, than the whole truth.

I make no assumption of having given in this book an exhaustive *exposé* of modern spiritualism, and I wish it as well remembered that I have no more prejudice against the good there is in that ism than I have against the good there is in any other ism ; but my experience with these people, which has been large, has invariably been against their honesty or social purity.

So far as there being anything about Spiritualism to compel awe or attract any but weak-minded or " weak-moraled " people, the assumption is simply absurd ; for the few illustrations given in the following pages will show how utterly preposterous the claim of supernatural power is, as applied to the *cause* of these " manifestations," which are not, in themselves, first-class tricks, but which, when made mysterious and enshrouded with the element of superstitious fear—which all of us in some measure possess—lead crowds of inconsiderate people into unusual eccentricities, if not eventually into insane asylums, as in some painful instances of which the public are already well aware.

In my exceptionally strange avocation I have been enabled to view this entire matter from the side which the public cannot reach—the side where the fraud of it all is so apparent that it becomes disgustingly monotonous and common ; and as a matter of duty to those who are half inclined to accept Spiritualism as a divine revelation and blessed experience, I have given but a single case—a sample of hundreds of others—which illustrates the despicable character of many, if not a majority, of Spiritualism's public champions and private disciples ; only adding that in this instance the picture does not show a thousandth part of the hideousness of the original.

The Judge Williams mentioned as having presided at Batavia, N. Y., is no myth, but an eminent jurist at present sitting upon the bench of one of the most important courts in the country. He has not only furnished a copy of his scathing remarks to the Winslow-Lyon jury upon their disagreement, as related, but will vouch for the correctness of much of this narrative, as most of the facts mentioned came under his personal observation.

I have given them to the public trusting they will fill some good place in the world, and assist in removing from the minds of those who are occupying the debatable ground regarding the question of the genuineness of Spiritualism and Spiritualistic "manifestations" the superstitious fear and the sensucus fascination which have heretofore bound and held them.

ALLAN PINKERTON.

CHICAGO, January, 1877.

THE SPIRITUALISTS

AND

THE DETECTIVES.

------◆◆◆------

CHAPTER I.

" Kal'm'zoo ! "—The Home of the Nettletons.—Lilly Nettleton.—A
wild Heart and a burning Brain.

MOST commercial and uncommercial travellers filling
the swift shuttles of transit between the East and
the West will remember that while passing through
Michigan, over the Central road, the brakeman has
shrieked the legend " Kal'm'zoo ! " at them as the train
rushed into one of the prettiest little cities in the country.
There is nothing particularly picturesque about Kalamazoo,
unless the wondering face of some harmless lunatic, on
parole from the Asylum which stands so gloomily among
the hills beyond the town, the solemn visage of some
Baptist University student, who with his toast, tea and
Thucydides, has become grave and attenuated, or the
plump form of some "seminary girl" who *will* look at

the incoming trains, and flout her handkerchief too, in spite of parents, principals, and all the proprieties, and the ordinary ebb and flow of the life of a stirring provincial town, may be so considered. Neither is there anything particularly interesting about Kalamazoo, save its native, quiet beauty. It meets life easily, and, like a happily-disposed tradesman, takes its full measure of traffic and enjoyment with undisturbed tranquillity, cultivating neat yards and streets, the social graces, and occasionally the arts, with a lazy sort of satisfaction that is pleasant to look upon and contemplate.

Standing at any street-corner of the city, you will see wide avenues of fine business houses or elegant residences, and, where the latter, a wealth of neatly-trimmed shrub-bery, and long lines of overarching maple trees merging into pretty vistas which seem to invite you beyond to the beautiful hills, uplands and valleys, with their murmuring streams, sloping farms and well-kept homes, where both plenty and contentment seem to be waiting to give you a right hearty welcome.

About twenty-five years ago, when the country was much newer, and the sturdy farmers that have made this great West blossom so magically until it has become the whole world's storehouse, were held closely to their arduous work by the hard hand of necessity and toil, a few miles up the river from the then little village of Kala-mazoo might have been seen a comfortable log farm-house which nestled within a pretty ravine sloping down to the banks of the lazily-flowing stream. It was a plain, homely sort of a place, but there was an air of thrift and cleanliness about the locality that told of earnest toil and its sure reward.

The farm was of that character generally described as "openings;" here a clump of oak, beech, and maple trees, there a rich stretch of meadow-land; beyond, a series of hills extending to the uplands, the bases of which were girted with groves, and whose summits were composed of a warm, rich, stony loam, where the golden seas of ripening grain, touched by passing zephyrs, waved and shimmered in the glowing summer sun ; while where the river wound along towards the villages below, there was a dense growth of elm, maple, and beech trees, standing there dark and sombre, save where the glintings of sunlight pierced their foliaged armor, like grim sentinels of the centuries.

This was the home of Robert Nettleton, a plain and uneducated farmer, who had several years before removed from the East with his family, and with them was slowly accumulating a competence for his declining days.

Robert Nettleton's family consisted of himself, his wife, and their three children. He was looked upon by his neighbors as somewhat erratic and strange, being repelling in his manner, and at times sullen and reticent. He went about his duties in a severe way, and at all times compelled the strictest obedience from each member of his family. On the contrary, his wife was a meek-eyed little woman, patient and long-suffering, and was looked upon in the neighborhood as a nonentity from her unre-

sisting, broken-down demeanor, save in times of sickness
and trouble, when she was immediately in great demand,
as she had little to say, but much to do, and had an effective method of noiseless, tender watching and nursing at
command, which was at all times ungrudgingly employed.

. The children consisted of one boy and two girls, the
eldest of whom, now in her eighteenth year, little dreamed
of the despicable commotion she was to create in after-
life, and was the reigning belle of the community, though
she always kept the country bumpkins at a respectful distance and was feared by fully as many as she was admired,
from her impetuous, imperious ways, that brooked no
opposition or hinderance. One would have to travel a
long distance to find a more attractive figure and face
than those possessed by this country girl. She was somewhat above the medium height, a living model for a
Venus, supple and lithe as the willows that grew upon the
banks of the winding stream, and so physically powerful
that she had already gained some notoriety among her
acquaintances through having soundly shaken the peda-
gogue of the district school, and afterwards pitched him
through the window into an adjacent snow-drift, where he
had remained buried to his middle, his legs wildly waving
signals of distress, until she had just as impulsively released him.

Although somewhat strange and unusual, her features,
while not strikingly beautiful, were still singularly attractive. Her head, which was large and seemingly well provided with faculties of quick perception, was covered with

a wondrous wealth of black hair, so heavy and luxurious as to be almost unmanageable, and which, when not in restraint, fell about her form, hiding it completely, nearly to her feet. Her forehead was full and prominent, while her eyes, large and rather deeply set, and fringed with heavy lashes, were of that peculiar gray color which at times may be touched by all shades, while a trace of blue always predominates. There was nothing worth remarking about other portions of her face, save that, critically examined, too much of it seemed to have got into her chin, and her upper lip had a strange habit of hugging her brilliantly white teeth too closely, and then curling upward before meeting the lower one, where sometimes crimson and ashy paleness played like quick and cruel lightning, a key to the slumbering devils within her. At these times, too, there was a certain light in her eyes that an observing person would feel a peculiar dread of awakening, though usually her face showed a complete repose, and it would have been difficult to decide whether she was a very ordinary or a very extraordinary character.

Still, with her magnificent figure and strangely attractive face, she was a young woman to strongly draw just two classes of men towards her—students of character and students of form. The first she invariably disappointed and repelled, always awakening the indefinable dread I have mentioned, while her presence among the latter class as swiftly opened the floodgates of passion to swiftly sweep the better nature and all good resolves before it. So, with her peculiarly unfortunate construction, it is

not strange that, on arriving at that period of life when
the almost omnipotent power of a self-willed woman begins to develop and hint at the possibilities beyond the
threshold of the strange life her inexperienced. feet had
just reached, Lilly Nettleton should have felt an oppres-
sive sense of littleness in the quiet community in which
she lived, and experienced a burning desire to cast these
humble associations from her, to compel admiration and
conquer whoever and whatever she might me   in the
wide, wide world beyond.

CHAPTER II.

DURING the summer the presiding elder of the Kalamazoo district decided to bid for the benighted souls that dwelt in Mr. Nettleton's neighborhood, and made arrangements to "supply" the school-house at the corners where Lilly had distinguished herself in giving the schoolmaster a cold bath in the snow-bank, with circuit-riders, or with young clergymen who had just graduated and were supposed to be in training for more extended fields of labor.

At that time the system of salvation as carried on by the Methodist Church—which must certainly be credited with a vast amount of push and energy in furthering its peculiar plan of redemption—outside of the large cities was almost exclusively one which necessitated the employment of circuit-riders, as they were then called, and are now called in some portions of the extreme west. They were usually men of great suavity of manner, personal bravery, unbounded zeal, and remarkable religious enthusiasm. They trusted principally in the Lord, but also placed implicit confidence in the extraordinary hospitality of the plain pioneer people with whom they came in contact, who, if not prepared to accept everything told them, responded to their strenuous efforts for their salvation by an unqualified welcome; so that the appearance of the circuit-rider, or "supply," was not only cause for unusual Bible catechism and hymn reading, but also a signal for culinary preparations on a grand scale, to which, as a rule, the hen-roost materially contributed.

Time and time again, in the early days, have I journeyed with these Gospel Knights-errant, listening to their interesting adventures, almost as strange as my own, and their simple tales of blessed experiences; often tarrying with them at their "stations," and for some good purpose, best known to myself, joining in their efforts to sow seed meet unto repentance as we crossed the beautiful streams and broad prairies of Illinois; and as we journeyed along so pleasantly together the thought that my comrade was giving his whole life to the work of saving sin-sick souls, while mine was as irrevocably devoted to bringing many of them to summary justice, has flashed across my mind with such startling force, that the dramatic nature of the life we live was presented to me more powerfully than I have since seen it shown before the footlights of any of the grandest theatres of the world.

As the Nettleton family had belonged to that church in the East, and had also attended service at the village when the roads and weather were favorable, they were, of course, leaders in the plan to secure "meetings nearer home; and when the good brother made his appearance one pleasant autumn Saturday afternoon, as was natural, he directed his faithful Rozinante to the comfortable log-house by the river, where both it and its reverend rider were given a genuine welcome.

The new preacher was none of your soiled, worked-out, toiling itinerants. He was a young clergyman, scarcely thirty years old, and just from college; tall, well-formed, with a florid, smoothy-shaven face, and plenty of hair and hallelujah about him. He could tell you all about the stars, and just as easily point out the merits or demerits in your plate of mutton or porter-house; and, being of this tropical nature, if there were two things above any other two things in life for which he had a penchant, they were a spirited nag and a spirited woman. In fact, he had accepted the ministry just the same as he would have accepted any other profession, merely as a makeshift, and had submitted to being ground through the theological mill, and afterwards to this backwoods breaking-in process, simply because his widowed mother, a Detroit lady, was immensely pious and also immensely wealthy; and if he should become a noted minister, he would get all her property, which otherwise would go to the good cause direct, but which, once in his hands, would enable him to gratify his elegant tastes and do as he pleased generally.

So, being a thorough judge of women, he was at once more interested in Lilly Nettleton than in the welfare of the souls of the Nettleton neighborhood; and after a bountiful supper had been disposed of, and the family were gathered upon the verandah for a pleasant chat with the minister in the long, hazy September sunset, and the Rev. Mr. Bland—for that was the young clergyman's name—had flattered Mr. Nettleton on the merits of his pretty farm, Mrs. Nettleton upon her elegant cooking, and the younger children upon their various degrees of perfection, he passed directly to the subject which most occupied his mind, and in a patronizing way, evidently with a view of attracting Lilly's attention without arousing the suspicions of her honest parents, said :

"By the way, Mr. Nettleton, your beautiful daughter here—ah, what may I call her ? thank you, Lilly ; and a very appropriate name, too—is the perfect image of a very dear friend of ours—my mother's and my own—in Detroit."

There was certainly a flush on Lilly's face deeper than could have been put there by the red glow of the setting sun. Mr. Bland did not fail to notice it either ; and as there was no response to his remark, he continued, occasionally glancing at Lilly, who, though apparently only interested in her needle-work, drank in every word that fell from the reverend gentleman's lips.

"In fact," said the minister, "the resemblance is quite striking, though I really think your daughter Lilly is the finer-looking of the two—indeed, has quite an intellectual face, and would, I am sure, make a thorough student."

"But she won't go to school here," interrupted Mr Nettleton ; while the strange light came into Lilly's eyes and the crimson and ashy paleness played upon the curled lips.

"But, Brother Nettleton, you must remember that we are not all similarly created. The world must have its hewers of wood and drawers of water, but it must also have its grand minds to direct——"

"I can do all the directin' necessary here," bluntly persisted Mr. Nettleton.

"Of course, of course," pleasantly continued Mr. Bland, talking *at* Lilly, though answering her father; "but I hope Lilly can some time have those advantages which would certainly cause her to shine in society——"

"And despise her home!" said Mr. Nettleton, bitterly.

The storm was still playing fiercely over Lilly's face, and her heaving bosom told how hard a struggle was necessary to restrain her from then and there saying or doing some reckless thing, and then rushing away into the woods and the night to escape the restraint that set so heavily upon her imperious spirit.

"No, I think not," replied Mr. Bland soothingly. "I am a pretty good judge of human nature, though a young man, and am sure that Lilly has a kind heart and will prove a blessing to your later years. Our dear Detroit friend was also a little spirited, but she is now one of the leaders of Sunday-school and church society, and is much sought after—yes, much sought after," repeated Mr. Bland slowly, as he saw its effect upon Lilly.

The clergyman's good opinion of their daughter made the simple parents really happy; but she knew as well as he what it was all said for, and she alread} hated **the** flippant Mr. Bland, for her quick woman's instinct—they never reason—had analyzed him thoroughly.   But her heart throbbed at the idea of being considered "fine-look ing," and her brain burned with the desire to also become "sought after.'   Y2s, young and inexperienced as she was, she was old in the crime of impure thought and unbridled ambition, and was ready to lend herself to any scheme, however questionable, that might offer release, or g·ve promise of the gratification of her passion for notoriJty, and ruling or ruining anything with which she came in contact.

After this the evening passed pleasantly to the old people, who, after a time, went into the house to attend to their several duties ; and also to the young people, Mr. Bland and Lilly, who, without any effort on the part of either, had arrived at a thorough understanding—so much so, indeed, that when the voice of Mr. Nettleton was heard apprising Mr. Bland that he would show him to his room whenever he desired to retire, he quietly stepped near tc where Lilly was sitting in the weird moonlight, and taking her pretty, warm hand within his own, said rapidly, but in a low voice :

"My dear Lilly, I have a deep interest in you ; your people cannot understand it, and, should they know it, would only suspect me, and watch and restrain you. *Make* an opportunity for us to be together alone.   I wiiJ remain until you accomplish it ; and—" Mr. Nettleton's step was now heard in the hall—"quick, Lilly ! do we understand each other ? "

She gave him a look that would have withered any but a lecherous villain as he was; but he met it in kind, as she whispered "Yes!" and added, disengaging herself as Bland stealthily stepped back and carelessly leaned against the door:

"What book did you say?"

"Ah, yes—'hem! 'Young's Night Thoughts.' It is a pure book, and would not only cultivate your mind, but aid you in the common duties of life. I will send it to you, and you can read it aloud to your parents. I know they will enjoy it too! Ha! Mr. Nettleton, excuse me Lilly, of course you will join us at prayers?"

She had been taught her first lesson, was an apt scholar, too; and as the man of God on his bended knees prayed that all blessings might descend upon this happy home, however much his cursed soul might have been stung by the devilish hypocrisy of the hour, there was not a pang of remorse in her heart for the bold step she knew she had taken.

Lilly did not attend service at the school-house on Sabbath, and made her appearance but once or twice during the day, feigning illness; but on Monday she was about the house fresh and rosy as ever, and the first opportunity that offered suggested to Bland the propriety of asking her out for a boat-ride on the river, which he did in the afternoon during Mr. Nettleton's absence, his meek wife thinking it a great honor to the family, and in her poor mother's heart, no doubt, praying that the good man might so soften her proud daughter's heart that she

2

might be bettered, and eventually led to the source of all good.

Whether he did or not, if the reader of this book could have followed the couple up the winding river to a secluded spot where the golden maple-leaves fell upon the stream and were borne away in silence, whatever of mad passion or reckless guilt might have been discovered, just before they stepped into the boat to float with the tide back to the dishonored home, a certain Rev. Mr. Bland might have been seen placing in Lilly Nettleton's shameless hand a roll of bills, and heard to say to the same person :

" Be sure, now—next Sunday night. Row down to Kalamazoo in this boat, and take the late night train for Detroit. Go to the Michigan Exchange Hotel, where I will meet you Monday evening !"

So the little neighborhood had had its "religious supply," but had also had its loss ; for, as the weird moonlight of the next Sunday evening fell upon the quiet log farmhouse, built strange forms among the moaning, almost leafless trees, and pictured upon the river's bosom a thousand ghostly figures, the scared form of a young woman stole away from her home, glided to the murmuring stream, sprang into the little boat, and was borne away to the hell of her future just as noiselessly but just as resistlessly as the river itself pushed onward to the great lakes, and was swept from thence to the ultimate, all-absorbing sea !

CHAPTER III.

TO the imagination of the wayward country girl Detroit was a great city, and as she was whirled into
the depot, where she saw the rushing river beyond, and
was hustled hither and thither by the clamorous cabmen,
a sense of giddiness came upon her, and for the first, and
undoubtedly last time, she yearned for the quiet of the old
log farm-house by the pleasant river.

Perhaps the old forms and faces called to her imploringly, pleading with her, as only the simple things of
home, however plain and commonplace, can plead with
the wandering one ; and in a swift, agonized longing for
the restfulness which the meanest virtue gives, but which
had forever fled from her, the thought, if not the words :

> " Of all sad words of tongue or pen
> The saddest are these : It might have been "—

sped through her mind in a pitiful way ; but just as she
had almost resolved to return to her parents, ask their for-
giveness, and disclose the character of the reverend vil-

lain, a man approached her, who, saying he was "from Bland," conducted her to a carriage in waiting and conveyed her to the Michigan Exchange Hotel, where she was fictitiously registered, and the clerk informed that her brother would call for her in the evening.

She had been assigned a very pretty room, elegantly furnished, and the windows gave her a view of the river and the shipping, with Windsor and the bluff hills of Canada beyond.   It was all beautiful and wonderful to her— the hotel a palace, the river, with its great steamers, vessels, and ferries—a fairy scene ; and Windsor, with the broken country beyond, all covered by the soft, blue, gossamer veil of early autumn—a beautiful dream !

With her thoroughly unprincipled nature there was a lazy sort of enjoyment in all this ; and when her dinner was brought to her room, as had been previously ordered by the hackman, and she was gingerly served by an ordinarily nimble waiter, but who took every possible occasion to illustrate the fact that he was cultivated and she was not, she received the attention in as dignified a manner as though born to rule, and had been accustomed to the service of menials from infancy.

The afternoon wore away, and as the gas-lights began to flare out upon the city, a gentle tap was heard at her door, and a moment after, before an invitation to enter had been given, the oily Bland slid into Lilly's apartment, closed the door after him, and turned the key in the lock. Then he walked right over to where Lilly was sitting upon the sofa, and took her in his arms, saying :

"Bland, am I to go to your mothers' as you promised?"—

" Well, I see my dearest Lilly has kept her word."

She allowed him to fondle her just long enough to dare to repel him gently, and answered :

" After what passed by the river, I could not do other wise than keep my word. Yes, your ' dearest Lilly' has kept her word. And what now, Mr. Bland ? "

Seeing that she was disposed to ask leading questions, he changed the subject laughingly.

" Why, some supper, of course," and immediately rang the bell, ordering of the servant, who appeared directly, a sumptuous spread, not forgetting a bottle of wine.

During the preparation of the meal Lilly stepped to the window, and pressing her restless face against the panes, seemed intently regarding the dancing lights upon the broad river, while Bland whistled softly, and warmed his delicate, pliable hands at the coals in the fireplace, which gave to the chilly evening a pleasant, cheery glow. Suddenly she stepped close to him, leaned her head in her left hand, her elbow resting upon the marble mantel, while with her right hand she firmly grasped his shoulder. She then said, in a quiet, determined way :

" Bland, am I to go to your mother's, as you promised ? "

She said this in such a resolute, icy way, and her hand rested upon his shoulder so heavily, that, for the first time, he looked at her as if satisfied that he had a beautiful tigress in keeping, and it might possibly require supreme will force to control her.

‘ No, Lilly, you will not go to my mother's.

“ Then I will go home.”

“ You will not go home.   You will remain here.”

“ Bland, no person on God's earth shall say ‘ will ’ to me.   That is just as certain as the course of that river ! ” and her long, trembling forefinger swept towards the rush-ing stream.

The appearance of the waiter with supper quieted the conversation, which was becoming stormy, and it was only resumed when Bland saw that Lilly was mellowing under the influence of the wine, which thrilled through her veins, pushing the rich, healthy blood to her cheeks, and lighting her great gray eyes with a wonderful lustre.   It could not be said that he loved the girl, but he had a mad passion for her which was simply overwhelming at these times when, untutored and uncultivated as she was, she became truly queenly in appearance.

It was a dainty little supper served upon a dainty little table, and they were sitting very closely together, and Bland, after feasting his eyes upon her magnificent form for a time, drew her into his arms impulsively, kissing her again and again, calling her endearing names, and prom-ising her everything that could come to the tongue of a talented man made wild by wine and a woman.

“ Lilly, you have crazed me—ruined me ! ” he said, ex-citedly.   “ You know what I profess to be—a Christian minister !   God forgive me for my cursed weakness, but you have me in your power ! ”

Although her face rested against his, and their hot

cheeks burned together, the old wicked light gleamed in her eyes, and the crimson and ashy paleness played upon the curled lip. If it all could have been seen by the reverend gentleman, it would have sobered him. The words ' in your power " had flung the lightning into Lilly Nettleton's face. Power, power, power ! No matter how secured; no matter what the result. The very word maddened her, made a scheming devil of her, but also made her ready for any proposition Bland might offer, as it swiftly came into her mind that the deeper she sank with him the greater would be her power over him.

"Well ?" she said, reassuringly.

"'Well ?'—I am at your mercy. A knowledge of what has passed between us would be my ruin; your ruin also. We have done what cannot be undone; yes," he continued passionately, and drawing her closer to him, "what I would not undo ! "

"Well?" It was tenderly said, and gave him courage.

"I am rich, or will be, Lilly."

"If you are careful," she added with a light laugh.

"Exactly. I can do a great deal for you, and will——"

"Conditionally ?"

"Yes, conditionally. The conditions are that you live quietly at an elegant place to which we will shortly be driven. You will be mistress of the place; that is, you will have everything you can desire——"

"Save respectability, Mr. Bland ?"

She was shrewder than he—in fact, his master already;

but hinted at the sale of her soul so heartlessly that it shocked even him.

"You had 'respectability' at home, Lily; and," glanc-ing at her plain garments, which were a burlesque upon her beautiful figure, "and old clothes, and surveillance, and restraint, and——"

"Bland," she said, springing to her feet with such vio-lence as to send him sprawling to the floor, from which he stared in amazement at her magnificent form, which trem-bled like a leaf, while the wicked lightning gleamed from her eyes, and swift shuttles of color flashed back and forth upon her lips; "Bland, be careful! Never speak to me again of the meanness of my home. The mean-ness of your black heart is a million times greater. You have something more than a country girl to deal with, sir; you have a woman and a woman's will. It is enough that I have sold my body and soul for what you can, or might, give me. I bargained for no contempt; and, Bland," she continued, advancing towards him fiercely as he regained his feet and retreated from her in dismay, "as sure as there is a heaven, and as sure as there ought to be a hell for such as we, if you begin it, I will kill you! Yes," she hissed, "I will kill you!" and then, woman-like, having passed the climax of feeling and expression, she threw herself on the bed for a good cry, while Bland, with wine and words and countless caresses, soothed her wild spirit, bringing her back to pliant good nature, where she was as putty in his dexterous hands.

CHAPTER IV.

SHORTLY afterwards a closed cabriolet containing
two persons was rapidly driven from the Michigan
Exchange up Wisconsin street, from thence into Griswold, and out towards the suburbs, finally drawing up before a neat cottage-house, where the lights, peeping around
the edges of the drawn curtains, showed the place to be
in a state of preparation.

A man and a woman quickly alighted from the carriage,
and as the woman, apparently a young one, though
closely veiled, stepped to the gate, opened it and waited
for her escort, the gentleman said in a low tone to the
coachman :

"James, drive to the house and inform mother that
while down town this evening I received an unexpected
call to Ann Arbor, to preach a funeral sermon over the
remains of an old student-friend at the University, and
that I may not be home until late to-morrow evening ;"

2*

then, after handing James some coin, "you understand, James?"

James thought he understood, grinned grimly, put the money in his pocket and drove away.

"Remember, Lilly," said Bland, stepping to the gate and taking her arm, "you are Lilly Mercer here."

"Yes, Bland."

"And you are never to mention anything regarding yourself to the lady who owns this place."

"I think I can keep my own counsel."

"And, if any inquiries are made here, by any person whatever, regarding myself, you are to be innocently and utterly ignorant."

"And what are you to do?" asked Lilly, naïvely.

"I?—why I am to do well by you."

"Just so long as you do that, Bland, you are perfectly safe!"

She had taken to dictating also; but it was a pretty little cottage and grounds, and a feeling of satisfaction at being their mistress, even if it necessitated being his mis-tress, came over her that made her affable and winning, if she did occasionally say things that hinted at a stormy future.

They strolled up the broad brick walk, he thrilled with his magnificent capture, and she just as satisfied with the power she had attained over one so high socially, and who stood in such near prospect of obtaining vast wealth. Instead of entering the house at its little front door with its highly ornamented porch, they opened the door of a little trellis-worked addition to the cottage, which was now covered by an almost leafless mass of vines, and passed to a side entrance, where a gentle pull of the bell caused the immediate appearance of a very fat and very flabby woman of middle age, who at once conducted them to a suite of rooms, consisting of a parlor and a large sleeping-room, between which, in place of the original folding-doors, had been substituted rich hangings suffi- ciently drawn apart to admit of the passage of one per- son, and which, with the tastefully draped windows, the deeply-framed pictures, the vari-colored marble mantels and fireplaces, the heavy, yielding carpet giving back no sound to the foot-fall, and the great easy-chairs into which one sank as into pillows of down, gave the rooms the hintings of such luxuriousness that Lilly was completely dazzled and bewildered with the unexpected elegance, and the, to her, never before realized splendor.

"Mother Blake," said Bland, " this is Lilly Mercer, who is my friend, and whom you are to make comfortable."

Mother Blake, as if realizing that her duties began whenever Bland spoke, majestically crossed the room, sat down beside Lilly and immediately kissed her very affectionately, merely remarking, " And a very nice girl she is, too, Mr. Bland."

"That'll do, mother. You may get us a sma'l bottle of wine, and then go to bed. It's getting late, and you know you need a good deal of sleep."

Mother Blake chuckled, and shook from it as though her enjoyment of any sort of pleasantry came to the surface only in a series of ripples over her great fat body, instead of in echoes of enjoyment from her great fat throat. But it might have been merely a habit with its origin in the necessities of her quiet mode of life ; and, doing as requested, only lingered to fasten back the curtain so that the low, luxurious bed came temptingly into view, after which she beamingly backed out of the room, wishing the couple " a pleasant night, and many of 'em ! "

If shame hovered over this pretty place, it did not pale the amber glow of the sparkling wine ; it came not into the ruddy coals upon the hearth, which gave forth their glowing warmth just as cheerily as from any other hearth in the broad land ; it never dimmed the light from the gilded chandeliers ; it put no crimson flush upon the faces which touched each other with an even flow of blood, nor quickened the pulses of the hands that as often met ; and God only knows whether, when, as sleep came down upon the city, and the man and woman rested in each other's arms upon the bed beyond the rich curtains (which, as the light in the fireplaces grew or waned, never contained one ghostly rustle or semblance), there was even a guilty dream to mark its presence !

But what of the inmates of the old log farm-house by the pleasant river ?

The morning came, and the agonized parents found that their daughter had gone. Robert Nettleton set his teeth and swore that he would never search for her, while his poor wife was completely broken and crushed, as much from the agonized fears that flooded into her heart as from the actual loss of her child.

The most dejected member of the household, however, was a new-comer, one Dick Hosford, who years before had drifted into the Nettleton family and had been brought up by them until, becoming a stout young man, he was borne away in the gold excitement with the "Forty-niners" to California, where by hard work and no luck whatever, being an honest, simple soul, he had got together a few thousand dollars ; with no announcement of his proposed return, had come back as far as Terre Haute, Indiana, where he had purchased a snug farm, and immediately turned his footsteps towards Mr. Nettleton's, arriving there the very morning after Lilly's departure, as he said, "to marry the gal, but couldn't find her shadder."

He was simply inconsolable, and it took off the keen edge of the parents' grief somewhat to find that another shared it with them, and even seemed to feel that it was all his own.

So it was arranged that the inquisitive neighbors should only know that Lilly had "gone to town for a week or two," while Dick Hosford should go to Chicago, and then back east as far as Detroit, making diligent search for something even more tangible than the "shadder" of the lost girl ; and as he said good-by to the Nettletons with quivering lips and suspiciously dimmed eyes, he added :

"Bob Nettleton, and mother—for you've always been a half-dozen mothers to me—don't ye never expect to see me back to these yer diggin's 'thout I bring the gal. I've sot my heart onto her'; and " with an oath that the Re-cording Angel as surely blotted out as Uncle Toby's, for it was only the clinching of a brave determination, "I'll have her if I find her in a——" He stopped suddenly as he saw the pain in their faces, shook their hands in a way that told them more than his simple words ever could have expressed, and trudged away with as little certainty of finding whom he sought, save by accident— or, if found, of securing the prize for himself, unless through her whim—as of ever himself becoming anything save the honest, faithful, gullible soul that he was.

At Detroit, Mother Blake had orders to provide Lily Mercer, her latest charge, with a suitable wardrobe and some fine pieces of jewelry, which was accordingly done; and in the novelty of her transformation, which really made her a beautiful young woman, her ardor of fondness for Bland was certainly sufficient to gratify both his vanity and passion to the fullest extent. But, to some women, both passion and finery must be frequently renewed in order to insure constancy; and while Bland was as hope-lessly in her toils as ever, as she had always despised him and now despised his offerings, which were neither so numerous or costly as at first, she became almost un-managable, caused Mother Blake great perturbation of spirit, and led Bland a deservedly stormy life.

CHAPTER V.

A FEW weeks later, one November evening, the first
snow-storm of the year came hurrying and skurry-
ing down upon the city. The streets seemed filled with
that thrilling, electric life which comes with the first snow-
flakes, and as they tapped their ghostly knuckles against
the panes of Lilly Mercer's boudoir, the weird *staccato*
passed into her restless spirit and filled her mind with
wild, reckless fancies. The storm had beaten up against
the cottage but a little time until it brought Bland with it.

He came to tell his Lilly, he said, that the cursed church
interests would compel him to go to the West, to be absent
for several weeks. In mentioning the fact he sat down
by the fireplace and gave her some money for use while
he was away, and also counted over quite an amount
which he had provided for his travelling expenses.

He also told her that he should leave the next evening,

and would, after a little time, of course, return for the night, as he could never go on so long a journey without spending the parting hours with his little bird, as he had come to call her.

His little bird had sat remarkably passive during all this, but now fluttered about him with cooings and regrets innumerable, and seemed to still be in a flutter of excitement when he had gone; for, after walking up and down the rooms for a time, she flung some wrappings about her, and quickly glided out among the pelting flakes that hid her among the hurrying thousands upon the streets and within the shops, until she as rapidly returned.

Within the warm nest again, there was a note to be written, and several feathery but valuable trifles to be got together. In fact, Bland's little bird was a busy bird, until when, at a late hour, he came back to its unusually tender ways and wooings, and was soon slumbering beside it.

Then the little bird became a great raven of the night, and stole quietly about the apartments, gathering together, quite like any other raven, everything that pleased its fancy, including even the money that was to have been used in the "cursed church interests," and the gold watch that ticked away at its sleeping owner's head, but not loud enough to awaken him, for he slept with a peculiar heaviness, and, strangely enough, with a folded handkerchief across his face. But the raven of the cottage, in a quiet way that ravens have, never ceased gathering what pleased it, until the early hours of morning, when, kissing its beak to the bed and the sleeper, and flinging upon the bed a little note which read :

A double exposé if you like.

Lilly "Mercer."—

took itself and its gathered treasures out into the storm and the night.

The storm was gone when the chloroformed man awoke, and the bright sun pushed through the shutters upon his feverish face. Slowly and with great effort he groped his way back to consciousness, and with a thrill of fear reached out his hand for his little bird, and to reassure himself that what was flooding furiously into his mind was untrue, and was but some horrible nightmare that her dear touch would drive away. But the place where she had lain was as cold and empty as her own heartless heart; and as he faintly called, "Lilly! oh, Lilly!" the very realistic voice of Mother Blake was heard in the hall, and her very realistic fists banging away against the door.

"Say, Bland! are ye all dead in there? Lord! it's broad noon!"

All dead? No; but far better so, as the Rev. Mr. Bland with a mighty effort sprang from the bed and saw the gas-light struggling with the sunlight, the dead ashes in the fireplace, and himself in the great mirror, a dishonored, despoiled, deserted roué, drugged, robbed and defied by the simple maiden from the log farm-house by the pleasant river.

'The same evening two persons on wonderfully different missions drifted into the depot and transfer-house at Detroit, and mingled with the great throng that the east and the west continually throw together at this point. One was a handsome, apparently self-possessed young lady, who attended to her baggage personally, and moved about among the crowds with apparent unconcern; though, closely watched, her face would have shown anxiety and restlessness. The other was a gaunt, though solidly built young fellow, whose clothes, although of good material, had the appearance of having been thrown at him and caught with considerable uncertainty upon his bony angles. He wandered about in a dejected way, looking hither and thither as if forever searching for some one whose discovery had become improbable, but who should not escape if an honest search by an honest, simple fellow as he seemed to be, could avail anything. By one of those unexplainable coincidences, or fatuities, as some are pleased to term them, these two persons—the one desirous of avoiding a crowd, and the other anxious to ascertain whom every throng contained—approached the ticket-office from different directions at the same moment.

He at the gent's window heard her at the ladies' window say to the agent, "Yes, to Buffalo, if you please;" and he jumped as though he had been lifted by an explosion. He peered through the window and saw her face at the other window, and without waiting to step around to her, yelled to the agent like a madman: "Say, you,

"Say, you?—mister?—dont give the gal that ticket! It's all a mistake!"—

mister !—don't give the gal that ticket. It's a mistake She's going 'tother way ;" and shoving his gaunt head and shoulders into the window and wildly gesticulating to the young lady, as the agent in a scared way saw the muscular intruder hovering over his tickets and money-box, he continued excitedly :

"Say, Lil, old gal ! Lil Nettleton !—Dick—Dick Hosford, ye know ! Ain't I tellin' the truth ? ain't it all a mistake, and ain't you goin' the other way—with *me*, ye know—yes, 'long with Dick ?"

Lilly Nettleton, for it was no other, nodded to the agent—who returned the money—and quickly stepped around to help Dick disengage himself from the window, and then quickly drew him away from the crowd which the little episode had collected, sat down beside him, and, heartily laughing at his ludicrous appearance, said, "Why, Dick, where under heaven did *you* come from ? "

"Lil, gal," said poor Dick, wiping the tears of joy out of his eyes, "I come all the way from Californy fur ye, found ye gone and the old folks all bust and banged up about it. Fur six weary weeks I've been huntin', huntin' ye up and down, here and yon, and was goin' back to Terre Haute, sell the d——d farm I bought fur ye, and skip back to the Slope to kill Injuns, or some-thin', to drown my sorrow, fur I told the old folks I'd bring ye back, or never set foot in them diggin's agin' ! "

Lilly looked at the great-hearted man beside her in a strange, calculating kind of a way, never touched by his tenderness and simple sacrifice, but moving very closely to him in a winsome way that quite overcame him.

"And I come to marry ye, Lil," persisted Dick, anxiously.

"To marry me, Dick?"

"Yes, and bought ye a purty farm at Terre Haute."

"A farm, Dick?"

"Yes, Lil, a farm, with as snug a little house as ye ever sot eyes on."

"But where did you get so much money? You never wrote anything about it."

"No, I wanted to kinder surprise ye; but I got it honest—got it honest; with these two hands, Lil, that'll work for ye all yer life like a nigger, if ye'll only come long with me and never go gallavantin' any more."

"And won't you ask me any questions or allow them —at home, Dick—to ask any, and take me just as I am?"

"Just as ye are; fur better, or fur wus, Lil."

"And marry me here, now, before we go home?"

"Marry ye, Lil? I'd marry ye if I'd a found ye in a ——; I won't give it a name, Lil. I didn't to them, and I won't to you."

She gave him her hand as firmly and frankly as though she had been a pure woman, and said, "I'm yours, Dick. We'll be married here, to-morrow."

She took charge of all the arrangements; called a cab which took them to the Michigan Exchange; sent Dick off to his room with orders to secure a license the first thing in the morning; wrote two notes to a certain person, one addressed to Mother Blake, and the other to *his* post-office box, ordering them posted that night; and went to her room to sleep the sleep of the just, which, contrary to general belief, also often comes to the unjust.

Early in the morning, Dick came with the license and suggested securing the services of a preacher; but Lily said that she had arranged that matter already, and had got a clergyman who, she was sure, would not disappoint them; and promptly at two o'clock in the afternoon courteously admitted the Rev. Mr. Bland, whom she had given the choice of officiating or an exposure, and who performed the ceremony in a pale, trembling way as the wicked old light gleamed in her great, gray eyes, and the swift shuttles of color played over her curled lip.

That night found the newly-wedded couple whirling back to Kalamazoo, where they arrived the next morning and were driven out to the farm-house, where they were joyfully welcomed, and where Dick Hosford in his blunt way announced that he had " found Lil workin' away like a good girl, had married her and took a little bridal ' tower,' and had come back to have no d——d questions asked."

So in a few days the young couple bade the Nettletons good-by and were soon after installed in the pleasant farm-house near Terre Haute, where the years passed on happily enough and brought them competence **and con** tentment and three children, who for a long time never knew the meaning of the strange light in the eyes, or the swift colors on the lips, of the mother who cared for them with an apparent full measure of kindness and affection.

CHAPTER VI.

ONE hot July afternoon in 186–, I was sitting in my
private office at my New York Agency, located
then, and now, at the corner of New Street and Exchange
Place, in the very heart of the money and stock battles
of Gotham, pretty well tired out from a busy day's work
in carrying to completion some of the vast transactions
that had accumulated during the war, and which were in
turn waiting for my professional services to unravel.

It had been a terribly hot day, and the city seemed like
a vast caldron filled with a million boiling victims; and
now that the day's labor was nearly over, I was principally employed in an attempt to keep cool, but finding
it impossible with everybody about me, settled myself in
my easy-chair at the window to watch the Babel of
brokers below.

From such an altitude, where one can look down
soberly upon these madmen and see their wild antics,
when for the moment they are absolutely insane in their
thirst for gold, never halting at the most extreme reck

lessness even though they know it may compel wholesale ruin, it is easy to realize how isolated cases occur
where the whole human nature yields to greed, and
sweeps on to the certain accomplishment of crime for its
satisfaction.

Just after a particularly heavy "rush" had been made,
resulting in a few broken limbs and numberless tattered
hats and demolished garments, and the bulls and bears
were gathered about in knots excitedly talking over their
profit and loss, and wiping the great beads of perspiration,
from their lobster-like faces, I noticed an important-
looking gentleman turn into New Street from the direction of Broadway, and after edging through the crowds,
occasionally halting to ask a question in the politest possible manner—the replies and gestures to which seemed
to indicate that he was seeking my agency, which afterwards proved true—this vision of precision and politeness
passed from my sight into Exchange Place, and in a few
moments after I was informed that a gentleman desired
to see me on very important business.

After ascertaining who the gentleman was, and already
knowing him to be a harmless sort of an adventurer, and
under the particular patronage of a wealthy Rochester
gentleman, I admitted him and he was introduced as Mr.
Harcout, of Rochester and New York.

Mr. Harcout was a character in his way, and deserving
of some notice. He was a tall, heavily-built, obese gentleman of about forty-five years of age, impressive, important, and supremely polite. His face was a strange com-

bination of imbecility and assumption; while his head, which was particularly developed in the back part, indicating low instincts that were evidently only repressed as occasion required, was consistent with the formation of his square, flat forehead, which sloped back at a suspiciously sharp angle from a pair of little, gray, expressionless eyes, which from the lack of intelligence behind them would look you out of face without blinking. His nose was straight and solidly set below, like some sharp instrument, to assist him in getting on in the world. His lips, though not unusually gross or sensual, had a way of opening and closing, during the pauses of conversation with a persistency of assertion that had the effect of keeping in the mind of the average listener that great weight should be attached to what Mr. Harcout had said, or was about to say; and at the same time, as also when he patronizingly smiled, which was almost constantly, disclosed a set of teeth of singular regularity and dazzling whiteness. A pair of very large ears, closely-cut and neatly-trimmed hair, and a whitish-olive complexion that suggested sluggish blood and a lack of fine organization, complete the sketch of his face, but could never give the full effect of the grandeur of his assumption and manners, which were a huge burlesque on chivalric courtliness. As he entered the room his gloved hand swept to the rim of his faultless silk hat, and removed it with an indescribably graceful gesture that actually seemed to make the hat say, "Ah! my very dear sir, while I belong to a gentleman of the vastest importance imaginable, be as

3

sured that we are both inexpressibly honored by this interview!" Nor were these all of his strikingly good points. He was a man that was always dressed in a suit of the finest procurable cloth, most artistically fitted to his commanding figure, and never a day passed when there was not an exquisite favor in the neat button-hole of his collar. When he had become seated in a most dignified and engaging manner, he had a neat habit of showing his little foot encased in patent leather so shining that, at a pinch, it might have answered for a mirror, by carelessly throwing his right leg over his left knee, so that he could keep up an incessant tapping upon his boot with the disengaged glove which his left hand contained ; and, with his head thrown slightly back and to one side, emphasized his remarks in a graceful and convincing way with the digit finger of his soft white right hand. Altogether he would have passed for a person of considerable importance and good commercial and social standing ; but to one versed in character-reading he gave the impression that he might at one time have been an easygoing clergyman, who had lapsed into some successful insurance or real estate agency that had been unexpectedly profitable ; or, at least, was a man who had thoroughly and artistically acquired the science of securing an elegant livelihood through the confidence he could readily inspire in others.

"Ah ! Mr. Pinkerton, I am very glad to see you—very glad to see you ; in fact, I take it as a peculiar honor, though my business with you is of an unpleasant nature,' said Mr. Harcout, settling into his chair with a kind of bland and amiable dignity.

I saw that he was making a great effort to please me, and told him pleasantly that it was quite natural for people to visit me on unpleasant business.

"Thank you, thank you," he replied in his rich, after-dinner voice, that seemed to come with his winning smile to his lips through a vast measure of good-fellowship and great-heartedness. "I feel that I am occupying a peculiar position, both painful and embarrassing to me : first, as the friend and agent of a wealthy man who is also an acquaintance of yours, and operates on the Produce Exchange, here ; and second, in being obliged to ascertain whether you will take our case without your becoming too fully aware of the particulars, in the event of your refusal."

"Well," said I encouragingly, highly enjoying his embarrassment and assumed importance, "if you will give me a general outline of the matter, I will take it into consideration ; and, in any event, you can rest assured that our walls have no ears to what our patrons have to say within them."

"Well, then," replied Harcout with a winning smile, "to be honest with you, Mr. Pinkerton, there's a woman in our case ; yes—though I'm very sorry to say it—the case is almost entirely a woman case."

' In that event, Mr. Harcout, I must plainly say to you that I don't like those cases at all. I have all the business that I can attend to, and even more than I

sometimes desire ; and I really think you had better se
cure the services of some other person."

"Pray don't say so ; pray don't say so, Mr. Pinkertoi.
Ah ! what *could* induce you to take the case ? "

" No sum of money," I replied, "unless I was fully assured that it was all right—that is, had the right on your
side. Almost without exception these cases with women
in them, where men become jealous of their mistresses,
mistresses of their men, wives of their husbands, husbands
of their wives, or when the lively and vigorous mother-in-
law lends spice to life, and, indeed, all those troubles
arising from social abuses, are a disgrace to every one con·
nected with them."

Harcout seemed quite disappointed that I did not ex·
press more avidity to transact the business he proffered,
but continued in his blandest manner :

" Still, supposing, although we were not altogether in
the right, we were endeavoring to defend ourselves
against a vile woman who had manipulated circumstances
so that she had us greatly in her power ? "

" I should still feel a great reluctance in taking the
case. All my life I have had one steady aim before me,
and that has been to purify and ennoble the detective
service ; and I am sure that all this sort of business is
degrading in the extreme to operatives engaged upon it."

"Very good, very good. But, Mr. Pinkerton, supposing the person pursued was worth two or three millions
of dollars ; that after the parties had met in a casual way,
and, through a strange and unexplainable feeling of ad-

miration mingled with awe which she had compelled in
him, she had acquired a familiarity with his habits, business, and vast wealth, and had from that time schemingly
begun a plan of operations to entrap him into marrying
her. working upon his rather susceptible temperament
through his peculiar religious belief, in order to gain
power over him, and then, failing to secure him as a husband, had for some time pursued a system of threats and
quiet, persistent robbery, constantly becoming more
brazen and impudent, until he could bear it no longer,
when he had refused to see her or submit to further
blackmail, whereupon she had heartlessly attempted his
social and financial ruin, by bringing a suit against him for
$100,000 damages for breach of promise of marriage?"

This extended conundrum flushed Harcout, and his
magnificent silk handkerchief came gracefully into use to
very gently and delicately absorb the perspiration that
had started upon his porous face.

"Mr. Harcout," I still insisted, "I should then require
to be unqualifiedly assured that the woman in question
was not a young woman who had really been led to be
lieve the promise of some man old enough to be her
father, and who should accept the consequences of his in-
discretion philosophically."

"Exactly, exactly," responded Harcout, quite uneasily, though with an evident endeavor at pleasantry; and
quite noble of you, too, Mr. Pinkerton! Really, I had
not anticipated finding such delicate honor among de
tectives!" and he laughed a low, musical laugh

which seemed to come gurgling up from his capacious middle.

I told him he might term it "delicate honor" or whatever he liked; that I had made thorough justice a strict business principle, and found that it won, too; but that, with the understanding that he had fairly represented the case, I would give it my consideration and apprise him of my decision the next day, giving him an appointment for that purpose; after which, while verbosely expressing the hope that I would assist him, he bowed himself out in a very impressive manner, passed into the street, which was now nearly as quiet as the Trinity Church-yard close by, and immediately went to the St. Nicholas, where he flourishingly reported the interview to the anxious millionaire, who thanked fortune for such a powerful and majestic friend.

CHAPTER VII.

IN the meantime I had a conversation on the subject with my General Superintendent, Mr. Bangs, in which we weighed the case thoroughly in all its bearings. I held, as I always do in such cases, if further investigation proved that the woman was one whose youth, or even inexperience, was such as to make it probable that she had been met by a man whose position had dazzled and bewildered her, and who, from his wealth and opportunities for exerting the immense influence of wealth, had led her to believe that he loved her, and had had such attention lavished upon her as had awakened in her heart an affection for him which should deserve some consideration, and that finally, after accomplishing his purpose, he had flung her from him, as was an every-day occurrence, it was a case which I could under no circumstances touch ; its justice ought only to be determined in the courts.

On the other hand, I argued that if this troublesome woman was grown in years, had arrived at a mature age, and had deliberately planned to secure a certain power over Harcout's friend in the questionable manner ascribed—had, in fact, used the " black arts " upon him, and in every manner possible fascinated him irresistibly, and wrung from him promises and pledges which no man in his sane moments would give, in order through this dishonorably-gained power to secure him for a husband—or worse, in the event of failing in this, of levying upon his wealth for the dishonor she had herself compelled, it was a case where I had a right to interfere in the best interests of society, as the professional female blackmailer is below pity, ought to be beyond protection of any sort whatever, has forfeited all the actual and poetical regard due her sex, and should be in every instance remorselessly hunted down.

This conclusion was easily arrived at ; for at each of my agencies all that is necessary for a decision upon a desired investigation is that my local superintendent shall sift the matter, to prove beyond the shadow of a doubt that the vast power of the detective service under my control shall not, under any circumstances, be prostituted to the assistance of questionable enterprises, or the furtherance of dishonorable schemes.

Accordingly, when Mr. Harcout wafted himself into my office the next day, like a fragrance-laden zephyr of early summer, I informed him that he could depend on my assistance to discover the history and antecedents of the woman; but that I should have to reserve the privilege of discontinuing the service, should it at any time tran·spire that my operatives were being employed for the pur·pose of discouraging a defenceless woman in securing the justice due her.

It was arranged that Harcout was to call the next day with his patron, the persecuted millionaire, and he also expressed a desire to defe; a settlement of the case in detail until that time, which was quite agreeable to me, as I wished to see the parties together and closely observe them, as well as their statements.

The next afternoon Mr. Harcout's elegant card was delivered to me, with the message that his friend was also with him. I ordered that they should be at once admit·ted, and in a moment the two gentlemen were ushered into my private office. I immediately recognized the elder of the two as J. H Lyon, one of the wealthiest ele·vator owners and millers of Rochester, a quiet, shrewd, calculating business man, who had amassed vast wealth, or the reputation of its possession, and its consequent commercial respect and credit.

He was a short, small-sized man, dressed in plain but rich garments, and wore no jewelry save a massive soli·taire diamond ring. His head, which seemed to contain an average brain, was solidly set on a great, heavy neck, that actually continued to the top of the back of his head without a curve or depression. His hair, and beard —which was shaven away from his lower lip to the curve of his chin—had a shaggy sort of look, though generally

3*

well kept, and were considerably tinged with gray; while his eyebrows were remarkably long, irregular, and forbidding. His eyes were medium-sized, of a grayish-brown color, and under the heavy shade of the brows somewhat keen and restless. His cheek-bones were quite prominent, and below them his cheeks sank away noticeably, which served to more strikingly show the upward turn of his nose and his full lips and broad, sensual mouth, which, with its half-shown, irregular teeth and ever-present tobacco-stains (for he smoked or chewed incessantly), gave him a face quite unlike those ordinarily supposed to be captivating to women. With his broad, bony hands, large, ill-shaped feet, and retiring, hesitating way, as if never exactly certain of anything, he was truly a great contrast to the pompous, elegant gentleman who seemed to have taken him under his fatherly protection.

Lyon slid into his seat in a nervous, diffident way; while Harcout, who had just drawn his chair between us, as if he desired it understood that he did not propose to yield his office of general manager of this vitally important affair under any circumstances, beamed on his friend reassuringly.

After a few remarks on the current topics of the day, and before they were themselves aware of it, we were getting along swimmingly towards an understanding of the subject-matter—Lyon, who had removed his cigar, fairly eating an immense amount of fine-cut as the voluble Harcout rattled away about the bold, bad woman who had entrapped him.

"Why, my dear Mr. Pinkerton, it's a terrible matter—an infamous affair! My friend here, Mr. Lyon, is quite nettled about it—I might say, quite cut up. You can see for yourself, sir, that it's wearing on him." This with a deprecating wave of his hand towards Lyon, who nervously gazed out of the window from under his shaggy brows.

I merely said that these things *were* sometimes a little wearing.

"But you see, Mr. Pinkerton, this is a peculiarly cruel case—a peculiarly cruel case. Hem! *I* know what is cruel in this respect, as I was once victimized by very much the same sort of a female, though she was *much younger*. Why, do you know, sir," and here the sympathetic Harcout's voice fell into a solemn murmur, "that my friend's beloved wife was scarcely at rest beneath the daisies when this Mrs. Winslow began worming herself into the confidence of my somewhat impressible friend here?"

I made no answer, and only took a memorandum of the facts developed, not forgetting Harcout's statement that he had once been victimized by very much the same sort of a female.

"She came to Rochester as a shining light among the exponents of our blessed faith——"

"And what may your religion be?" I asked.

"We believe in the constant communication between mortals and the occupants of the beautiful spirit home beyond the river."

"Exactly," said I, noticing the remarkable develop ment at the back of their heads and about their mouths.

"And our friend here, Mr. Lyon," continued Harcout, with his eyes devoutly raised to the ceiling, "met her at one of our pleasant seances."

I made another note at this point.

"To be frank—'hem ! it's my nature to be frank—' then turning his face to me and raising his eyebrows inquiringly—"I suppose, Mr. Pinkerton, it is quite desirable that I should be so ? " To which I responded, "Necessarily so," when he resumed : "To be frank, then, Mr. Lyon was wonderfully interested in her. In fact, the woman *has* a strange power of compelling admiration and even fear—shall I say fear, Mr. Lyon.?"

"Guess that's about right," said Mr. Lyon tersely.

"Admiration and fear," repeated Mr. Harcout, as if thinking of something long gone by, while Lyon chewed more fiercely than ever. "Indeed, Mr. Pinkerton, she's a superb woman—a superb woman ; but a she-devil for all that !"

I noticed that Harcout's fervor seemed to have come from some similar experience, and I noted both it and his heated estimate of Mrs. Winslow, although he remarked that he had never met her.

"Well, my friend here was irresistibly drawn to her, and he has told me that for a time it seemed that he had found his real affinity. You felt that way, didn't you, Lyon ?"

Lyon nodded and chewed rapidly.

" But for a long time the more my friend endeavored to secure her favor, the more she seemed to draw away from and avoid him, though constantly making opportunities to more deeply impress him with her most splendid physical and mental qualities. My friend recollects now, though he gave it no attention at the time, that she shrewdly drew from him much information regarding his family affairs, habits, business relations, and wealth ; and as she was, or pretended to be, a medium of great power, at those times when he sought her professional services she worked upon his feelings in such a peculiar manner as to completely upset him."

Here Mr. Lyon offered an extended remark for the first time, and said : "The truth is, Mr. Pinkerton, this is a subject that I am particularly tender upon. I think under certain circumstances I could really have made the woman my wife ; " then turning to his agent, he said, " Harcout, cut it short."

" But," Harcout protested, " we can't cut it short. Mr. Pinkerton wants facts—he must have facts. Well, at one time Mr. Lyon felt a real affection for the woman, which does him honor—is no disgrace to him ; but after a time began to suspect, and eventually to feel sure, that Mrs. Winslow was playing a deep game ; indeed, had originally come to Rochester for that purpose ; and while he still regarded her highly on account of her fine qualities, refrained from seeking her society, which at once seemed to awaken a violent and uncortrollable passion for him in her heart. She sought him everywhere and compelled him to visit her frequently, lavishing the wildet affection upon him, which he delicately repelled —delicately repelled; and, as she represented herself in straitened circumstances, charitably assisted her just as he would have done any other person in want—any other person in want; but, you see, Mrs. Winslow presumed upon this, accused him of having broken her heart, and was now cruelly deserting her after he had taught her to worship him."

Mr. Lyon's nervous face presented a singular combination of pride at his own powers, chagrin at his predicament, and a general protest that the tender privacies of a millionaire should be thus disclosed.

"In this way," continued Harcout, "she so worked upon his kindly feelings that he really gave her large sums of money—large sums of money."

"A good deal of money," interrupted Mr. Lyon.

"But finally," pursued Harcout, "my friend saw that he must discontinue his charity altogether, and through my advice—hem! through my advice, he did. Mrs. Winslow then became very impudent indeed, and annoyed my friend beyond endurance, until he was forced to refuse to recognize her, and gave orders that she should be denied admission to his office. But, being a very talented woman—— "

" She *is* talented," said Lyon, with a start.

"She has found means to continue her operations against him incessantly, demanding still larger sums of money, ard has engaged counsel to act for her. Hem !

—undei my advice, quite recently Mr. Lyon, by paying her five thousand dollars, secured from her a relinquishment of all claims against him, rather than oblige a public scandal. But now Mrs. Winslow claims that this was secured by fraud, and after making another fruitless demand for ten thousand dollars, which—hem ! Mr. Lyon resisted through my advice, last week began suit against him for one hundred thousand dollars for breach of promise of marriage. And a hundred thousand dollars is a big sum of money, Mr. Pinkerton."

"A big sum of money," echoed Lyon.

"But of course," continued Harcout, inserting his thumbs in the arm-holes of his vest and looking the very picture of injured virtue, "Mr. Lyon cares nothing for that amount. It is the principle of the thing. It is the stain upon his good name that he desires to prevent— and these juries are confoundedly unreliable."

"Confoundedly unreliable," repeated Lyon, chewing nervously.

"Therefore," said Harcout, "really believing, as we do, that we—hem! that is, Mr. Lyon, of course—is the victim of a designing woman who really means to wrongfully compel the payment of a large sum of money and ruin my friend in the estimation of the public, we are anxious that you should set about ascertainiug everything concerning her for use as evidence in the case."

After asking them a few questions touching facts I desired to ascertain, the interview terminated with the understanding that Harcout should act for Mr. Lyor unqualifiedly in the matter, and call at my office as often as desirable to listen to reports of the progress of my investigations into the life and history of Mrs. Winslow. I was satisfied that not half the truth had been given me, and I was more than ever convinced of this fact when Lyon called me to one side as the lordly Harcout passed out, and said to me hurriedly :

"Don't be too hard upon the woman, Mr. Pinkerton. You know we are *all* liable to err ; and—and, by Jupiter ! Mrs. Winslow is certainly a most magnificent woman—a *most* magnificent woman," and then chewed himself out after his courtly henchman.

CHAPTER VIII.

AS the interview related in the previous chapter occurred on Friday, and I could not attend to the matter at once, I was obliged to wait until the following Sunday evening, when I quietly took the western-bound express, which brought me to Rochester the following noon, where I engaged rooms at the Brackett House under an assumed name, and immediately began a preliminary examination on my own account, having directed my New York Superintendent to inform either Lyon or Harcout, in the event of their calling at the agency, that I could not be seen regarding their matter for a few days, as I had suddenly been called South on important business.

My object in doing this was to look over the ground at Rochester myself, and get an unbiased idea of the whole matter, so that I could properly proceed with the work, being satisfied that this was the only way to secure a basis to operate upon, as I was sure that I had not go' at the bottom facts in the late interview. I invariably insist on having all the facts, and always take measures to secure them before any decided move is made.

As a rule, however, in cases of this kind, it is almost impossible to secure what the detective absolutely needs from the parties from whom the information should come; as it is a principle of human nature possessed by us all, to be very frank about our merits, and quite careful about mentioning anything that might be construed into either a lack of judgment or principle.

I found that the New York papers were already publishing specials concerning the matter, with solemn editorials regarding the perfidy of man, the constancy of woman, and the general cussedness of both; and that at Rochester the knowledge of the commencement of the suit had just got into the papers, and consequently, into everybody's mouth; and was creating a great sensation, as Lyon was known to the whole city as one of its richest citizens, "though a little off on Spiritualism lately," as the talk went; and Mrs. Winslow had also become quite notorious from her magnificent figure and winning manner, her equally notorious mediumistic powers, and through her prominent connection with the more *material* believers in spiritual phenomena; or, to be plain, that vast majority of so-called spiritualists whose only visible means of support are in excellently humbugging their brethren or sisters, or any other portion of the gullible world with whom they come in contact.

Nearly every Rochester paper contained the advertise

ment of Mr3. Winslow, trance medium, and I concluded that either the lady had been unusually successful in her trance business, or that her levies upon Lyon had been remunerative—perhaps both—to pay for such extensive advertising.

After dinner I took a stroll and found that the lady occupied very luxurious apartments on South St. Paul street, near Meech's Opera-house, a location well adapted for her business. I also ordered a carriage and drove out to Port Charlotte—a magnificent drive through a lovely country dotted with fine farm-houses and the splendid suburban residences of wealthy Rochester citizens—and, as a casual stranger, inspected Lyon's warehouses and elevators, the largest and most expensive at the Port, returning to the Brackett House in time to eat a hearty supper.

After supper, without any effort, and without disclosing my identity, I got into conversation with the genial landlord of the house, who gave me—as a part of my entertainment, I presume—a rich account of Lyon's business relations, and particularly of his personal habits, painted in entirely different colors than by the blarneying tongue of Harcout; and also spoke of the latter as "a d——d barnacle," who had in some unexplainable way fastened himself upon Lyon and was living like a prince off the "old fool," as he called him. He also told me confidentially that he believed Mrs. Winslow to be a woman of questionable character; as, when she first came to the city, she had stopped at his hotel, and had advertised her mediumistic powers so largely that it had brought a class of men there whom he thought, from his personal knowledge of their habits, to be more interested in inquiries into the mysteries of the *present* than of the hereafter, until he had become so anxious as to the reputation of his house that he had informed the lady of the preference of her absence to her company ; wherupon she had raised such a storm about his ears that he was only too glad to compromise by letting her go, bag and baggage, without paying her bill, which was a large one and of a month's standing.

I also gained from him the opinion that she had been married a half-dozen times, or as often as had suited her convenience ; and that he had only a day or so previous conversed with a gentleman from some part of the West, who had told him that somebody in Rochester had assisted her in procuring her a divorce from her husband. I made a note of all these points after I had retired to my room, and felt quite satisfied with the day's work.

The next day, with a gentleman at the hotel with whom I had become acquainted, representing myself as a person of means who might possibly make an investment at Rochester, I visited Lyon's mills, and incidentally became quite well informed as to his financial and social standing.

The latter was a little peculiar. His wife, a most estimable lady, had died a few years previous, and it appeared that during her life the Lyon family were among the aristocrats of the city ; but at her death, and

Lyon's subsequent dabbling in Spiritualism, they had been gradually dropped from the visiting lists, and nothing remained of the former home circle save a gaunt, grim mother-in-law, who vainly waged war against the loose habits, laxity of morals, and general degeneracy that had come with the new order of things.

I also secured the addresses of all the professional mediums, fortune-tellers, and astrologers of the city, and during that day and the next visited their rooms, claiming to be a devoted believer in Spiritualism, having my fortune told at various places, and picking up a good deal of information regarding the fascinating Mrs. Winslow, which tended to prove her a remarkably talented woman, capable of not only attending to her mediumistic duties, but also of carrying on litigation of various kinds in different parts of the country. My investigations also showed that these different " doctors " and " doctresses," claiming to perform almost miraculous cures and their ability to foretell the fates of others through the aid of this supernatural spirit-power, were quite like other people in their bickerings and jealousies, and, as a rule, they gave each other quite as bad names as the public generally gave them ; and that Mrs. Winslow could not have been considered exactly the pink of perfection if judged even by those of her own persuasion, as one vaguely hinted at her having played the same game on other parties. Another was sure she had been a camp-follower during the war. Another assured me that she had similar suits at Louisville, Cincinnati, and St. Louis. Still another was quite certain that she was only a common woman. Altogether, according to these reports, which were easily enough secured, as her case against Lyon was the engrossing subject of the hour at Rochester, it appeared that the ravishing Mrs. Winslow held her place, such as it was, in the world more through her supreme will power, and the respect through fear she unconsciously inspired in others, than through any of the tenderer graces or a superabundance of personal purity.

From cautious inquiries and the wonderful amount of street, saloon, and hotel talk which the affair was causing, I also ascertained that Mrs. Winslow had made her appearance in Rochester some years before ; some said from the east, and some from the West, but the preponderance of evidence indicated that it had been from the West ; that she had at once allied herself with the spiritualists of the city, and Lyon had first met or seen her at one of their seances or lectures; that he had at once yielded to her charms, and begun visiting her for " advice," as it was sarcastically reported, continuing the visits with such frequency and regularity as to hasten the death of his wife, after which event he had given his new affinity nearly his entire attention until she had come to be commonly considered as his mistress ; that she had frequently boasted among her friends that she was to become Lyon's wife, and was even by some called Mrs. Lyon, to which pleasant designation she made no mur mur ; that she had made a common practice of visiting Lyon at his offices in the Arcade, where she had been treated with considerable deference and respect by his employees ; and that during this period Mrs. Winslow had made several trips to the West, evidently at Lyon's insti-gation, and through his financial aid.

I fonnd also that she was as truly a believer in the farces others of her profession enacted for her benefit as she was in the mediumistic power she had persuaded her-self that she possessed, and was consequently a regular attendant at all the meetings and seances held in the city; and as there was one to be held that evening at Washington Hall, I decided to attend for the purpose of getting a good view of the lady with whom, for a time, we should be obliged to keep close company. Accord-ingly, at half-past seven o'clock I found the hall, which is but a few blocks above the bridge on Main Street, and after purchasing a ticket of a sleek, long-haired individual with deft fingers and a restless eye, passed into the room, where there was already quite a number of the faithful, all bearing unmistakable evidences of either their peculiar faith, or the character of their business.

As the exercises of the evening had not yet begun, those present were gathered about the hall excitedly dis-cussing the great sensation of the hour, which was partic-ularly interesting to them, as the parties to it were both of their number, and from what I could gather they were about evenly divided in their opinion as to the merits of the case—the male portion of the assemblage warmly espousing the cause of Mrs. Winslow, and the female portion as eagerly sympathizing with "poor dear Mr

Lyon," and roundly condemning the naughty woman who had ensnared him and was so relentlessly pursuing him.

I was sure the naughty woman had now arrived, as theie was a sudden twisting of necks and buzzing of "That's her—that's her!" "There's Mrs. Winslow!" and "Yes, that's Mrs. Lyon!" an.l the females that had given Mrs. Winslow such a bad reputation a few moments before, now pressed around her with sympathizing inquiries and loud protestations of regard, quite like other ladies under similar circumstances. But the lady appeared to be quite unconcerned as to their good or ill feeling towards her, and swept up the aisle with a regal air, taking a seat so near me and in such a position that I was able to make a perfect study of her while apparently only absorbed in the wonderful revelation that fell from the trance-speaker's lips.

She appeared to be a lady of about thirty-five years of age, and of a very commanding appearance. She was not a beautiful woman, but there was an indescribable something about her entire face and figure that was strangely attractive. It was both the dignity of self-conscious power and the peculiar attractiveness of a majestically formed woman. It could not be said that there was a single beautiful feature about her face, though it attracted and held every observer. Her head was large, well formed, and covered with a wavy mass of black hair marvelous in its richness of color and luxuriance. Her complexion was a clear, wax-like white, singularly con trasting with he: hair, delicately arching eyebrows, and long, dark lashes, which heavily shaded great gray eyes that were sometimes touched with a shading of blue, and occasionally glowed with a light as keen, glittering, and cold as might flash from a diamond or a dagger's point, which seemed to work in sympathy with the rapid movement of her thin nostrils, and the swift shuttles of crimson and paleness that darted over her curled upper lip, which, notwithstanding this singularity, touched the full, pouting lower one with a hint of wild and riotous blood.

Although Mrs. Winslow was a woman who, being met in the better circles of society, would have wonderfully interested every one with whom she came in contact, in the circle within which she moved, and which, unconsciously, seemed to be far beneath her, she surely commanded a certain kind of respect, with a touch of fear, perhaps ; and in any circle of life was undoubtedly one in whom the ambition for power was only equalled by the remorseless way with which she would wield it after it had been gained.

Not once during the whole evening did she by any movement of her person or motion of her features give any further indication of her character ; and I could only leave the hall and return to my hotel, and from thence immediately to New York, with the thorough conviction that Mrs. Winslow was a remarkably shrewd woman ; had systematically fastened herself upon Lyon with the view of beccming his wife, or compelling him to divide his immense wealth with her ; would give us plenty to attend to,

4

and had easily gained a wonderful power over Lyon;
which, even after her repeated piracies upon him, and the
evident knowledge he possessed of her villainous·char-
acter, was yet strong upon him.

CHAPTER IX.

ON my return to New York I found that the splendid
Harcout had been using the interim in a suc-
cession of heated rushes from the St. Nicholas Hotel to
the Agency, where he had given my superintendents and
clerks voluminous instructions as to how the investigation
should be conducted, and, in explaining his idea of how
detectives should work up any case, permeated the entire
establishment with his fragrant pomposity. He was
also quite impatient that nothing had been done in "our
case," as he termed it, and I could only pacify him by
assuring him that it should be given my immediate attention.

As soon as I could dispose of Harcout I held another
consultation with my General Superintendent, during
which the information I had secured at Rochester was
analyzed and recorded, and which, with some other facts
already in possession of the Agency bearing on the case,

we decided to be sufficient to warrant a conclusion that Mrs. Winslow was not Mrs. Winslow at all, but somebody else altogether, and had had as many *aliases* as a cat is supposed to have lives. It was also quite evident, the more we looked into the matter and searched the records, that certain other cities of the country had suffered from the much-named Mrs. Winslow, and in many instances in a quite similar manner to that of the Rochester infliction.

Running through all the strange chain of evidence that the records of our almost numberless operations gave, there were also found items which told of a female not alto-gether unlike Mrs. Winslow, and there were in them all traces of a woman absolutely heartless, cold, calculating, cruel; now here under one name and in one guise, now there under another name and in another guise, but for-ever upon that unrelenting search for power and with that remorseless greed for gold, and also showing as truly a trace of spiritualism, of lust, and of licentiousness.

Of course the result of it all was only a question of time; only a question of duration in villainy and shrewd human deviltry; a mere question of how long supreme depravity would wear in a constant war upon fairness, purity, and the conscience of society. It never wins—it always loses, and, as certain as life or death, good or evil, reaches its sure punishment here, whatever may be the result in that undiscovered territory of the future which the preachers find happiness and good incomes in quarrelling over. But as my long experience with crime and criminals had proven to me the fact that one desperately bad woman brings upon society vastly more misery than a hundred equally as bad men, and being equally as certain that Mrs. Winslow was an exceptionally bad woman, I felt no regret whatever in becoming her Nemesis, and even experienced a peculiar degree of satisfaction in inaugurating a crusade against her as a pitiless, heartless, dangerous woman, utterly devoid of conscience, and without a single redeeming trait of character.

I accordingly detailed two of my operatives, Fox and Bristol, to proceed to Rochester in charge of Superintendent Bangs, whom I gave instructions to locate the men so that they could keep Mrs. Winslow under the strictest surveillance, and make daily reports in writing to me concerning her habits and associates, and operations of any character whatever, using the telegraph freely if occasion required. I also instructed him, after the men were located in Rochester, and he had followed up the clue I had got for him as to Mrs. Winslow's western exploits, to proceed to the West, taking all the time necessary, and ascertain everything possible favorable or unfavorable to the woman; as I held it to be not only a matter of utmost importance to thorough detective work, but also a principle of common justice, that any suspected person should receive the benefit of whatever good there is in them.

For these reasons I have always fought against the system of rewards for the capture and conviction of supposed criminals. There could be nothing more absolutely unjust. Under that system, through a combination of circumstances, an innocent party is often deemed guilty of crime, and the detective, anxious to secure professional honor and large remuneration for small work, begins with the presumption of guilt, and industriously piles up a mountain of presumptive and circumstantial evidence that times without number has sent innocent persons to the felon's cell or the hangman's noose.

On arriving at Rochester the following Monday, Bangs took rooms at the National Hotel, opposite the court-house—a house more a resort for persons in attendance at the courts, and people visiting Rochester from neighboring towns, than for fashionable people or commercial travellers ; while Fox settled himself at a little hotel nearly opposite Mrs. Winslow's rooms on South St. Paul street, and Bristol found a home at a little saloon, restaurant and boarding-house, kept by three old maids named Grim, who were firm believers in Spiritualism—probably from never having got any satisfaction out of life from any other religion—under Washington Hall, on East Main street, a place given up to variety shows, masked balls, sleight-of-hand performances, seances, and other questionable entertainments ; so that they were all within easy communication, and could work to advantage. It was also arranged that the reports of Fox and Bristol should be put in Mr. Bang's hands, by a mode of communication which would prevent their being seen together, before being forwarded to me, so that their observations might be of assistance in his securing necessary information for his western tour.

While Bristol and Fox were watching the movements

of the gay madam, familiarizing themselves with the city, and getting on an easy footing at their boarding-houses, Mr. Bangs set to work to ascertain if possible in what part of the West Mrs. Winslow had operated.

He first visited Mr. Lyon at his office in the Arcade, introducing himself as Mr. Clement, one of my operatives, not giving his correct name, as the newspaper reporters were flying around at a great rate for items, and the appearance of a man so well known by reputation as Mr. Bangs would have given their overcharged imaginations an opportunity to flood over several columns of their respective papers. After being seated in Lyon's private office Mr. Bangs, as Mr. Clement, began the conversation :

" Mr Lyon, I am directed by Mr. Pinkerton to ascertain if possible from you whether Mrs. Winslow has ever informed you of having at any previous time resided in the West ? "

Lyon gave Bangs a cigar, lighted one for himself, and after puffing away vigorously for a little time, replied : " Mr. Clement, I think she has done so, but I can't recollect what the information was."

" Couldn't you call to mind anything that would be of some little assistance to us, Mr. Lyon ? "

" No," he nervously answered ; " no, I think not. I have put this whole matter away from me as much as possible."

" We have positively ascertained," continued Bangs, looking searchingly into Lyon's face, " that she recently secured a divorce from a former husband. We also know that some one here in Rochester rendered her substantial assistance. That person found, tracing her history would be comparatively an easy matter."

Lyon moved about uneasily, and finally through the clouds of smoke about his head puffed out, "Indeed!"

"Yes," replied Bangs, "and, Mr. Lyon, if we could get at the exact truth about this part of it, I am sure it would not only greatly facilitate our work, but also greatly lessen the expense of the operation."

Lyon sat for a little time twisting his shaggy gray whiskers, and finally said: "Mr. Clement, I insist on not being worried about this business; perhaps Harcout didn't make that point quite clear. Harcout *is* a little flighty, but a noble fellow though, after all. I don't hardly know what I would do without Harcout, Mr. Clement; he takes the whole thing off my shoulders, as it were."

Bangs saw that Lyon could have given him just what information he needed, and also saw with equal certainty that he had fully decided to throw the matter off his mind entirely, and compel us to gain whatever necessary by hard work. He was also now satisfied of the truth of my conviction, that Lyon had assisted Mrs. Winslow in this divorce matter, and had been very much more intimate with her than he even desired us to know. So he bade him good-day, returned to his hotel, and telegraphed for instructions. I directed him to go ahead and use his own judgment altogether, also suggesting that he should visit the different clairvoyants and mediums, with a view of getting further information which might be secured from their almost ceaseless chatter upon the subject.

As Rochester is as full of mediums as a thistle of thorns, this was a kind of investigation which necessitated the expenditure of considerable time, and three days had elapsed before any information of a satisfactory nature was secured. He had expended quite a little fortune in having his "horoscope cast," his fortune told, and his fate pointed out with such unerring certainty by male and female seers of every name, appearance and nature, that if any two of these predictions had borne the slightest possible resemblance to each other, he would have been horrified enough to have taken a last leap into the surging Genesee like poor Sam Patch. But he persisted in the face of these terrible revelations until he had found a certain Dr. Hubbard, who proved to be one of the jolliest of the profession he had ever met. The Doctor was a pleasant gentleman, and proved more pleasant than ever when Mr. Bangs informed him that he did not desire any fortune-telling, predictions or horoscopes, but was interested in the subject of Spiritualism, and had been directed to him as one likely to give some information that could be relied on, for which he would liberally remunerate him.

As Mr. Bangs had some choice cigars, which he divided with the Doctor, and the Doctor had some choice brandy, which he divided with Mr. Bangs, they at once became easy together, and taking seats at the window overlooking

4*

Main street, while watching the crowds below, were soon chatting away quite unlike two people very badly affected with spiritualistic tendencies.

After a little time, however, the Doctor looked pretty sharply at Bangs, and suddenly asked: "Well, who are you, anyhow?"

"Who am I?" returned Bangs smilingly, "well, to be frank, I am Professor Owen, of the Indiana State University."   Bangs never blushed at the libel on the kind old man bearing that name and title, and continued, "It is our vacation now, and I am travelling a little in the East investigating this subject.   My brother is an enthusiastic believer in it, but I wished other testimony."

The Doctor seemed to think that the Professor took to the brandy and cigars quite too familiarly for an educator, but the explanation satisfied him, and he asked: "Professor, you want the whole truth, don't you?"

" Nothing but the truth," responded Bangs.

Doctor Hubbard blew out a long series of rings and expressively followed it with " Humbug !"

" It can't be possible," persisted Bangs.

" It oughtn't to be possible," urged the Doctor, "for a man of your probable talent and position to be engaged in investigating what one visit to any one of us should show to be the most infernal fraud ever practised upon the public !" said the Doctor heatedly.

Bangs expressed himself as surprised beyond measure.

" Well," continued the Doctor earnestly, "you came to me like a man, didn't you?"

Bangs assured him that he was quite right.

"And you came fair and square, without any ifs and ands, didn't you ?"

"All of that," responded Bangs.

"And," continued the Doctor helping himself to the brandy, then excusing himself and pushing it towards Bangs, who partook sparingly, "you didn't want any fortune told, or predictions, or horoscopes, or any other ncnsense ?"

"Exactly," said Bangs.

"And you said you'd pay me liberally for information, didn't you ?"

"Yes, and I'll be as good as my word," replied the assumed professor.

"Well, then," continued the Doctor in a burst of good feeling, brandy and honesty, "you see in me an unsuccessful physician, a disciple of Æsculapius without followers. I graduated with high honors, hung out my sign, sharpened my tools, moulded my pills, drank a toast to disease, but waited in vain for patronage. As this became monotonous," continued the Doctor, taking another pull at the brandy bottle, then wiping the mouth and passing it to Mr. Bangs, who excused himself, "I glided into a 'specialist.' It required too much money to advertise, and the papers slashed me villainously besides. *Then* I became a Spiritualist—it's the record of every one of us. You can see," and the Doctor waved his hand towards the cosy appointments in a satisfied way, "I am pretty comfortable now."

"Yes, quite comfortable," said Bangs, wondering what the Doctor was driving at.

"So I am an enthusiastic Spiritualist," resumed the happy physician, "for its profession has provided me with necessities, comforts, and even luxuries."

"Do you really effect any of the marvellous cures you adveitise?"

"Most assuredly," he replied.

"And may I ask how?" interrogated Mr. Bangs.

"In the good old-fashioned way—salts, senna, calomel, and the blue-pill," said the Doctor, laughing heartily.

"And is not the aid of the spirits essential to your cures?"

"A belief, or *faith*, that such an agency is used, does the whole thing, Professor."

"And is there no such thing?" persisted Bangs.

"Just as much of it as there is faith in it; no more and no less."

"Then the whole thing's a humbug, as you say?"

"Just as thoroughly as is that woman," said the Doctor stoutly, pointing to Mrs. Winslow, who at that moment was seen in the street below, being driven towards the suburbs in a neat phaeton.

Bangs, becoming suddenly interested, though repressing himself, carelessly asked, "Who is she?"

Here the Doctor executed a grimace which might mean a good deal, or nothing at all, and said tersely: "She's a bouncer; don t you know her?"

"No."

"Wҍy, that's Mrs. Winslow, old Lyons' soothing syrup; and old Lyon's one of the children—'teething,'" added the Doctor with a hearty laugh. "But she's a tigress!"

Mr. Bangs leaned out of the window, took a good look at the tigress, and then, as if endeavoring to recollect some former occurrence, said: "I believe I have seen her somewhere before."

"Quite so, quite so; undoubtedly you have."

"And I think in the West, too," replied Mr. Bangs, trying hard to remember, and handing the doctor a fresh cigar.

"Exactly—Chicago, St. Louis, Cincinnati, Louisville—everywhere, in fact. One might call her a social floater, and not be far out of the way either. She used to live at Terre Haute."

"Terre Haute? Why, of course! I knew I had seen her somewhere."

"Yes, she lived a few miles out, up the Wabash river, for years. Her husband's name was Oxford, or Hosford, or something of the kind."

"Yes?" said Bangs.

"Yes," replied the Doctor; "I didn't know her personally, but I knew *of* her there. That's where she first went off the hook—and—and became one of us."

"Is she a remarkable character?" asked Mr. Bangs.

"A remarkable character? Why, sir, she's a wonderful woman—a perfect Satan. I wouldn't have her get after me," said the Doctor, shaking his head protestingly "for ten thousand dollars!　Why, sir, that woman has ruined more men, and broken up more families than you could count."

"And is *she*, too, a spiritualist?" asked Mr. Bangs.

"A spiritualist?　Why, of course she is; and, what is more, I sometimes think she really believes in her own mummeries."

"What has become of her family?" asked Bangs.

"Oh, gone to the devil, I presume, just like everybody she has had anything to do with—just as old Lyon is certain to do, too."

"Then this Oxford or Hosford is not living at Terre Haute now?"

"Couldn't tell you that," replied the Doctor; and then, suddenly returning to the subject and putting the brandy-bottle into a little closet with a slam as footsteps were heard coming up the stairs, "can I be of any further service to you?"

Mr. Bangs thought not, handed the good Doctor a five-dollar bill while remarking that he would call again, both of which evidences of good feeling pleased the latter immensely, and took his departure quite well pleased with the result of his inquiries into the wonderful subject of modern Spiritualism.

CHAPTER X.

WHILE Superintendent Bangs is on his hunting expedition in the West, we will follow the fortunes of Mrs. Winslow in the beautiful city of Rochester.

There is hardly a city in the country better adapted for either the pursuit of pleasure or wealth than Rochester. Everything combines to make it so. It nestles in one of the most beautiful valleys in the world, like the nest of a busy bird in a luxuriant meadow. There is the sound of pleasant waters, the roar of a mighty cataract, the din of two score busy mills, the music of the spindles, the cogs and the reels, the clash and the clangor of the factories, the thunderings of the forges, and the footfalls of a hundred thousand happy, contented people who have wrung competence and even luxury from the hard hand of necessity and toil.

From the summit of Mount Hope Observatory, an elevation of nearly five hundred feet above the lake, there is a grand picture whereon the eye may rest. At your feet,

and to the north, lies the busy city with the noble Gene·
see winding rapidly through it, lending its half-million
horse-power force to the needs of labor, then plunging a
hundred feet downwards, eddying and rushing onward,
plunging and eddying again and again, until it sobers into
a steady current northward towards Ontario through a
deep, dark gorge, looking like an ugly serpent trailing to
the lower inland sea where can be seen the city of Charlotte, formerly called Port Genesee, the port of Rochester,
beyond which, on a clear day, may be seen countless
dreamy sails, and steamers with their trailing plumes of
smoke, and still beyond appears the dim outlines of the
far-off Canadian shore. To the east, as far as can be dis-
cerned, lies a country of the nature of "openings"—
beautiful groves of trees, magnificent farms, with the
almost palatial homes of the owners, who have become
rich from the legacies of their ancestors with the added
thrift of scores of fruitful years. Southward for a half
hundred miles, stretches the beautiful valley of the Genesee, dimpled by lesser valleys and a hundred sparkling
brooks, and dotted by field and forest and numberless
groups of half-hidden houses, with outbuildings full to
bursting with the fruitage of the fields ; while to the west
along the lake are low ranges of sand-hills, and south of
these extending nearly to Lake Erie is a beautiful prairie
country, while with a glass can be traced the ghostly mist
perpetually hovering above Niagara.

If this scene be inspiring to the looker-on, the intrinsic
beauty of the city, its unusual life, its fine public build

ings, business houses, and splendid private residences; its clean macadamized streets and broad, brick walks, shaded with the trees of half a century's growth as in many of the famous Southern cities; its numberless little parks or " places," owned in common by the proprietors of the handsome residences which surround them, and filled with rare shrubs, flowers, beautiful fountains and costly statuary; the vast *parterres* of flowers in the suburbs, sending in upon every summer wind an Arabian wealth of exquisite fragrance; the large summer gardens, where beer and Gambrinus reign supreme; the enticing promenades, and the splendid drives in every direction from the city—would give any one not completely at war with every pleasant thing in life a genuine inspiration of pleasure and a more than ordinary thrill of enjoyment.

It is little wonder, then, that Mrs. Winslow found Rochester a profitable field for operating in her peculiar double capacity of a dashing adventuress and a trance medium. She found there not only men of vast wealth, but of vast immorality, as is quite common all over the world, and hundreds of firm believers in spiritualism, which was a special peculiarity to Rochester. Among the first number there were many who sought her for her charms of figure and manners, which were certainly powerfully attractive, and which yielded her an elegant income without positive public degradation, as no man of wealth and position feels called upon to make known his own peccadilloes for the sake of exposing the sharer of them, even though she be a dangerous woman :

and consequently there was only that universal verdict of evil against her which society quite generally, and also quite correctly, pronounces on forcibly circumstantial evidence.

Her apartments were elegant, and even sumptuous; and though there was a quite general understanding of her character among the epicurean gentlemen of the city, she held them aloof with such freezing dignity that they seldom presumed upon her acquaintance, and were even possessed of a certain respect for her unusually rare shrewdness in preserving her reputation, such as it was; so that her rooms, so far as the public were able to ascertain, were only frequented by those who believed her to be able to allay their sufferings, or open the gates of the undiscovered country to their anxious, yearning eyes.

A large amount of money had been paid her by Lyon to prevent a scandal. The last sum was known to have been five thousand dollars, and it was quite probable that if there had been an intimacy so ripe as to have warranted the payment of this amount, still larger sums had doubtless been expended in maturing so tender a relation. In any event it was ascertained by Bristol and Fox that Mrs. Winslow had for some time been living in elegance, though at the same time carefully, being g ven to no particular excesses, and it was a matter for considerable speculation whether she was now in the possession of much money or not.

Fox affected the quiet, well-bred gentleman, expended sufficient money among the boarders to make them talk ative, and even confidential, and in this way learned a great deal about the madam's habits and peculiarities that was afterwards useful, though of no particular moment at that time; while Bristol, who was a florid, well-kept Canadian gentleman of about forty-five years of age, of a literary and poetical turn, and with an easy habit of falling into the manner and brogue of an Englishman, Scotchman, or Irishman, made himself immensely popular with the old maids under Washington Hall, who in turn were enamored with his good physical parts and blarneying tongue, and were at any time ready to confide to him all they knew, and, in fact, a great deal more; so that, as he professed to be an ardent Spiritualist, he was enabled to become well informed concerning the leading persons of that persuasion in the city, of whom he forwarded a complete list, with something of a history of each; and while not becoming known to or personally familiar with any one of them—which would have destroyed his usefulness, he was yet able to keep track of nearly all that was said or done within the charmed circle; as after each lecture, or seance, the economically-built and antiquated maidens would retire to a little snuggery behind the restaurant, to which they would invite the sympathetic Bristol, who was old enough to protect them from scandal, and then and there, while easing their by no means ravishing forms of portions of their garments preparatory to the night's virtuous repose, over strong toast and weak tea would rattle on in such a bewildering way about the events of the evening and the good or bad characteristics of the faithful, that Bristol figuratively, if not in fact, sat at the feet of a trinity of oracles.

His reports showed that while Mrs. Winslow was accepted among their number without question, still there was but little known about her previous history. I felt satisfied that this was true, and had only stationed Bristol and Fox at Rochester for the purpose of keeping me informed of her every movement, knowing well enough that after Bangs had got a good start he would follow up her trail in the West as remorselessly as I myself would have done.

Mrs. Winslow seemed to be absolutely without associates, either from a confirmed habit of suspicion of everybody which she seemed to possess, or from a resolve to maintain as good a character as possible until the Winslow-Lyon case should be heard in court, so that her evidence, and particularly her reputation, might not be impeached or broken down ; and it required the constant attention of both Bristol and Fox to discover in her anything of even a suspicious character, as the nature of her mediumistic business—allowing as it did scores of visitors daily access to her rooms, only one being admitted to the trance-room of her apartments at a time—gave her a vast advantage over them.

It was evident that she had in a measure persuaded herself that she had a genuine cause of action against Lyon ; or, that if she had not, she had fully determined to make a big fight under any circumstances, as both the prestige secured by the presumption of some shadow of a claim which the mere pressing of it in court would give, and the assistance to her which even a tithe of the damages she claimed would be, would not only give her a degree of importance and respectability which would greatly assist her in future operations, but would also yield her the means for future comfort, without this terrible continued struggle for gold and the happiness it is supposed to command.

How vain such a hope ! and how strange that, with the bitter reminder of countless never-realized ambitions before them, the adventurer and the criminal will go on and on, still clinging to the shadow of a hope that by *some* exceptional freak of fortune in their favor they may gain the peace and quietness they so agonizedly long for, but which is just as irrevocably decreed to be forever beyond their reach as were the luscious fruits to escape the touch and taste of the condemned and tortured Phrygian king.

And right here, were I a preacher—being only a *doer*, however—I would show the criminal neglect of parents, teachers and preachers in forever warring for reformation, and never battling against the numberless packs of little foxes of pride and covetousness of society, which drive weak natures into a constant struggle to excel in power and display, eating away at the vines until the life, like the fields, is left barren and desolate, or is only a vast waste of thorns and noxious weeds. My records are full of lives wrecked upon the glittering rocks built by false pride and vanity and the greed for gold which society, and even the aristocratic systems of modern religion compel. Whatever may be preached, all this cursed assumption of what is not possessed without years of honest, sturdy toil, is practised in the pulpit, the pew, the palace, and the povety-stricken hovel, permeating every stratum of business, society and religion, until honorable action is at discount, dishonesty commands a premium of gain and lachrymose sympathy, and the whole world is being swiftly driven into a surging channel of fraud, crime and debauchery that will require generations of something besides splendid hypocrisy and luxurious cant to restrain and purify.

With this digression, which I cannot well avoid, as it contains the convictions based upon long years of close observation and peculiar experience, I will return to the woman whom my operatives found so difficult to analyze and trace out.

Bangs's visit to Dr. Hubbard showed that she had a habit of driving out. Bristol and Fox became acquainted with this fact at once and transmitted it in their reports. It appeared that the carriage and driver were secured at a livery stable near the opera house, a short distance from her rooms and Fox's boarding-house. I instructed Fox to ascertain to what points these trips were made, and if any one ever accompanied her. Careful inquiries at this stable elicited nothing, as Mrs. Winslow's custom was valuable, and even her driver proved close-mouthed upon the subject. Accordingly, after Fox had discovered the general direction taken by Mrs. Winslow and the usual streets frequented at starting, he strolled out State Street and from thence into Lake View Avenue, which is but a continuation of State Street. After he had walked some little distance he was pleased to find that he had company in the person of a dapper little blond gentleman who was somewhat in advance of him, but who, though apparently enjoying the morning air, seemed both apprehensive of being followed, and desirous of the appearance of some one for whom he was waiting. His make-up gave him something of a foreign air, and was the most exquisite imaginable. He was a slender, tender nymph of the male order of fairies, with a face as delicate as a woman's, with large, blue, expressive eyes, long, luxuriant hair, and as neat a little moustache as was ever waxed to keep it from melting away altogether. If his face and figure were neat enough for a millinery window, his clothing was a model even for a Poole. His lustrous silk hat scarcely outshone in richness his faultless dress-coat, which was buttoned low, exposing a perfect duck vest, a spotless shirt-front and a low, rolling Byron collar, with a delicate flowing tie ; while his pantaloons, which were of a mellow lavender color, seemed only to increase the effect of his shapely legs, and by their graceful swell at the instep only to stop to disclose a foot perfect enough for a model. His jewelry consisted of a modest solitaire diamond pin, and a large seal ring which he wore upon the little finger of his left hand.

For some reason Fox felt interested in him, and resolved, though looking for a quite different person, to watch him closely. So he passed him without giving him an opportunity of seeing his face, and, taking a position in the bar-room of a small beer-garden a little way beyond, where he had a good view of the avenue, waited for developments which were not long in taking place, as the neat little fellow arrived at the garden a few minutes after Fox, and shortly after Mrs. Winslow's carriage was seen coming from the direction of the city. Fox saw that he was bringing two birds down with one stone, and anxiously watched Mrs. Winslow and the little fop, feeling satisfied that their meeting at the garden was pre-arranged, for as soon as her carriage came in sight, he had noticed a look of satisfaction come over the man's face, and when it was driven up to the door he stepped out nimbly, smiling and bowing like a brisk wax figure at a show.

The driver was at once discharged, and after watering the horse, immediately started towards town on foot, occasionally looking over his shoulder with a sardonic smile on his face, as if pleased at the loving meeting at the garden, as that sort of thing probably brought him many an honest penny ; but no sooner had the driver turned his back on the place than Mrs. Winslow said :

" Come, Le Compte, get me a glass of brandy."

Fox thought that pretty strong for a lady who had been damaged a hundred thousand dollars by breach of promise of marriage, but held his peace, and a paper before his face, while her admirer danced into the bar and procured two glasses of brandy, which he took to the carriage upon a little tray.

"My dear, you were a little late, eh?" said Le Compte.

"Ah, a French divinity," thought Fox.

"Le Compte," replied Mrs. Winslow, handing him a bill with which to pay for the refreshment, and paying no attention to the little fellow's remark, "tell that d——d Dutchman that if he don't get some better brandy, I'll never pay him another penny!"

Fox also thought this pretty strong for the pure, broken-hearted maiden Mrs. Winslow's bill of complaint against Lyon showed her to be, and he accordingly made a note of the same, as her friend returned to the bar-room and paid for the liquor, while saying to the land-lord that the madam desired him to say that the brandy was perfectly exquisite in flavor.

Presently Mrs. Winslow called out, "Come, Le Compte, get in here!" when he ran out with the alacrity of a carriage spaniel, sprang into the carriage, took the reins, and drove away towards the country, looking like a pretty daisy in the shade of a gigantic sunflower.

5

CHAPTER XI.

MANY other conveyances were passing to and fro, and Fox's first impulse was to secure a seat in some one of them and follow the couple in the direction they had taken. But he recollected that it might cause either Mrs. Winslow, or the little fellow at her side to know him again, which would prove disastrous, and he was consequently obliged to apply his pump to the important little Dutchman who owned the half-way house, and who was busying himself around the cool, pleasant bar-room, making the place as attractive as possible, and singing lustily in his own mother-tongue.

" Good morning to you ! " said Fox cheerily, stepping to the bar in a way that indicated his desire to imbibe.

" Good mornings mit yourself," answered the lively proprietor, getting behind the bar nimbly ; " Beer ? "

"Yes, thank you," replied Fox, ' a schnit, if you please. Won't you drink with me?"

"Oh, ya, ya; I dank you; I dank you;" and there were as many smiles on his honest face as bubbles upon his good beer.

The glasses touched, Fox said, "Here's luck!" and the landlord met it with "Best resbects, mister!"

In good time two more schnits followed, and as the landlord was each time requested to join with Fox, he was so pleased with his liberality and apparent good feeling that he beamed all over like a sunny day in June.

"You have a beautiful place here," said Fox.

"Oh, so, so!" answered the landlord with a quick, deprecatory shrug which meant that he was very well satisfied with it.

"I was never here before."

"No?—So? I guess mebby I don't ever have seen you. Don't you leef py Rochester?—no?"

"No, I live in Buffalo, and I just came over to Rochester on a little business. Having plenty of time, I thought I would stroll out a bit this morning."

"Ya, I get a good many strollers dot same way. Eferypody goes out by der Bort."

"The Bort?"

"Ya, ya, der Bort—Bort Charlotte."

"Is this the way to Charlotte?"

"To be certainly. When you come five miles auf, **den** you stand by der Bort, sure."

"And so that is where the big woman and the little man were going?" asked Fox carelessly.

"Sure, sure," said the landlord with a knowing wink; and then taking a very large pinch of snuff, and laying his forefinger the whole length of his rosy nose, added with an air of great importance and mystery, "I tell you, py Jupiter, I don't let somebody got rooms *here !*"

"That's right, old fellow!" said Fox, slapping the honest beer-vender on the shoulder. "Be unhappy and you will be virtuous !"

"Vell," continued the Teuton, excitedly lapsing into nis own vernacular, *"es macht keinen unterschied;* I don't got mein leefing dot way. I—I vould pe a bolitician first !"

Fox expressed his admiration for such heroism, and purchased a cigar to assist the landlord in his efforts to avoid the necessity of either renting rooms to ladies and gentlemen of Mrs. Winslow's and Le Compte's standing, or of accepting the more unfortunate emergency of becoming a "bolitician."

Then they both seated themselves outside the house, underneath the shaded porch, and chatted away about current events, Fox all the time directing the conversation in a manner so as to draw out the genial Teuton on the subject which most interested him, and was successful to the extent of learning that Le Compte was what the landlord termed a "luffer," evidently meaning a loafer; that several months before, they came there together desiring a room, which had been refused; but he had directed them to the Port, where they had evidently been accommodated, as they had after that, until this time, regularly went in that direction, always stopping at his place for a glass of his best brandy ; and that they had also always came there together until within a few weeks, since when, for some reason, this Le Compte had walked out to the hotel, where she had overtaken him with her carriage and driver, when the driver would be sent back to the city, and Le Compte taken in for the drive to Charlotte, as Fox had seen. He also learned that on their return, which was generally towards evening, the driver met them at the same place, when the latter took the reins, and Le Compte, somewhat soiled from his trip, walked into the city.

Fox concluded that there would be no better time than the present to learn something further concerning Le Compte, and after enjoying himself in the vicinity for a short time, came back to the hotel, took a hearty German dinner, and after another stroll secured a room for a short nap, as he told the landlord, but really for the purpose of observation. About six o'clock he saw the driver coming to the hotel from towards Rochester, and in about a half an hour afterwards noticed the carriage containing Mrs. Winslow and Le Compte coming down the road from Charlotte. The couple seemed very gay and lively, and drove up to the hotel with considerable dash and spirit. They both drank, as in the morning, while the driver resumed his old place by the side of Mrs. Winslow ; and as they were about to depart, Fox heard the woman say to Le Compte: "No, not again until Saturday; I'll try to be a little earlier." Then the carriage went away, Le Compte loitering about for a few minutes, after which he started off on a brisk walk towards town.

As the evening was drawing on, Fox hurried down to the bar-room, paid his bill, and bidding his host good-by, trudged on after the little fellow, keeping him well in sight, though remaining some distance behind to escape observation, but gradually closing in upon him, until, when they had arrived within the thickly settled portion of the city, they were trudging along quite convenient to each other.

The lamps now began to flare out upon the town, and the gay shops were lighted as Fox followed his man in and out, up and down the streets. Le Compte first went to a restaurant just beyond the Arcade in Mill street, where he got his supper, and afterwards promenaded about the streets in an aimless sort of a way for some little time, after which he returned to the Arcade and seemingly anxiously inquired for letters at the post-office. He got several, but was evidently either disappointed at what he had received, or at not receiving what he had expected. In any event he cautiously peered into Lyon's closed offices, as if hoping to find some one there. Disappointed in this also, he went directly to State Street, near Main, where, after looking about for a moment, he suddenly disappeared up a stairway leading to the upper stories of a large brick block. Fox quickly followed, and was able to catch sight of the little fellow just as he was entering a room at the side of the hall. He waited until everything was quiet, and then approached the door. The light from the single jet in the hallway was not sufficient for the purpose, but with the aid of a lighted match he was able to trace upon a neat card tacked to the door the inscription :

B. JEROME LE COMPTE,

POSITIVE, PROPHETIC, HEALING AND TRANCE MEDIUM.

Psychrometrist, Clairvoyant, and Mineral Locater.

As Fox had succeeded in "locating" his man, he returned to his boarding-house, wrote out his report and posted it, and after carelessly dropping into the restaurant under Washington Hall, where he took a dish of ice-cream and found means to inform Bristol of the latest development, he returned and retired for the night well satisfied with his day's work, and fully resolved to be on hand for Saturday's sport at Charlotte.

I received Fox's report the next noon, and not a half-hour afterwards the splendid Harcout cam: rushing in.

"Pinkerton, Pinkerton," he exclaimed excitedly, "here's something which we must attend to at once—at once, mind you, or—bless my soul ! I'm afraid I left it at the St. Nicholas. How could I be so careless !"

Harcout grew red in the face and plunged into all his pockets wildly, utterly regardless of his exquisite make-up, until quite exhausted.

" Why, Harcout, you're excited. Tell me what's the matter, my man," said I, reassuringly.

"Matter? matter? everything's the matter. Here's something which should be acted upon at once, and like an ass I've left it at the hotel. I'll go back and get it immediately."

"Get what?" I asked him.

"Get a letter that I just received from Lyon. He's there all by himself, and they will draw him into some terrible confession. But I—I must get the letter," and Harcout grabbed his hat and gloves and started.

"Hold on, Harcout," I called to him, "what is that you have in your hand?"

"In my hand? Oh, just a private note I got in the same mail."

"Just look at it before you go," I suggested.

Harcout stopped in the door, examined the letter, pulled another from the inside of the envelope, and blurted out sheepishly : "Ah, bless my soul !—Pinkerton, this is just what I wanted. Here, quick, read them both."

I took the letters as Harcout sat down and fanned himself with his glove, and saw that they were dated from Rochester on the previous day. The first one was from Lyon, in which he stated that he had received the enclosed letter in the morning, probably shortly after Fox had strolled out Lake View Avenue, also expressing a desire that Harcout should submit it to me for advice as to the best course to be pursued, and have the reply telegraphed. The enclosed letter was from Le Compte to Lyon, insist-ing that he should immediately come to his rooms to receive information of the greatest importance. I did not let Harcout know that I had any information concerning Le Compte, but I saw that that portion of Fox's report which stated that he had followed Le Compte to the Arcade the previous evening, where the latter had anxiously inquired for mail, and after that had taken a peep into Lyon's offices, agreed with Lyon's letter as to the time when Le Compte probably expected an answer from him.

I was at loss to know what the dapper little fellow was driving at—whether he and Mrs. Winslow were after further blackmail, or whether he had secured some confession from her while she was lavishing her favors and money upon him, which the treacherous little villain was endeavoring to make bring a good price through Lyon's superstitious faith in the power of those who claimed supernatural powers and a profession of Spiritualism.

I at once decided to go to Rochester and interview this new apparition in the field in company with Lyon, and accordingly told Harcout that I would do so, and would immediately telegraph to Lyon to that effect; upon which he trotted away, announcing his determination to also telegraph, so that Lyon might see that he was "attending closely to our case," as he termed it.

As soon as he had left, I indicted a dispatch to Lyon, asking him to make an appointment with Le Compte for an interview on the next afternoon, when I would be there to accompany him; and after getting my supper took the evening train and arrived at Rochester the next noon.

5*

After taking dinner at the Waverly, I immediately proceeded to Lyon's offices. He seemed worried and anxious to see me, and felt extremely alarmed about the whole matter, having as yet kept it from his attorney. I had him send a message for him at once, and in a few minutes we were all three in consultation. His attorney, a Mr. Balingal, thought we were doing just right, and, on leaving, privately informed me that in no event should I allow any person that professed mediumistic powers to remain with Lyon alone, as he would be certain to do something which would in some way compromise the case.

A few minutes after Lyon's attorney had left, we took different routes, arriving at the hallway leading to Le Compte's rooms on State street at about the same time, ascending the staircase together. A negro, who had borne a second and a more imperative message to Lyon, was in waiting at the top, and smilingly showed us along the hall in the direction of Number 28, which afterwards proved to be Le Compte's seance-room. The little fellow himself here stepped out of an adjoining room with a very insinuating smile upon his face, which suddenly changed to a look of disappointment as he saw that Mr. Lyon had rather solidly-built company.

As Mr. Lyon entered the room, this Monsieur Le Compte undertook to close the door in my face; but I shoved myself into the room, and told the mineral locater, etc., that I was a friend of Mr. Lyon's, and insisted on being one of the party

Lyon began timidly looking around the gas lighted room—though it was not after three o'clock—which was filled with the ordinary paraphernalia for compelling awe and fear : "I understand you have some business with me. My name is Lyon."

"Yes, yes," he replied, "I have great business with you. But I can only make you my *one* confidant, Mr. Lyon."

"Oh, well, well, now," I interrupted, with some assumed bravado, "this sort of thing better play out before it begins. I am Mr. Lyon's friend, and whatever you have to say to him will have to be said before me. Isn't that so, Mr. Lyon ?"

Lyon assented feebly, and Le Compte asked : "Will you make me the pleasure of your friend's name ?"

"No matter, no matter," said I quickly, for I knew how weak Lyon was. "I am here as my friend's friend. He has nothing to say in this matter. You will have to inform me of your business with Mr. Lyon."

Le Compte suddenly arose from his chair, locked the door and put the key in his pocket. He then went to the windows, which were slightly raised on account of the heat, closed them, and lowered the curtains so as to shut out the light completely. Just as he had completed the work, which took him but a moment, I said to him sharply : "See here, sir, you will make this room uncomfortably warm for yourself as well as us, if you are not careful. Don't send us to perdition before our time, Le Compte."

He made no answer, and looked exceedingly meek; but I saw that he was determined to endeavor to play upon Lyon's feelings for future profit, even if the present interview offered none. He immediately seated himself at a table opposite us, and said to Lyon : " The clairvoyant state I will go into before anything I can reveal."

" Mr. Le Compte," I interrupted, noticing that Lyon was already weakening before the scoundrel's assumption, " if you have got anything to say to Mr. Lyon, go on and say it with your eyes open, like a man. We won't be humbugged by you or any one else ! "

He did go on now, and with his eyes open, and said : "Well, gentlemen, I know of this lady who troubles Mr. Lyon, and learn of much witnesses for his help. But the clairvoyant state gave it to me."

" No, no, my young fellow," said I, " we don't pay for that kind of evidence. If you have any evidence in your possession which will be of benefit to Mr. Lyon, I am prepared to receive and pay for it ; but clairvoyant evidence isn't worth a cent!"

" Well," he replied, somewhat ruffled, " I can go on the jury and swear clearly of this ! "

I then told him I was satisfied that he did not know the first principles of law and evidence, and that the probability was that he had no evidence in his possession at all. I spoke in a very loud tone of voice, and evidently frightened the little fellow considerably.

" You are much intractable—a much intractable man," he responded. " I could tell about you greatly to con vince you of my power; but it is impossible in double presence."

"All right," said I. "Mr. Lyon, I don't see as you have anything to do with this interview, and I want you to go right back to your office and remain there until I come!"

Lyon got up in a scared kind of way, and started hesitatingly towards the door, looking appealingly at me; but I paid no attention to it, and the little Frenchman instantly arose and politely showed him out, saying in a low voice: "My dear Mr. Lyon, it will be for your great interest to make appointment without the boor."

"Lyon will do nothing of the kind, you little villain," I said, as I saw he was shrewdly arranging for future business. "The 'boor,' as you are pleased to term me, has the whole charge of this business, and you will transact it with him or nobody."

Le Compte flushed, closed the door without another word, locked it, and put the key in his pocket.

I turned on him savagely with: "My friend, what do you mean? If you make a single treacherous motion, you'll never get out of this room alive!"

I was now thoroughly mad, and am sure that the little jackanapes saw it and felt that I might possibly serve him as he deserved, for he quickly and tremblingly said, "Oh, if that is the case, I have no objection if you the key hold; but in clairvoyant state we shall be alone and locked."

There was a bed in the room, and I suggested that he

looked flurried and had better take a rest upon it while going on with his story; but he seated himself at the opposite side of the table, and began putting his hands upon his eyes and drawing them away with an indescribably graceful, though rapid gesture. This he continued for some little time, when he brought his hands down upon the table with considerable force. Then he began the old humbug about my having had trouble with some one, somewhere in the United States, at some time or other about something; that there was another man of uncertain size, peculiar complexion, unusual hair, singular face, and a strange, general appearance; and that this difficulty was about money, he thought it would amount to from five hundred to one thousand dollars, and that I would receive this sum within a few weeks. As I said that this was absolutely true, he was greatly encouraged, and went on for some time in an equally silly and foolish manner. I stood it as long as I could, and finally said:

"See here, my friend, you and I must talk business!" upon which he was wide awake and quite ready to enter into earthly conversation.

"Well, sir, what *could* you want?"

"I want this nonsense stopped," I replied rising, at which he also jumped up nimbly.

"Well," he said, "this woman"—evidently referring to Mrs. Winslow, though no name had been mentioned—"once lived in Iowa with wrong names!"

"Oh, nonsense!" I replied, "I know that already."

"But," he continued quickly, I can furnish you the

name of another man—very rich, very rich he is, too—who should be by law more her husband."

"Well," said I angrily, though now fully believing the little fellow for the first time, "write this out fully ; give me the man's name, business or occupation ; his place of residence, his standing, etc. ; how he became acquainted with this woman and under what circumstances they lived together, and when and where ; and when you give me the information, if I find it reliable, I will pay liberally for it. If not, I won't pay you a cent. Now, do we understand each other ? "

" I think we do," he answered timidly.

"Le Compte," said I sternly, " there's no use of your practising this clairvoyant game any longer. You won't get a dollar out of it ; not a dollar. I understand all about it as well as you do. Now, have a care about yourself, sir, or one of these bright days you'll be coming up with a sudden turn."

I now started towards the door; but the persistent scamp seemed anxious to still keep me, on some manner of pretext, and stood holding the key in a confused, undecided way.

" Open that door, you villain ! " I demanded ; " open it at once, or you'll get into trouble."

He started suddenly, put the key in the lock, and then turned to me and asked : " Won't you give me opportunity to show you I do not swindle. Just let me make some few little passes over your head. I will sure put you to sleep quickly ! "

"I am not sleepy, nor do I need sleep now, thank you. I had a good nap about an hour since," I answered, laughing at the little fellow's annoyance. "Now open that door!"

Le Compte shrugged his handsome shoulders despairingly, unlocked the door, and as I passed out of the no less than robber's den—though under the guise of a mediumistic and spiritualistic blackmailing headquarters--he said: "Well, sir, I will think of this statement a great deal; but you are a very untractable man; a very untractable man—what might I call your name?"

"Oh, anything you like, my little man!" I replied pleasantly; "but mind, we won't have any more of this silly business. It won't pay, and you will certainly get into trouble from it. You may send the statement to George H. Bangs, at the post-office, by Monday noon, and if it is what you represent it to be, and reliable, you will be paid for it; but you may be very, very certain, Le Compte, that it will prove extremely unprofitable to you if you attempt any more of this humbuggery upon Mr. Lyon!"

With this admonition I left Le Compte's, and soon found Lyon in his office. We arranged that he should pay no further attention to either Le Compte's or any other person's communications concerning this case, but should at once turn them over to his attorneys, who should immediately forward them to me after reading them, as I was satisfied that if Le Compte had any evidence he would never swear to it when the case was tried, and only desired to blackmail Lyon on his own account, while playing the necessary male friend and confidant to Mrs. Winslow, who for some reason seemed to have a strange and unexplainable liking for the little Monsieur, although exercising great care that her passion for him should not become a matter for public knowledge and comment.

CHAPTER XII

AT last the promised Saturday came, and there were
at least three people in Rochester who looked
forward to a pleasant day, and were up betimes that they
might get an early start. Mrs. Winslow, from her sumptuous apartments, looked out upon the streets and the
glorious morning as if it had come too soon—as it always
does to those who have not clean hearts and clean lives—
and, *en deshabille*, gazed down through her rich lace curtains upon the early passers stepping off with a brisk
tread to their separate labors, with a look of contempt.

Nature had been wantonly generous with Mrs. Winslow,
and as she stood there in her loose morning robes, the
first soft breaths that come with the sun from the far-off
Orient playing hide-and-seek among the sumptuous hangings of her room, and giving just the least possible motion
to her matchlessly luxuriant black hair, while the mellow
and golden rays of the sun, which was just peeping over

the roofs and the chimneys, shimmered upon her through the curtains, lighting her great gray eyes with a wondrous lustrousness, heightening the fine color of her face, and giving to her voluptuous form an added grace—this utterly lone woman had not in her heart an iota of tenderness for, or sympathy with, the glories without, and was as dead to every good thing in life as though carved from marble by some sculptor, as she really had been carved from stone, or ice, by nature. As she stood there by the window, regarding the passers with such a wise and ogreish air that Fox, behind the blinds in his window opposite, could not but couple her in his thoughts with some splendid beast of prey—if Mother Blake or the voluble Rev. Bland could have seen her, the years that had passed would have been swept away, and in the mature woman and the conscienceless adventuress would have been recognized the raven of the Detroit cottage, that, as Lilly Nettleton, in a habit that ravens have, glided noiselessly about the other sumptuous apartments, gathering together what pleased its fancy—not forgetting the money which was to have been used in the cursed church interests, and a gold watch, which the raven wore to this day—and then, kissing its beak to the heavily sleeping man, for all the world like a raven, had passed out into the storm and the night.

In a few moments she retired from the window, and after dressing passed out upon the street, and went to the falls for a short walk and an appetite, and then went to the Washington Hall restaurant, where she had quite fre quently taken her meals since she had incidentally learned that Bristol was a retired Montreal banker, as gossip had it now among the Spiritualists; and it was evident that persons of that grade of recommendation weie of peculiar interest to Mrs. Winslow. For hours of dalliance, the aristocratic though impecunious popinjay, Le Compte, would more than answer; but when it came to a matter of serious work, and when a new source of income was to be sought, Mrs. Winslow, being a shrewd and able professor of the art of fascination which secured her an independent and elegant livelihood, in connection with her ability to compel a large number of people to pay her for guessing at what had befallen them and what might befall them, she invariably sought gentlemen on the shady side of life, with judgment and discretion, who knew a good thing when they saw it, and who were both able and willing to carry their bank accounts into their aged knight-errantry.

Lyon was not a handsome man, but he had vast wealth. His weazen face, his grizzly hair, his repulsive, tobacco-stained mouth, were naught against him. His passion for her had brought her thousands upon thousands of dollars—would bring her, she hoped, as much more. Here was Bristol. He was not handsome, he was not a Canadian Adonis, he incessantly smoked a very ugly pipe fully as old as himself. But he had some way got the reputation of being "a retired Canadian banker" among these people, and Mrs. Winslow's heart warmed towards him the way it had towards a hundred others when she had wanted them to walk into her parlor as the ancient spider had desired of the fly.

So she had begun weaving a shining web of loving looks, of tender glances, of dreamy sighs, and of graceful manœuvres of a general character about the unsuspecting Bristol, that resulted in pecuniary profit to the old maids, who, nevertheless, with the quick instinct of three jealous women of economical build and mature years, had already begun to hate her as a rival, and pour into Bristol's alert ears sad tales about the splendid charmer, all of which were properly reported to me by the " retired Montreal banker," who had suddenly found himself a prize worthy to be sought for, and fought for, if necessary, by four determined women, one of whom hungered for his supposed wealth, and three of whom possessed the more desperate, life-long hunger whose appeasing is worth a severe struggle.

After her breakfast, which, unfortunately, had not given her an opportunity for bestowing a graceful nod or a winning smile upon Bristol, whom the old maids had furnished a superb breakfast in his own apartment, Mrs. Winslow returned to her rooms and seated herself at her windows, where she read the morning paper for a little time. She then disappeared from Fox s sight for a half-hour or so, when, just as he was about leaving his watch at his window he noticed her descend the stairs, and, after looking cautiously about for a moment, deposit a card behind her own sign, which was attached to the frame of the outer doorway leading to her rooms. As soon as she had

retired, and before she could have returned to her windows, Fox slipped down and out across the street, and
removing the card from its novel depository, saw written
upon it:

" Le Compte :—Will be at the Garden with carriage at
ten, prompt.

" MRS. W."

Fox had no more than time to return the card to its
place when he saw the person to whom it was addressed
turn into St. Paul street from East Main. He accordingly got back to his old post as rapidly as possible, and
watched the young Frenchman saunter along towards the
hallway as if carelessly taking his morning walk. He was
irreproachably dressed, as usual, and was daintily smoking
a cigarette with that inimitable grace with only which a
Frenchman or a Spaniard can smoke. After arriving at
the hallway, as if undecided whether he would go farther
up the street or not, he leaned carelessly against the sign,
and in a moment had deftly whipped the card out of its
hiding-place. He then started up the street saunteringly,
and when about a half-block distant, read the card, which
seemed to give him much pleasure, as he smilingly wrote
something upon it, and after walking a short distance,
turned suddenly and walked rapidly back, dexterously depositing the card in its strange receptacle, without
scarcely varying his pace or direction, and quickly passed
on to Main street, turning down that thoroughfare.

Fox noticed that Mrs. Winslow had witnessed this incident from her windows, and at the moment when her form had disappeared, he swiftly stepped across the street and read the reply, which ran thus :

"Your announcement makes pleasure in your lover's soul, and your name is saluted by the lips of

"LE COMPTE."

Fox had just time to slip into a tobacconist's for a cigar when Mrs. Winslow came down stairs, took the card out of its resting-place, and after going down the street for some slight purchase, returned to her rooms and prepared for the drive to Charlotte.

At half-past nine Mrs. Winslow's carriage arrived and in a few minutes after she was leisurely riding down Main street, and from thence out through State street and Lake View Avenue towards the Port. As I had nothing to do until Monday's interview with Le Compte, and time hung heavily upon my hands, I had decided to make one of the party.

I knew the direction Mrs. Winslow would take, and so securing a position on the corner of Main and State streets, I had but a little time to wait before I saw the gay madam pass, and also noticed Fox at an opposite corner evidently making sure of her direction ; for, as soon as he saw her carriage turn down State street, he immediately started for the depot, from which a train left for Charlotte at ten o'clock, so that he could be at that place, under any circumstances, some time before the happy and unsuspecting couple should have arrived.

At about train-time Fox bought a cigar and took a seat in the smoking-car, while I purchased a cheap edition of one of Dickens's stories and settled myself down in a ladies' car.

The trip to Charlotte was soon made through a beautiful country where the farmers were busy stacking their grain, threshing, and, in some instances, turning the black loam to the sun that it might early mellow for the next year's seed-time, and in a half-hour we were at Charlotte, where the beautiful lake is seen at one's feet, with its rippling waves dotted here and there by a hundred dreamy sails and lazy steamers from as many waiting ports.

Fox immediately made inquiries of the villagers where he could find the road leading into Charlotte from Rochester, and started out towards it from the depot at a brisk walk, while I waited until he had got well under way, when I took a short stroll among the warehouses and shipping of the harbor, and then went to the only hotel of any importance the place contained, where I knew Mrs. Winslow and Le Compte would be likely to stop, and engaged a room in the front part of the house, where I resumed my story and waited, like Micawber, for " something to turn up."

I had been engaged at my book but a short time when I saw Fox come up the street towards the hotel at a rapid pace, flushed and perspiring freely as from a very long and rapid walk, and but a moment afterwards also saw the dashing Rochester turnout whirling up to the hotel.

'The arrival at the hotel of the couple bore out the truth of the statement of the little Dutchman, contained in Fox's report of his trip to the half-way house, as the habitués of the house seemed quite accustomed to their presence and the employees stepped about nimbly, as they generally do at hotels as a greeting to good custom ers, and they generally do not when persons of common appearance arrive.

As good luck would have it, after a few moments had elapsed, " Mr. and Mrs. Jones, of Rochester," as Fox saw they had registered, were ushered into a room adjoining my own, and between which, as is quite common at hotels, there was a door, which might be opened for the purpose of throwing the rooms *en suite,* as occasion required.

Although I was prevented from seeing the couple, their voices, which were both familiar to me, could not be mis-taken ; and I could not restrain a smile as I listened to the little Frenchman's voluble and peculiarly-constructed expressions of endearment, and the coarser, but none the less tender, responses of the virtuous Mrs. Winslow, whose life had been shattered, heart smashed to atoms, and good name defamed, by the tyrant man in the person of the weak but wealthy Lyon, and to think how much nearer I was to the quarry than Fox himself, who in this instance was making noble efforts to bring down his game without "flushing" it.

For the sake of the public whose servant I have been for the last thirty years, I would blush to put on paper what I know to have occurred in the adjoining room, and

6

which only served to further convince me of the depths of infamy to which she had sunk; and I will pass on to those things only necessary to acquaint the reader with my plan of operation to bring her into the public notoriety and scorn which she had years before only too richly deserved.

But a short time had elapsed after Mrs. Winslow and Le Compte had been given their room when I heard Fox's footsteps coming along the hall. He passed their room slowly, evidently locating it, and after a few moments stealthily returned and listened at the door. He then stole away, but returned again with a bold, firm step, as though conscious of being on legitimate business, walked right up to the door and gave the knob a quick turn, as if he had intended to at once walk into the room.

The door did not open, however, and Fox stepped back as if surprised, saying : " Why, I can't be mistaken ; the register surely said Room 30 !" while within there were quick, though smothered exclamations of surprise, fright, and rage of an unusually profane nature.

Fox immediately returned to the attack as if certain that he was in the right, and knocked at the door sharply.

There was no response but the quick hustlings about the room, from which I, as an attentive listener with my ear close to the key-hole, learned that the inmates were preparing for discovery.

Fox knocked again, this time louder and more persistently than at first.

I now plainly heard Mrs. Winslow ordering Le Compte

under the bed among the dust, bandboxes, and unmention
ables, at which he protested with innumerable " *Sacrès !* "
But she was relentless, and finally, seeing that he would
go no other way, took him up like a recalcitrant cur and
flung him under bodily.

Again Fox attacked the door, shook the knob furiously,
and knocked loud enough to raise the dead, following it
up with : " Say you ?—Jones ? Why in thunder don't
you open the door ? "

At this Mrs. Winslow plucked up the courage of desperation, and asked in a loud and injured voice, " Who's
there ? "

" Why, me, of course ; Barker, Jones's partner.   I
want to see Jones ! "

" What Jones do you want ? " asked Mrs. Winslow, to
get time to think further what to do.

" Jones, of Rochester, of course," yelled Fox. " Two
ship-loads of spoiled grain's just come in ; don't know
what to do with 'em."

" Sink 'em ! " responded Mrs. Winslow, breathing
freer.

" Where's Jones ? " persisted Fox, banging away at the
door again.

" There's no Jones here, you fool ! " answered the
woman hotly.

" Yes there is, too," insisted Fox. " Landlord told me so."

" Well," parried the female, raising her voice again,
" Jones ain't in the wheat trade at all ; he's a professor of
music ; and besides that, he ain't in here, either."

"Oh, beg pardon, ma'am," said Fox apologetically. "It isn't your Jones I want *this time*, then. Hope I haven't disturbed you, madam," and he walked away, having clinched the matter quite thoroughly enough for any twelve honest and true men under the sun.

Mrs. Winslow stuck her head out of the door, launched a threat, coupled with a well-defined oath, against Fox, who was leisurely strolling along the hall, to the effect that he ought to be ashamed of himself for "insulting a defenceless woman in that way, and that if he came there again she would have him arrested." To which he cheerily responded, " No offence meant, ma'am ; 'fraid the wheat'd spoil, ye see ; " and as he went whistling down the stairs, she slammed the door, locked it, drew the trembling Le Compte from under the bed, and amid a chime of crockery set him upon his feet again with a snap to it, and then threw herself into a rocking-chair and burst into tears, insisting that she was the most abused woman on the face of earth, and that Le Compte, with his " *Sacrès !*" and "*Diables !*" hadn't the sense of a moth or the muscle of an oyster, or he would have followed the brute and given him a sound beating !

Not desiring to be seen by Fox, I ordered my dinner sent to my room, as did the unhappy couple in the adjoining apartment, who seemed to be greatly put out by the intrusion, and who were for an hour after speculating as to the cause of the interruption, and as to whether it was accidental or not.

"We mustn't come here any more, Le Compte," said the woman dolefully.

"And for why, my angel precious?" anxiously asked the man.

"Why, do you know," replied Mrs. Winslow with earnestness, "I sometimes really believe I am being watched!"

"No, that was impossible!" said Le Compte, with a start.

"And sometimes," she continued, paying no attention to him, "it seems as though I could not stand this terrible keeping up appearances any longer."

"You should have pleasure in the appearance," responded Le Compte insinuatingly, "it breaks him down already. He is now like one weak infant."

"That's so, that's so," she answered quickly, in a tone of vengeful joyousness. "I'll bring the old devil to my feet yet. I'll crush him out and ruin his fortune, if it takes me all my life. I'll get the biggest part of it, too; and then, Le Compte, we'll get out of this cursed country and enjoy ourselves the rest of our lives."

"Yes, in Paris, the magnificent, the beautiful, the sublime! Then we will live in one heaven of love. Oh, beautiful, beautiful!" cried the little Frenchman excitedly.

"There, Le Compte," said his companion, suddenly becoming practical again, "don't make a fool of yourself! Take this bill and go down and get a bottle of wine; and mind you, don't keep the change either."

As the train returned at two, and I had but little time to reach it, as soon as Le Compte had come back with the wine and they had become sufficiently noisy to admit of it, I quietly left my room, paid my bill, went to the train, avoiding Fox entirely, and, with him, was soon again in Rochester, leaving the roystering couple at the little hotel at Charlotte building their vain dreams and air-castles about crushing out Lyon—which would have been an easy matter if left to himself—their beautiful, magnificent, and sublime Paris, and their " one heaven of love " within it.

As soon as Fox stepped from the train I quietly handed him a slip of paper directing him to make his report to me at the Waverley House, where I was stopping under an assumed name, which he assured me he would do, without a word being spoken or even a look of recognition being passed.

Although the public may not be aware of it, this is an absolute necessity in detective service. Though I employ hundreds of persons as detectives, preventive police, and in clerical duties, at my different agencies, on no occasion and under no circumstances is there ever on the street, or in any public place whatever, the slightest token by which the stranger might know that there had ever been any previous communication between any of my people.

On the next day, Sunday, Lyon called to see me at the hotel and brought with him two notes from Le Compte— one having been received late Saturday afternoon, and the other delivered at his house that morning—both imperatively insisting that Lyon should come to his rooms and leave that " untractable man " behind.

I complimented him extensively on his having refrained from visiting the winsome little villain who seemed determined to get Lyon within his power. He solemnly pledged his word that he would have nothing whatever to do with the man, and would bluff him in every advance that he made ; and in order to clinch it, I read him choice extracts from Fox's report regarding the Charlotte party of the day before, interspering it with a few of the still choicer items that had come under my own observation.

" My God ! " exclaimed Lyon, as I concluded, " are they *all* that way ? "

" Your experience and mine," I smilingly replied, " would almost point to the fact that a very decided majority of them are."

CHAPTER XIII.

NO jury in the land would render a verdict against a
man on the unsupported evidence of a woman
whose character was so vile as we had already found
Mrs. Winslow's to be ; and I would have paid no further
attention to the little Frenchman, had I not suspected
from his expensive style of living, and from Mrs. Winslow's injunctions to him regarding not swindling her in
so small a matter as a bottle of wine, that his necessities
and cupidity might cause him to make some tangible dis-
closure regarding her, that would give us a clue to other
information against her further than that which Bangs
would probably secure in the West, as I never use detective evidence when it can be avoided, and knew that
a perfect mountain of criminal transactions could be eventually heaped up against her which could be secured from
reliable parties, who could have no other possible interest

in her downfall than a desire to promote the personal good of society.

Le Compte did not desire to see me again, and had made strenuous efforts to prevent it and secure a surreptitious interview with Lyon instead. Failing in this, at the last moment, I had received a very terse note from him to the effect that he did not desire to transmit any statement by mail, but would take it as an honor, etc., if I would call at his place at ten o'clock, Monday morning, which I did, finding the little fellow in a gorgeous dressing-gown, freshly shaved, and in a neat and orderly state generally.

"Well, my young friend," said I, "I suppose you have decided to give me some information this morning."

"Do I get good pay?" he asked in response.

"You will get good pay if you have a good article for sale," I replied.

"Humph!" he responded, with a soft shrug of his delicate shoulders.

"Are you ready to make such a sale?" I asked.

"But where comes my money?" inquired Le Compte, suspiciously.

"It is right here," I answered, slapping my pocket in a hearty way.

"But suppose it shall stay there, then where is Le Compte?" he persisted with a doleful look which was irresistibly funny.

"It *will* stay there," I replied, "in case you attempt to play any of your tricks, my little fellow."

6*

"How shall I then know I am to be paid?"

"You will have to take my word for it."

"But I have not pleasure in your acquaintance; how can I be sure?" he continued anxiously.

"Le Compte, swindler as you are, you *know* that I am an honest man. This quibbling is utterly foolish and sim‧ple. I am acting entirely for Mr. Lyon in this matter, and should you write to him or call upon him a hundred times, you would get nothing from him but a bluff. Here are your two notes," I continued, producing them, "one written Saturday, the other yesterday. The only response you got to them was, silence—and this interview. I thought we understood each other already."

I saw that he was still undecided about saying whatever he might have to say, and tenacious of sustaining his professional reputation as a clairvoyant. I might have easily frightened him into submission by the slightest reference to the occurrences of the previous day, but knew that this would have the effect of putting Mrs. Winslow on her guard, as she was already becoming suspicious and anxious, and preferred getting at his communication in the ordinary way. After he had sat musing for a time he suddenly asked:

"How great will be my pay?"

"What do you think the information is worth?" I said.

He looked at me as if fixing a price in his mind that I would stand, and replied:

"Certain, a thousand dollars."

"That is a good deal of money, Le Compte," I said

"*You little villain!*" *I shouted, advancing upon him threateningly:—*

pleasantly. "I hardly think you can divulge a thousand dollars' worth. But if you can give me reliable information of a satisfactory character, I think I could pay you three hundred dollars.

"Now?" he inquired, suddenly.

"Oh, no, oh, no," I replied as quickly; "no, sir, *not* until we find the information you give is reliable."

This dampened the little fellow wonderfully, but he finally said: "Well, the evidence is certain, but I must offer it to you by clairvoyance," and he immediately arose and began darkening the room as on the previous interview, which act I interrupted by stepping to the window he had just darkened, and jerking the curtain as high as it would roll, opening the window, and flinging the blinds open with a slam.

"You little villain!" I shouted, advancing upon him threateningly, "I will wring your neck if you don't stop this contemptible nonsense!" while he slunk into the corner, like the mean coward that he was. I could scarcely keep my hands off the little puppy; but recollecting that I was there for quite another purpose, I said:

"Le Compte, this is the last time I shall come here, and it is the last time you will have an opportunity of making a dollar out of any information you may possess. Now, sir," I said, savagely, starting towards the door, "you will give it to me, trusting entirely to my honor to pay you for it, or you will never get a cent for it on earth."

The little fellow turned towards me imploringly, with a

"Please don't go.   My dear sir, you are so greatly abrupt We have no men like you in La Belle France."

"Heaven knows, I hope but few *like* you," I responded. "Now, which is it, yes, or no?   I will give you just thirty seconds in which to answer," and I timed him, thoroughly resolved to do as I had said.

Before the expiration of the time mentioned, Le Compte sat down, and with a despairing shrug of the shoulders, said "Yes."

I immediately returned, sat down in front of him, and said, "Well, Le Compte, now go ahead with your story like a man."

"What must it be like?" he asked innocently.

"What must it be like?" I repeated, aghast.   "Why, you don't intend to manufacture a story for me against this woman, do you?"

"Oh, no, no, never.   But I must know first how bad it must be, when it is worth three hundred dollars, which you call such great money?"

"Well," said I, all out of patience, "if you know of any occasion when this woman has been with any man as his wife, or his mistress, and can give names, dates, and places, and under what circumstances, and this information on examination proves so reliable that we can get other witnesses besides yourself—persons of credibility and reputation—to testify to it, I will pay you three hun dred dollars.   Isn't that plain enough?"

"Will you put it to paper?"

"No, sir, you have my word for it, that's all."

Le Compte tapped the floor with his delicate foot a moment, and I saw the impostor was in real misery. He had a sort of affection for the woman, which she had more than reciprocated. He could lean on the strong, daring nature she possessed, and go to her with all his troubles and disappointments and get help. She had promised him that, as soon as she had mulcted Lyon of the hundred thousand dollars, he should share it with her in his own beautiful Paris. All his self-interest laid in and with the woman ; but need for money was pressing, and there were a million other women as impressible to his charms as she had been. Here was an opportunity to make a few hundred dollars by betraying her ; but in doing so he still might not get the money, and she might at once discover from what source the information had come, and he knew enough about Mrs. Winslow to be sure that she dared any mode of revenge that best suited her fancy, and he had a wholesome fear of her. I could see that all these things were flitting through his mind, as plainly as the reader can see them upon this printed page, and to some extent pitied his weakness and indecision.

"Or," said I encouragingly, "as you undoubtedly know Mrs. Winslow intimately, and are very much in her company, if you know of any occasion when she had, while here in Rochester or in the vicinity, say Batavia, Syracuse, or Port Charlotte, for instance, gone with some one of her many favorites, and under an assumed name— Brown, Jones, or anything of the kind—to a hotel where they had been assigned a room, and had occupied it together for several hours, and you could put us on track of persons of reliability who would be willing to come into court and swear to such facts—I presume there are many persons who could and would with whom you are acquainted—I would pay you the amount named at once."

This was cutting pretty close to a tender subject, and before I had half finished my remarks he started, and looked me in the face in a suspicious, apprehensive manner, eyeing me closely until I had finished. But my manner and looks betraying no knowledge on my part of any such facts hinted at, he relapsed into a puzzled, nonplussed look that was really ridiculous.

"No, no," he said slowly and cautiously. "I have no such valuable evidence. That would be much more worth than a thousand dollars—much more worth. But I can do what you first say, and rest me on the honor of your word."

"Go on, then," said I.

"Well, we shall go back almost a year. I met first Mrs. Winslow at Port Charlotte, when she was from Canada returning."

"Did she formerly live in Canada?" I asked.

"No, not for a great time; but has had much travel and friends there. I first see her at Charlotte. I go there to take a boat. She comes from the boat there. Lyon meets her, and I think her his wife, he is so much happy. I like her so much that I do not take the boat. I follow her back to the city here, and find her beautiful rooms, when I discover she is not Lyon's wife, but his mistress ; but I still have for her admiration, and one day she comes to me for her future in clairvoyance."

"And then she became your mistress ?" I inquired, smiling at his earnestness.

" No, no, no—never ! " he replied quickly, growing red as a rose ; "I became her *friend !* "

Le Compte did not know how near he came to expressing the truth while endeavoring to avoid it, but continued :

"I became her friend, and we came to each other for advice. She has great faith—great faith," repeated Le Compte, with much emphasis on the expression, which seemed to please him, "in my clairvoyance powers. I give her much comfort. She gives me great confidence of her affairs, and shows me how rich Lyon makes her. I see her often—very often, at the Hall and here in my apartments. She gives me much confidence of her affairs still, and 1 am informed when she makes Canada some visits. She goes much to Canada, and I ask her why ? She does not tell me, but laughs in my face, and shows me much money, which she ever brings back. I shake my finger at her so (illustrating), and say to her : 'You cannot hide from Le Compte,' which she answers : 'No, I will not. I go for money. See !'—when she would shake many bills in my face—' I make him come down, too !'"

" Did she give you the man's name ? "

"I *got* it," continued Le Compte proudly, " with much wine—*and* clairvoyance !"

"Oh, confound your eternal clairvoyance!" said L
"I want the facts."

"But I got facts *with* clairvoyance," persisted the im·
perturbable Le Compte. "Little by little, patience by
patience, at the end I got confession from her——"

"Which was? "——

"Which was," continued Le Compte, taking his time,
"that Mrs. Winslow had got great power over a Toronto
merchant with much wealth and great family, by name
Devereaux."

"How long had she known him?"

"I know not that—five, four, three years, I will think."

"Did you ever see this Devereaux?"

"Oh, no, no—never; but it is all certain that I speak.
Here," continued Le Compte, stepping nimbly to a sec·
retary and producing a photograph, which he handed to
me, "here you will find the face of Devereaux. Many,
many times I have seen the color of his money."

"And does Mrs. Winslow visit Canada for the purpose
of meeting this man still?" I asked.

"Certain," he answered promptly; then, after a little
pause, as if doubtful of the propriety of what he was
about to say, but finally resolving to earn his money, if
possible, "and she shall go there once more in the next
week."

I began to think that the little Frenchman had really a
good article for sale, and made full memoranda of all the
main points. I asked him some further questions, the an·
swers to which showed conclusively that Mrs. Winslow

had made a full confidant of him concerning the Canadian affair, at least; that she had secured a vast amount
of money from Devereaux at the same time that Lyon
was breaking her heart; and that, whether Devereaux
was fated to go through the same final experience as Lyon,
or not, that he had undergone and was undergoing the
same preliminary experience.

At the close of the interview I informed Le Compte
that his information was quite satisfactory, and that it only
remained for me to prove its correctness in order to permit the payment of the money, which, however, should
necessarily be on the additional condition that he at once
secured for us information as to the date on which the
madam was to make her profitable little pleasure-trip to
Toronto.

This he agreed to do, and I left him; not, however,
until he had anxiously requested to know more about me,
and where and when he was to receive his money. I told
him that I was a travelling man; that I had no permanent
residence, was here and there all over the country; but
that the moment we ascertained the truth of his statements, which would be very soon, he should be compen-
sated.

I communicated to Lyon the facts elicited during this
interview, which completely overwhelmed him with the
perfidy of human nature in general, and woman in particular; but gave him considerable encouragement concerning the progress of our work; and after directing
Bristol, through the post, to continue playing the *rôle* of

the banker, and to keep himself in preparation for tele-graphic instructions, returned to New York.

All this time Bristol was in clover. The three old maids, Tabitha, Amanda, and Hannah, had looked him over and saw that he was a good man to tie to. Here was a man, they agreed, who had come in among them a perfect stranger, and yet so possessed was he of a frank, winsome way, and such a reliable, honorable demeanor had he exhibited towards them, three lone and defenceless women as they were, that they had instinctively felt that they could trust him; nay, even more, they were sure that they could lean upon him, as it were; take him into their confidence; share their joys with him, rely on him to sympathize with them in all their sorrows—in fact, make of him a sort of an affectionate Handy Andy—a good-natured and attractive attaché to their affections, and a profitable sign-post to their business.

Neither had any man ever before received such signs and tokens of a deep-seated and ineradicable affection.

Every morning he was awakened from his virtuous slumbers by the delicious music of a bird-training organ, which was wound in turn by the maidens and set inside his door, where, "in linked sweetness long drawn out," it galloped over the harmonies with: "Then you'll remem-ber me," "Don't be angry with me, Darling," "Who will care for Mother Now?" "Bonnie Charlie's Noo Awa'," "Annie Laurie," and like tender airs, until the poor man cursed the Three Graces of Washington Hall restaurant, and the detective service, threadbare.

After this delicious reminder of languishing love he was served with a breakfast fit for a king, at which Tabitha, Amanda, and Hannah in turn presided, and which was always graced by a large bouquet of flowers whose language and fragrance only breathed of love.

On these occasions the conversation never failed to turn upon Bristol's merits, the old maids' loneliness, and the superiority of women without physical beauties, but full of soul, over those more fortunate in flesh but wanting in spirituality. This was an advertisement for their own establishment, and a drive at Mrs. Winslow; and Bristol always acknowledged the force of the argument.

Whenever Mrs. Winslow took a meal at the restaurant, which had now become a frequent occurrence, just so certain was Bristol's corresponding meal served in the little snuggery, where, however busy they might be, one of the ancient ladies kept him good company and quickened his digestion with sparkling humor and witty jest, such only as can course through the flowery avenues of an aged spinster's mind, made fresh and blooming by the wild fancy of the second childhood of love's young dream; and at night, when the busy day was over and the vulgar public shut out by the well-bolted front door, the little snuggery always held the same wise old company, where Bristol, ripe in age and experience, passed an hour with the ladies over tea and sweetmeats, or wine and waffles, surrounded by the thrilled and blushing trio, who, preparatory to retiring, discovered to him as many of their combined charms as modesty would allow, and in their tender hearts built plans for the future when they would bodily possess Bristol—at least one of them, if the laws of society did prevent his making a sort of blessed trinity of himself for their benefit.

This course of procedure angered Mrs. Winslow. *Her* heart also yearned for the retired banker, and when she saw how securely he was being kept from her grasp by the wily old maids, she immediately began preparing a plan the execution of which would foil them, and eventually give her the coveted game all to herself. To this end she walked to and fro past the restaurant, and finally attracted the attention of Bristol while the old ladies were busily engaged elsewhere, and motioned to him in so imperative a way and with such earnestness, that he slipped out of the place, and at a careful distance followed her in the direction of the Falls Field Garden, where lovers often met and where there was no danger of interruption.

CHAPTER XIV.

SUPERINTENDENT BANGS arrived at Terre
Haute in good time, and found himself in one of
the greatest centres of Spiritualism in the world.

The very air seemed charged and surcharged with the
permeating power. People watching incoming trains
had a listless, far-away look, as though watching for the
dim spirits which were constantly expected from the other
land, but which never came. The clamorous cabmen
raised their sing-song voices as if only expecting, though
more than desiring, only shadowy freight. The regular
loiterers had long hair, cadaverous faces, and large, lustrous eyes, and where females appeared, they were generally in pinched faces, flowing hair, long pantaloons and
short gowns, as if ready for a grand Amazon-march upon
the gullible public.

On the way to the hotel every other stairway held the
sign of one or more clairvoyants, mediums, or astrologists,
and every manner of business seemed to have the ghostly

trail upon it. The pedestrians upon the streets, the men at their counters, the workmen at their trades, the women at their various employments, the common laborers at their most menial toil, each and every, from the highest to the lowest, seemed to have a weary, listless air, as if constant wrestling with communicating spirits healthier and more robust than themselves, had left a chronic exhaustion upon and with them.

At the hotel the register was thin and ghostly, the office was deserted and dreary, the meals were served in a listless, dreamy way, as if the guests were ghosts and the waiters not so good. In fact, the whole place and everything in it was tinctured with the common craziness, and gave the healthy, wide-awake stranger the impression of having suddenly come upon a community of mild lunatics, who were quite happy in the conviction that they were directing the affairs of both earth and heaven, and establishing pleasant, intramural relations between their chosen Hoosier City and the beautiful City beyond the River ; all of which would be very pleasant and profitable if anybody had ever come back from the undiscovered country to give us its geographical outlines, define its limits, or explain any profit that has accrued from becoming a monomaniac on a subject that has no relation whatever to the common needs and duties of life, and has never been known to give to the world or its society a single healthful, helpful nature or intellect.

Mr. Bangs was neither pleased with the hotel, or able to get much information while there, and consequently changed his quarters to Mrs. Deck's boarding-house, a long, rambling brick building, that at one time had been a fine residence after the Southern style. It was covered with moss and vines, and had a snug, pleasant appearance, while everything about the house had an air of quaint, attractive restfulness. Every person who has ever been in Terre Haute for a few days' stay, as Bangs was, will remember the genial old soul who presided over the destinies of this particular boarding-house—the fat, garrulous, whimpering, but kind-hearted Mrs. Deck ; her charming daughter, the blooming Belle Ruggles, by a former and more fortunate marriage, with her fair face and wealth of golden hair, flitting about the house—which was also the abode of spirits, mysterious materializations and unexplainable rappings—like a good, sensible spirit that *she* was, and letting her good sense and kind ways into the cobwebbed rooms and dark places, like an ever-changing though constant flood of sunlight ; and " Old Deck," as the boys called him, who believed in another kind of spirits still, and, when opportunity offered, became so full of them that he held a grand and extended " seance " on his own account.

People not only sought Mrs. Deck for good board, but for reliable neighborhood gossip ; and Mr. Bangs, learning of her reputation as a repository of news as well as a liberal dispenser of creature comforts, changed his quarters from the hotel to her place, and found from a few days in her company that she was a sort of historian, having at her tongue's end numberless incidents connected with the growth of the city and the family relations of **every** class of people in or near it.

He learned from her where the Hosfords had lived, but could get nothing particular regarding the woman herself, as Mrs. Deck had never seen her, and only knew of her by reputation, which she was sure had been good.

Mr. Bangs at once went into the country neighborhood where the Hosfords had lived, and found that they had removed to some point in Wisconsin, near Sheboygan Falls, the neighbors had heard, but he could not find that there had been a single trace of trouble at Terre Haute. All those who had known them spoke of them both in the highest terms. They had both been staunch members of the Methodist Church, and though plain, quiet farmers, had been considered prominent people in the neighborhood.

Hosford was remembered as a slow-going, easy-conditioned, good-natured fellow, but as honest as the day was long ; and no one had ever known aught against his wife, save that some of the old gossips thought that she had brought too much jewelry and fine clothing into the neighborhood with her. This, however, she had judiciously kept out of sight as much as possible, and, as far as could be learned, had led in every respect an exem. plary life.

From this point Mr. Bangs proceeded to Kalamazoo. The Nettleton family were gone, no one knew where ; but here he was told of the escapade to Detroit of Lilly Nettleton years before, enough of which had floated back to her native place—coupled with the old people's later sorrows, which were largely dilated upon—to account for the breaking up of the family and its members being scattered broadcast.

Accidentally at Kalamazoo, in conversation, with the clerk at the Kalamazoo House, who had formerly been employed at Detroit, and who was "up to snuff,' as he termed it, Bangs learned of Mother Blake, who had informed the clerk of Bland's unfortunate experience with one Lilly Mercer. He also got from the clerk a description of Mother Blake sufficiently comprehensive to enable him to find her if she were still at Detroit, where he at once proceeded.

On arriving in that city he went to the Michigan Exchange Hotel, and, through the courtesy of the proprietors, was allowed to look up the records of the house.

It was fifteen years previous that the man who said he was "from Bland" met Lilly Nettleton at the depot and had taken her to the Michigan Exchange to meet the reverend circuit-rider ; but after he had got at the dusty records he found on the register, evidently in the handwriting of a clerk: "Lilly Mercer, Buffalo, Room 34," under date of August 15, 1856, and also the names of "R. J. Hosford, Terre Haute, Room 98," and "Lilly Nettleton, Kalamazoo, Room 34," in a cramped and almost illegible hand under date of November 28th of the same year ; and on the next day's page, in the same hand : "R. J. Hosford and wife, Terre Haute, Room 34."

The next step was to hunt up Mother Blake, which was

7

not a very hard matter, as women of her character gener·
ally run in the same noisome rut, until they are swept
from the great highway with other pestilences of life, and
pass from bitter existence and infamous memory; and
after one or two evenings running about among the
demi-monde he found the woman—quite an old lady now,
but nearly as well-kept and quite as jolly as ever, presid·
ing over a group of soiled divinities at a neat retreat **on**
Griswold Street.

Through the purchase of a vile bottle of wine the old
lady's lips were opened, and her tongue began a perfect
gallop about Bland and Lilly Mercer.

She gave the latter the reputation of being one of the
shrewdest women she had ever met, and laughed until the
tears came into her eyes over the way in which she had
" played it " on Bland, who had picked her up for a fool,
and had himself been terribly sold.   Then she launched
into vituperations towards the young minister, who had accused her of "standing in " with the girl in the robbery,
when she had been as badly fooled as himself.   Whatever
she had been and was, she said, there wasn't a dishonest
hair in her head; which assertion Bangs had reason to
believe to be literally true, as he noticed that she wore a
wig.

She then in great glee told him how she had "got
even " with Bland by "giving him away" to the papers,
which had soon taken the feathers out of *his* cap, she remarked with much satisfaction, broken his mother's heart,
who died and willed all her property to the good cause of

furnishing the heathen with an occasional fat missionary steak, and finally drove Bland out of Detroit, when he had gone to some Eastern city and, under another name, with his fine manners, airy ways, and good clothes, was playing it fine on some old Spiritualist millionaire out our way.

When the vision of the magnificent Harcout—which was almost a constant one, as he rushed into my office on the slightest pretext whatever, big with his own importance and unusually full of enthusiasm over "our case"—flitted before my eyes, it gave to me. additional romance in the work, in the sense that here, after many years, the man whom Mrs. Winslow in her early career had so magnificently duped, had unconsciously become one of her most relentless pursuers.

But it was a matter for speculation whether Harcout knew her to be the person who had so neatly taken him in, or whether he had risen to this condition of fervor in his work merely to impress Lyon with his useful friendship. I inclined to the latter opinion, however, as I was satisfied that if he had known with whom he was dealing he would have given up all expectations of continued favor and patronage from Lyon, and left Rochester as hastily as he had, as Bland, departed from Detroit.

Bangs also asked her if she had ever seen Lilly Mercer since that time.

Of course she had seen her, just at the close of the war. One day as she was crossing the river in the ferry, coming back from Windsor, she had met her face to face.

Mother Blake said that she seemed wonderfully glad to meet her, and wanted to borrow some money, which she had refused. She then gave her her card, upon which she was called some Madam or other, a clairvoyant, and she had some shabby rooms on Wisconsin Street, near the theatres. She was still young and pretty, Mother Blake said, and she easily persuaded her to come and live with her, which she did, "and," continued the old woman, with a withering look at the girls, "low down as she was, she made more money in a day than any half-dozen women I ever had." The old lady further said that she had only remained with her long enough to get some fine clothing and money together, when she started for the East.

She had never seen her since, but she had heard that she had several times passed through the city towards Chicago, always returning to the East, however, and also always richly dressed, and having every appearance of living in clover. "Let her alone to get along," concluded the old lady; "she'll live like a queen where another, a million times better than she, would starve."

From Detroit, Bangs proceeded to Chicago, and from thence to Sheboygan Falls, Wisconsin, where it required but a few minutes' inquiries to put him on track of the Hosfords.

Hosford had come there from Terre Haute several years ago, bought a fine farm a few miles out, and had, as far as could be ascertained, lived a comfortable sort of life for about a year, when trouble began.

Mrs. Hosford, from the good member of society which she was supposed to be, or really had been, suddenly embraced Spiritualism, and began running about the country with any old vagabond tramp of this kind that came along; and from the hard-working, economical woman she had been, she had become a spendthrift, a drunkard, and a prostitute. Hosford had moved away, and after considerable time and inquiry, it was ascertained that he had gone to Oskaloosa, in Iowa, determined to get away from old associations as far as possible, and had taken their three children with him, which she had vainly endeavored to secure.

Bangs spent several days here in hunting up evidence. There was plenty of it—mountains of it. Merchants and other business men of the town would button-hole him, take him into some retired place and tell him how this man had been caught *in flagrante delicto* with Mrs. Hosford, how that man had confessed to having been caught in her toils, and how some other person had been made a suspicious person in the society of the place, through some peccadillo with the dashing *Madam.*

All these persons referred to told of all the other persons who had divulged their weaknesses, until it seemed to Mr. Bangs, after remaining a few days in the vicinity, that the entire male portion of the community were implicated. But securing promises of depositions was quite another thing. Mr. A. was a married man, belonged to the church, had extensive business relations, and, while he would like to assist in the noble effort to show up the infamous woman, he really could not, you see, place himself in so delicate a position.

Mr. B. was not a member of any church, but had the reputation of a high order of morality. While he could not but acknowledge the justice of the request, and hoped that Mr. Bangs would have no trouble in securing all the evidence he needed, which would be a very easy matter, still he did not see how he could consistently compromise himself by going on record as a common adulterer.

Mr. C. was neither a churchman, nor did he claim a high order of morality; but if he had good luck, he would in the spring marry a very pretty girl of the village, and if she should ascertain that he had previously been so generous with his affections in another direction, he was satisfied that his dream of future bliss would be dissolved in thin air at once.

And so on through the entire village directory. There were pointed out scores of persons who had the knowledge desired, were all willing to help him secure *some other person* for sacrifice, and all equally enthusiastically hoped that her suit against Lyon would end in an ignominious failure; but declined, with thanks, the proud honor of exposing their own weaknesses, for even the extreme honor of assisting in her downfall.

CHAPTER XV.

A Chicago Divorce ' Shyster."—Hosford found.—His pathetic Narrative.—More Facts.

MR. BANGS was in no hurry to leave Sheboygan
Falls, as he found that he was in a fruitful field
for information, and he continued garnering it in and
stacking it away industriously.

It appeared that Hosford's wife, not content with dis-
gracing his name, had soon developed her old and never-
satisfied greed for money and any sort of power that might
be wielded mercilessly ; and it was evident that she had
money, for she immediately began dressing with much elegance and travelling about the country extensively.   The
probability was that she had still retained the money
stolen from Bland, and had also, during her years of
economy, carefully added to it until she had secured a
large sum, as she had occasion to use a good deal of
money in a certain transaction, which quite thoroughly
illustrated her unprincipled and revengeful character.

When Hosford had removed from Indiana to Wisconsin, he had purchased a larger and a finer farm, and had
been obliged to give a mortgage upon it for several thousand dollars, to be used in making necessary improve

ments. This had been paid off with the exception of about three thousand dollars, which amount, as soon as Mrs. Hosford had begun making it lively for her husband, and had left him for the purpose of wedding Spiritualism and all that the term implies, she immediately produced and bought up the mortgage, placing it in ex-Senator Carpenter's hands for foreclosure; but poor Hosford, struggling under his heavy load of desertion, disgrace and persecution, managed to raise the money and take it up, thus preventing the villainous woman from turning him out of his own home, which she had deserted and desecrated.

This had proven too much for even the patient Hosford to endure, and he had set about getting a divorce. But this was a harder thing to do than he had anticipated. Although he was in possession of nearly as much information as Bangs had secured, it was impossible to obtain definite evidence against her. Her terrible temper, her unscrupulousness, her unbounded and almost devilish shrewdness, and the swift and sudden principle of revenge that seemed only equalled by her greed for money, compelled thorough awe and fear among those from whom Hosford had expected assistance, and the result was he did not get it, and he was obliged to let the suit for divorce go by default. After this every petty annoyance that could occur to the woman's mind was visited on him. She would write him threatening letters; forward him express packages of a nature to both humiliate him and cause him fear; run him in debt at every place where she could force, or "confidence," merchants into trusting her ; hire a carriage and secure some male companion as vile as she, with whom she would proceed to her old home, and in the presence of her agonized husband and helpless, innocent children, threaten him with every conceivable form of punishment, including death, and engage in profanity and drunken orgies that would have disgraced the lowest brothel in the land.

Mr. Bangs learned that after this sort of procedure for a considerable period, she suddenly disappeared. Hosford took this opportunity to dispose of his farm and remove with his motherless family to Iowa. Mr. Bangs could not learn at Sheboygan what the woman's history had been during that period, but vague rumors had floated back to the place that she had become an army-follower, which was quite probable ; but at the close of the war she had assumed the role of an abandoned adventuress, and had wandered about the Pacific Slope until she had made too extensive an acquaintance for her safety in that section, and from thence had wandered through the country towards the East, seeking for any kind of prey ; and being hunted from place to place, under countless *aliases*, until she had in a measure retrieved herself, as far as money matters were concerned, and being careful of herself physically, had regained her good looks which her former terrible dissipation had almost destroyed, and had eventually so insinuated herself into the affections of a rich somebody that she had been furnished money with which to secure a divorce from

7*

Hosford, which had been granted in Chicago about a year and a half previous ; when she had come on to Sheboygan Falls and while there made her boasts that she would soon marry one of the richest men in New York State, as soon as his wife died, which wouldn't be very long she had hoped and believed.   Besides this, the rumors went, she had failed to marry that richest somebody in New York State, and papers had been seen containing an account of the woman and Lyon, her suit against him, and the fact, which particularly interested her old neighbors, that she had engaged no lawyer whatever, but had drawn and filed the bill of complaint herself.

In fact, the entire community were in a state of great excitement over the woman who was also creating much excitement in the East, and each person had his or her story to tell of some striking peculiarity or previous adventure of the madam's, and it required a great amount of sifting and careful work for Mr. Bangs to secure what he came for.

After a few days, however, he had worked so judiciously that he had got pledges from several responsible citizens that they would give their depositions as to her general character and reputation for chastity, or rather, want of it, whenever a commission should be forwarded to a certain lawyer of the city whom he engaged to take them.

From here he at once proceeded to Iowa, only stopping at Chicago long enough to secure a transcript of the divorce which had been granted in that city so noted for divorces, that one shyster alone secured seven hundred and seventy-seven of these desirable instruments from the period between the great fire and the close of the year 1875, from whence he immediately proceeded to Oskaloosa, where he soon became acquainted with parties who had known the woman, though under as many different *aliases* as she had visited cities of that State.

She had invariably advertised herself as a medium and female physician, and had swindled every one with whom she had come in contact, from the editor to errand-boy, from one end of the State to the other, and had gained even a worse reputation there than in Wisconsin. He ascertained that Hosford was not living at Oskaloosa, and before going through the same experience in listening to countless tales of the woman's depravity as he had in Wisconsin, he decided to proceed to his place, which was near Monroe, twenty-nine miles distant. He procured a conveyance and drove out to Hosford's farm, arriving at the place about dusk, where, after he had stated his business, he was invited to remain over night, and made comfortable.

Although a farmer, Hosford had everything cozy and pleasant about him, had married into a very respectable family, and had secured a most agreeable wife, who was caring for his children—two bright girls and a boy, from twelve to fifteen years of age—with almost the tenderness and affection of an own mother. After supper Hosford sent his family into another part of the house, and expressed himself as ready to give any information in his power.

He had not yet heard of the suit against Lyon, and when Mr. Bangs told him, he seemed astonished beyond expression, and after a little time said that he had often tried to think of some Satanic scheme that the woman *would not* dare to undertake if it occurred to her, but he had failed to imagine any. But with the record, especially for personal purity, behind her that Mrs. Winslow possessed, he could not but be particularly startled and surprised at her supreme self-possession and audacity. After a little further desultory conversation, Mr. Bangs told him that the Agency had all the necessary information regarding their early career, and of their subsequent history up to the time when they left Terre Haute, and probably a great deal after that time, and asked Hosford if he would be willing to go over the whole matter, giving the outlines of their troubles, what brought them about, and what had been their result.

He was the same old Dick Hosford—abrupt, kind, generous, with perhaps some of the old "forty-niner" roughness worn off and a toning-down of his whole nature, that his keen sorrows had given him ; but he was quite as impulsively reckless, and just as impulsively tender, and he began his story in a kind of weary way, that, to one knowing his history, was really sad and touching.

"Well, sir," said Hosford, "I knew the gal had been doing wrong at Detroit, but for all these hard years in Californy I had been working, savin', and goin' through danger with the purty pictur ahead that the bright girl I had left by the river would one day make me a happy home. I worked like a nigger, and it was sometimes up and sometimes down with me out thar—mostly down, though. But I struck a good lead one day, and worked close till it panned dry. I didn't have much aside some of them fellows out thar; but instead of runnin' it down my throat, givin' it to cut-throat gamblers, or flingin' it away on vile women, I started full chisel for the States. I come to Terre Haute, as you know, and spent nearly all my dust buyin' a little farm. Then I started fur Nettleton's, whar I expected heaven—but found hell!

"It bust me all up like, and I wandered about the old place jest as though I had went to sleep happy and waked up in a big grave that I couldn't get out of. The old folks themselves wasn't any more cut up than me; but I thought as how I wasn't doin' anything to help matters, 'n only making *them* more trouble. So I thought and thought what to do, and finally made up to go a-huntin' her, 'n told the old folks I wouldn't come back 'thout her.

"It all come over me then what she was doing; but I only thought to get her back for the old folks' sake Well, sir, I went to Chicago, and hung around that dog-goned city fur a week 'r two; but no Lil. Then I come back, lookin' everywhere, askin' everybody, an' peerin' into every place; but no Lil. Firally, I got to Detroit, and I went into every one of those places where I feared she *might* be; but no Lil. Do you know where I found her?"

Mr. Bangs told him he did, and how.

"Well, sir," continued Hosford, "I was utterly discouraged, 'n was goin' to go back and sell the place, and get away from the country altogether; but when I saw her all so rosy, fixed up so gay, and got to be such a grand sort of a woman, I just caved in altogether and wanted her for myself more 'n ever. I thought she had a good heart, and that I loved her enough to always be kind to her—as God knows I was—and thought *that* might keep her right. I never asked her a question, 'n wouldn't let the old folks. Everybody makes mistakes, ye know, and it kind of makes people wild to let 'em know *you* know it, and to badger 'em with questions. Well, she had lots of good sense, and took off her finery before we got to the old folks', who were 'most crazy with joy that we had come back together as man and wife. We stayed at Nettleton's a few days, then went direct to Terre Haute. I don't believe a man ever had a better wife 'n she was to to me while we lived there. We never mentioned the old times, and were very happy, as the children kept comin' along. The silks and jewels she got at Detroit were all put away, 'n I never saw 'em, till one day I come home unexpected and found the children shut out in the yard, and my wife afore the lookin'-glass, all rigged out in her old finery, an' lookin' herself over and over, while countin' a big pile of money that I had never seen before. I got a good look at her, but went whistlin' about the house for a long time, so as to let on that I didn't see her, and to give her time to get her old clothes on agin.

"It seemed as if right there and then the clouds begun hangin' over the house. I didn't say a word about it, and made everything as cheery as I could ; but begur tryin' to think what had set her goin', and after a few days found that she had been attendin' some of those Spiritual meetings down to town, and one of the Doctors come up to our place and stayed a few days, representin' himself as a good Methodist.

"I knew it wouldn't do to stay there any longer, an' so we moved to Wisconsin, I makin' her think it was healthier 'n where they had no ager. Well, sir, after we got there everything was pleasant and happy agi'n till the Spiritualists begun overrunnin' that country too, and she commenced her tantrums at once. I didn't oppose her goin' to them meetin's, but told her I hoped she wouldn't get mixed up with 'em too much ; but 'twas no use. The devil had come into the house in that shape, and though I prayed hard that it might leave, it got worse and worse, till the children were 'most crazy with fright and sorrow. I didn't know what to do. She run me in debt, slandered me, disgraced me. She would not only run about the country with those terrible people, but she took to her old life, which was worse than everything else. I tried every way to reform her ; but she was bound to go her vile way, and I could stand it no longer.

"You know the rest up there. After she had been gone some time and had got the divorce in Chicago, I come here with the children, to try and get away from it all. You have seen my wife. She ain't a purty woman.

She is pure and good though, and I prayed to God that the shadder would never come here. But 'twasn't any use. It seemed as though my prayin' never helped things much! We hadn't more 'n got settled here, when I heard of her travellin' through the country—you know how. Some way she found me out here, and I haven't had much peace since.

"One time she came here and left a trunk full of nice silk dresses and things. After a time, wife and I looked into it and found over two hundred keys of all kinds, besides pistols and knives. She came and took it away soon after, accusin' us of stealin' some of her things, and threatened to have us arrested. A few months afterwards she went up to Newton, the county-seat, and swore out a warrant for our arrest on the charge of assault and battery, and got subpœnas out for all the folks across the way. The Sheriff came down here to serve his warrant and subpœnas, and at Monroe learned something about the woman, so that by the time he got here and talked it over with us, I come to the conclusion she wanted to get us away and then steal the children; so we took them all along, left one of the neighbors to take care of the house, and went to Newton to stand trial. Sure enough, she didn't appear agin' us, but did come here in a carriage fur the children, awful drunk, and come near shootin' the man that was taking care of the place!"

Bangs here asked Hosford whether he had ever seen her since or had heard from her.

"I have seen her but once," he replied. "But I have

heerd about her doin's, time and time again. She come here one day in a carriage, dressed fit to kill ; and the first I see, she was tryin' to get the children into the carriage with her. I ordered them to come in, when, with an oath, she put her hand to her bosom as if to draw a pistol.

"I got mad at this, and told her that if she had come to that agin, *I'd* have a hand in too ; and as soon as I turned into the house as if to get a pistol—I only had an old rusty one with a broken lock, but had an idea that I could some way use it—she blazed away at me, the ball going through the front door and driving the splinters into my clothes. As she didn't know whether she had hit me or not, she drove away at full gallop, and I've never sot eyes on her since."

The poor fellow seemed to say this with an inexpressible sense of satisfaction and relief. He had had more than his share of her general depravity forced upon him, and the respite from it, though short, was very dear to him.

Bangs got from Hosford the names of parties in contiguous towns who could give him definite information about Mrs. Winslow, while he offered to come to Rochester himself, if his presence was required ; and after a good night's rest and an early breakfast, Mr. Bangs returned to Monroe. After a few days' travel and inquiry he secured a thousand times more information than necessary to compel the retiracy of the splendid Mrs. Winslow from her then public and profitable field of operations, after which he returned to New York, well satisfied with the result of his by no means pleasant labors.

CHAPTER XVI.

BACK in the streets of Rochester, Bristol followed
Mrs. Winslow with much wonderment and some
anxiety as to the result, not sure as to whether any of the
three lovely women had noticed his leaving at the call of
their hated rival, and cogitating what the woman might
want with him.

They soon arrived at the Garden, the woman frequently looking back to assure herself that the retired banker
was following her, and finally passed into the Fields and
took a booth, where she ordered a bottle of wine, which
gave her right to its occupancy for an indefinite period ;
and as soon as Bristol sauntered in, she signalled him to
join her, which he did with great apparent hesitation and
diffidence, and the general appearance of a man guilty of
almost his first wrong intent, but yet with strong resolution to not let it get the better of him.

She did not remove the delicate lace veil from her face,
and it blended the pretty flush which the exercise had
heightened with her naturally clear complexion in a most

artistic way, and toned the light in her great gray eyes into a languid lustre, very thrilling to behold when one knows there is a clean life behind such beauty, but as dangerous when transformed into a winning mask covering the perdition in the heart of a wicked woman, as the dazzling power of the Prophet of Khorassan.

Bristol was a very courtly sort of fellow, and received a glass of wine from the neat hand with considerable grace, though inwardly wondering what it all meant. Their wine-glasses touched, and the cheap nectar was drunk in silence, Mrs. Winslow only indulging in those little motions and changes of features that some women believe to be attractive and fascinating, and which really are so to many susceptible people ; and though Bristol might ordinarily have succumbed to the charms of the accomplished woman before him—and had he been the retired banker she supposed him to be would probably have done so—as the sedate, elderly, and capable detective, he only pretended to be smitten, and coyishly acknowledged her loving glances with more than ordinary ardor.

Finally, the fair woman, after modestly biting her lips for a time, began tapping the table with the handle of her fan, and looking Bristol full in the face, suddenly said :

" Mr. Bristol, aren't you a little curious why I wanted to see you ? "

" Any man who is a man," replied Bristol earnestly, "could not but have a pardonable curiosity when so fair a woman as Mrs. Winslow claims his attention ! "

" There, there," said she laughing, and extending her

hands across the table as if in a burst of confidence, "let us wave formalities; let us be friends."

Bristol took her proffered hands rather stiffly, but held them as long as was necessary, as they were pretty hands, warm hands, and hands that could grasp another's with a good show of honesty, too.

"There is no reason why we shouldn't," he said gallantly, as she poured out another glass of wine.

"Only one," answered Mrs. Winslow archly. "The three Graces don't like me, and they are bound we sha'n't meet. Now," she continued, again tapping the table nervously with her fan, and then raising her fine eyebrows and looking at Bristol half anxiously, half tenderly, and altogether meltingly, "*I* feel as though we had been acquainted for years. Don't think me bold, Mr. Bristol, but I have had you in my thoughts much—possibly *too* much," she added with the faintest trace of a blush; "but if I could feel that this—I was going to say attachment, though that would be quite improper, and I will say—unexplainable regard I have formed for you was in the least measure reciprocated——"

Bristol interrupted her with: "I think I can assure you that it is, at least, in a proper measure."

"Then," she continued, apparently radiant with happiness, "as I was about to say, I am sure it could be arranged so that we could be more in each other's society. You know who I am?" she abruptly and almost suspiciously asked.

Bristol was almost put off his guard by the sudden

change of the subject, but parried the question with: "Certainly not; at least no more than through what I have been told at the restaurant."

Tears started in her well-trained eyes, but she impetuously brushed them away and followed the pretty piece of acting with: "Oh, Mr. Bristol! I fear we may never be to each other what we might have been if these three old hags—I mean old maids—had not poisoned your mind regarding me. Let me tell you," and she took hold of his collar and drew the reluctant detective towards her, "they are trying to get your money—your vast wealth. Let a comparatively unknown friend whisper in your ear, '*Beware!*'"

Bristol started, adjusted his glasses, grasped Mrs. Winslow's hand, and, as if very much frightened and extremely grateful, said heartily and with great fervor, "My dear madam, for this kindness I am yours to command!"

The woman evidently felt assured from that moment that she had made a conquest; but her varied experience and professional tact, as well as her native shrewdness, prevented her from expressing too great gayety over it, and she proceeded to inform Bristol how keen and shrewd the old ladies under Washington Hall were; how in confidence they had told her that they would compel him to marry one of them, and were going to draw cuts to determine which should carry off the prize; and when that was settled, if he did not marry the fortunate person willingly, their combined evidence would bring him down, or despoil him of a great portion of his wealth, which, she had no doubt, he had acquired by long years of honest toil.

Bristol expressed himself aghast at the depravity of women, and told Mrs. Winslow that it seemed to him that the nearer the grave they got the more terrible their greed and hideousness became.

Mrs. Winslow murmured that *she* was not so very, *very* old.

"Quite the contrary," said Bristol, gallantly, "and even when you become so, I am sure—very sure, that you will prove a marked exception."

An expression of pleasure flitted into her face, succeeded by one of evident pain—pleasure, probably, that she had made another dupe as she supposed; pain, that in one swift moment there had flashed into her mind some terrible picture of her cursed, lonely, homeless old age, when the whole world should scoff at her and thrust her from it, like the vile thing that she was and the hideous thing that she would surely become; both followed by the set features, where the cruel light came into her eyes and the swift shuttles of crimson and ashy paleness shot over her curled lips—the outward semblance of the inward tigress, that, though diverted for an instant by some little sunlight-flash of either tenderness or regret, never could be won from its irrevocably awful nature!

But it was all gone as soon as it had come, and she sat there, to all appearances a handsome woman, as modestly and carefully as possible encroaching upon the grounds of a first after-marriage flirtation, and in a few

"Do you believe in affinities, Mr. Bristol?"—

moments pleasantly said : "I have become so interested in you, Mr. Bristol, that I have found myself asking the question : Why is it that this gentleman is continually in my mind? until, do you know, I have such a curiosity about you that I shall be perfectly delighted to get better acquainted with you."

Bristol gracefully acknowledged the compliment by stating to her that he himself, since he had seen her, had had a strange feeling that he should know more about her, and the presentiment was still so strong upon him that he was now quite sure that he *should.*

"Ever since I saw you I have felt that we should become intimate," continued Mrs. Winslow radiantly.

"And I may myself confess that ever since I saw you, Mrs. Winslow, I really *knew* that I should be obliged to search you out and remain near you."

Mrs. Winslow blushed and coyishly asked : "Mr. Bristol, do you believe in affinities ?"

"Most assuredly."

"So do I, and as we have sat here together, it has seemed to me that the good spirits were hovering over and around us, and had been, and were even now, whispering to us the sacredness of the affinity which surely must exist between us."

Mrs. Winslow said this in a kind of rhapsody of emotion, which betokened both an air of sincerity derived from frequent repetition and long practice, and a sort of superstitious belief in what she herself said ; and then poured out another glass of wine for each, while Bristol remarked as he drank, that of late years these spirits had been a great source of comfort to him, and that their free circulation was a good thing for society.

An hour or two was pleasantly beguiled in this manner, but Bristol hardly knew what course to pursue, and began to feel that in the absence of instructions he might become altogether too familiar with the charming woman who was making such an effort to please him. But he dare not cause her to become angry at him, for that would destroy his usefulness, and she seemed bound that he should admire her; so, as he had been directed by me to continue the *role* of the "retired banker," he concluded it would be better to humor Mrs. Winslow in the belief that he was-smitten by her, as she showed great anxiety that it should be so. Accordingly, when she proposed that he should call at her apartments that evening, he acceded to the request with such a show of pleasure that Mrs. Winslow could not restrain her gratification, but rose and terminated the interview by slapping Bristol heartily on the shoulder and calling him a "dear old trump, anyhow!" And Fox, who was reading the morning paper over a glass of beer at a little table not more than ten feet distant, looked in blank astonishment at Bristol, as if fearing that the woman had really bewitched him; while little Le Compte, who stood at the entrance beyond, looked the very picture of abject jealousy as he saw his darling lavishing endearments upon a man old enough to be her father.

Mrs. Winslow passed out of the Fields, and noticing Le Compte, who was retreating as rapidly as possible, beckoned to him, and when he had approached her near enough for her to speak to him, gave him a few quick, angry words that sent him at a rapid pace over the railroad bridge in the direction of his rooms; while she, after a parting smile at the beaming Bristol, who stood radiantly in the Fields' entrance, walked into St. Paul street, and from thence back and forth past the restaurant, where the three deserted old maids might witness her stride of triumph; while Bristol joined Fox at a retired spot under the shade of the trees overhanging the brink of the precipice rising from the gorge of the Genesee River, and explained the status of affairs which had all unconsciously to himself drawn him from his quiet work into an awful whirlpool of love and all that the term implied. Fox felt much relieved at this information, and at once proceeded home, while Bristol, with a guilty look in his face, returned to the little restaurant, where he found a dispatch from me stating that Mrs. Winslow intended going to Canada two days later, as I had been very positively informed by Le Compte, and directing him to in some manner keep her company and never let her make a move or meet a person without his knowledge.

Bristol hardly saw how he was to do this, but concluded that it might be best to wait until after his interview with his charmer in the evening, so that he could also forward the result of that with his regular report; and after expressing unbounded regret at being obliged to part from the three graces and a little card-party they had arranged, he proceeded to Mrs. Winslow's apartments,

8

which had seemingly been specially arranged for his reception.

The mistress of the place was most elegantly attired, and greeted the "retired banker" with such grace and marked esteem, that Fox, at his lonely window opposite, almost felt jealous of the attention bestowed upon his comrade by their mutual quarry.

If ever a woman endeavored to make herself irresistibly winning, it was Mrs. Winslow on that night. She threw off all reserve at once, and was all smiles, pleasant words, and pretty ways. The rooms were most beautifully arranged, and where splendid flowers failed to furnish aroma, the delicate odors of art took their place. A very shrewd woman was Mrs. Winslow—a woman who was supreme in the art of providing *bijouterie* to appeal to the sensuous in men's natures. In her conversation, which apparently was lady-like enough when guarded, there was always more suggested than said. The tone, the smile, the eye, the gesture, the touch—every movement, glance, or sound, betokened an unexpressed *something* ready at any moment to be brought forward to crush down a weakening resolution, and sweep from existence so much of good or purity as might come into her baleful presence. She had rich game in Bristol, she thought. Why could she not work this with the Lyon case, bring to a successful termination a half-dozen other cases she was working up, secure a big pile of spoil at one time, and then with her little Le Compte glide away to *La Belle France,* where with his wit and her winning ways and wisdom, she might yet amass vast wealth in levying upon the personal and family pride of the thousands of rich numskulls who annually throng the gay capital.

And so to any man but a duty-doing detective that evening would have been a thrilling one. As it was, it was a hard one for Bristol, who knew that Fox's lynx eyes were upon him from across the street, who had to invent legend after legend regarding his life, his present and his imaginary future, and who was obliged under any circumstances not only to please the woman, but to preserve himself blameless—two things to ordinary men quite difficult to manage.

During the hour that Bristol remained with her she intimated to him the propriety of his securing another boarding-place, so that they might enjoy each other's society without the annoyance to which the old maids would subject them both should he remain there. He had wanted to make a change, Bristol said, but his long and varied experience had made him cautious, and he never gave up one good thing until he had secured a better. How would as pleasant a place as this do, Mrs. Winslow wanted to know? She had been thinking of renting the entire flat, she said, and then re-renting it to select parties, like Mr. Bristol, who were willing to pay a good price for a really luxurious place in which to live.

Bristol was apparently flattered by her regard for him, which had, of course, alone suggested the matter to her mind; but, being an elderly gentleman of conservative habits, he required time to think the matter over. In any

event, it couldn't but be a pleasant theme for contemplation.

In fact, they got along famously together ; so much so,
indeed, that before Bristol had taken his departure, Mrs.
Winslow had pressed him to accompany her on a trip of
both business and pleasure to Toronto, and had so
urgently presented the request that he had half consented
to go, and was quite sure that he would be able to do so,
unless some unexpected business transaction should
detain him.   In any case, he would be able to inform her
by the next afternoon, he said, as he gallantly bade her
good-night, and observed Le Compte scowling upon him
from the dark end of the hall beyond.

Bristol hastened to the post-office and added the events
of the evening to his daily report, which reached me the
next afternoon, when I telegraphed to him to proceed
with Mrs. Winslow, as her friend ; but while pleasing her
by feigning extreme regard, to be discreet, and not put
himself too much in her power, nor to allow her to advance any of her other schemes by a sort of exhibition of
him as her champion and protector.

Mrs. Winslow was made very happy by Bristol's accept-
ance of her invitation, and, at her suggestion, they took
the train for Port Charlotte as strangers—Mrs. Winslow
informing Bristol that the " old scoundrel," meaning
Lyon, was having her watched, she believed, but she
would outwit him at every point ; but on arriving at the
Port the loving couple got together quite naturally, and
soon after were on board a steamer bound for Port Hope.

It was one of those dreamy, hazy days of early September, when the disappearing shore seemed to gradually take upon itself a tint of blue as deep as that of the sky above and as pure as that of the waters below, which on this day was almost as smooth as a mirror, only broken by long, far-reaching swells that seemed to have neither beginning nor end, but which here and there swept away in endless ribbons of liquid light, while the trailing wake of the steamer seemed in the pleasant sun like some marvellous and limitless lace-work flung across the water in wanton richness and profusion.

It was a lovely day for love, and to an unprejudiced observer Bristol and Mrs. Winslow improved it. At Charlotte the woman spoke of the matter in such a way that Bristol understood that she would not object to make the trip as his wife, but he innocently failed to catch the meaning of her covert invitation, and was only the attentive admirer during the entire trip. But in the cabin, or seated coyishly together under a huge sunshade upon the forward deck, they were as fine a couple as one would care to see, while the woman seemed unusually affectionate and agreeable.

Arriving at Port Hope after a few hours, the couple took the night train for the West, and arrived at Toronto at midnight, being driven to the Queen's Hotel. They had become so confidential and intimate by this time that Mrs. Winslow again suggested the propriety of travelling under more intimate relations than they had done, but was again carefully diverted from her purpose by the assumed innocence of the venerable detective, who saw that her real purpose was to secure evidence of having travelled as his wife, in order to have a future power over him, as she certainly believed him to be a man of great wealth.

She had told him that she had business that would prevent her seeing him during the next day, at which he expressed extreme regret, and they retired to their separate apartments for the night.

CHAPTER XVII.

AS Mrs. Winslow had said, she was not to be seen the next morning; and Bristol, after breakfasting early, came to the conclusion that he should also be busied for the day following my instructions to watch her every movement.

He ascertained the number of her room and leisurely strolled through the hall until he located it, when he at once took a position where he could observe any movement in or out of the door. At about ten o'clock he noticed a waiter enter her room as if by summons, in a few minutes pass out smiling, and shortly afterwards return with a very large glass filled with some sort of liquor. Soon after he brought her breakfast, and about a half-hour later he saw that the dishes were being removed from the room, and, lying on one edge of the tray, an ordinary envelope, from its puffed condition evidently containing a note. He felt sure that this would give him the overture to the day's performance; but how to secure it was another thing entirely. He could not take the letter from the tray, as it rested on the front edge which projected over the boy's shoulder, and was consequently immediately before his eyes. He probably would not be able to bribe him into letting him have it, for the letter might require an answer, and he would fear getting into trouble. Bristol was standing at the end of the hall, by the window overlooking the street, while the waiter was approaching the stairs which descended to the lower floors near him. The boy had reached the second step going down, and it was Bristol's last opportunity.

"Stop!" he said excitedly to the boy. "Here, give me that tray," and he pulled it from the boy's shoulder and rested it upon the stair-rail. "I'll take care of this. Run down to the street, now, quick, and get me a this morning's paper. There's a newsboy right in front of the house. Here's a half-dollar; keep the change!"

The boy seemed startled at the action, but Bristol had been so impetuous about it; that he had relinquished the tray and started down stairs, but, recovering himself, came back and reached his hand up as if to take the letter.

"Tut, tut," said Bristol angrily, picking up the letter and carelessly putting it in his pocket without looking at the address, "I'll take care of everything until you get back; get along with you now!"

Bristol was noted for his benign and fatherly appearance, and, after another good look at him, the waiter took a brisk trot down stairs, leaving the detective in possession of the letter. He hastily put the tray upon the floor, and whisking the letter from his pocket, saw that it was addressed with a pencil, to " J. Devereaux, No. —, Yonge St.," and marked " Personal."   It was but the work of an instant to open it, and but of a moment to read it, as it was short and to the point, and ran as follows :

QUEEN'S HOTEL, TORONTO, Sept. 6, 186–.

DEVEREAUX––I am hard up.   I need one thousand dollars, though five hundred will do, but I must have that amount at once.   You have intimated that you would not help me any further.   I have merely to say to you that if you do not either call with, or send the money, during the day, I will cause you to reflect as to whether your busi ness and social reputation are not worth to you and your estimable family immeasurably more than the trifle named.   Exercise your own pleasure about the matter however.

MRS. W.

Bristol copied this upon the back of the addressed en- velope in less than a minute, and in a minute more had the note enclosed in another envelope and addressed in a handwriting sufficiently similar to that of Mrs. Wins- low's to answer every purpose, and had just got into a calm and bland position with the tray, when the boy came up the stairs, three steps at a time, gave the paper a toss into the hall, jerked the letter out of Bristol's hand, and after giving him a look that had considerable resentment in it, strode down the stairs with his tray on his shoulder and his letter in his pocket, in a very offended and digni fied manner.

8*

But as Bristol was on this kind of business at Toronto he thought he n.ight as well ascertain where the little fel low went ; and, taking a position a half-block distant from the hotel, was obliged to wait but a little time before the waiter came down and started off on a brisk walk down the street.

He waited until the boy had passed him, and then fol·lowed him in and out the streets until he saw him sud·denly turn into a large wholesale house on Yonge street, when he rapidly lessened the distance between them, ar·riving in front of the place as he saw the boy hand the note to a thin old gentleman, who took him aside and nervously questioned him for a few minutes, after which he nodded to him as if assenting to something, or direct·ing the boy to return an affirmative answer to whoever had sent the note, or whatever it contained.

The boy walked briskly back to the hotel, and Bristol only remained long enough to notice the old man—who was evidently the Devereaux of whom Le Compte had informed me, and whose name Bristol had so recently written—walk tremblingly towards the door as if over come with some sudden faintness, and in a sort of vacant, listless way tear the note into little bits and fling them piecemeal upon the stones of the street, hurling the last bunch of pieces upon the pavement with a violent, agon·ized action, as if he would to God he could dispose of the dark and relentless shadow across his life as quickly and as effectually !

All Bristol now had to do was to ascertain when Dev·

ereaux called, and, if possible, to overhear what was said at the interview.

But this might not be so easy a matter to accomplish as securing the contents of the letter addressed to the latter. After studying the matter over for a little time, but without any definite decision what to do, he found himself strolling along the hall where Mrs. Winslow's room was located, and noticed several rooms standing open and being put to rights after the departure of guests. Among this number was one next to that occupied by Mrs. Winslow, and, taking the number, he immediately repaired to the office and had his baggage changed to that room, where, after dinner, with a few cigars and some fresh reading matter, he comfortably and leisurely waited for developments.

The day dragged along, and both Bristol and Mrs. Winslow became anxious.. The latter paced back and forth in her room, and every few moments went to the door, and even passed out into the hall, going as far as the stairs and peering anxiously down, while the waiter at frequent intervals was summoned to provide her courage and patience of a liquid character. Finally, however, Bristol noticed that she had either concluded to take a short nap, or was determined to wait patiently, for quite a period of silence elapsed in her room, which he took advantage of to steal quietly out into the hall, leaving his door ajar so that he might re-enter it noiselessly as occasion required.

It was not long before the occasion presented itself, for

Bristol had got no more than to the end of the hall when he saw Devereaux ascending the stairs from below. He quietly stepped behind the curtains that trailed from the lambrequin over the window, and watched the old man as he came up the stairs.

He was a little, gray, withered old man. Almost all his strength was gone, and he certainly had but a few more years to use what little strength was left. His hair was almost white, and his face was quite as colorless, while the weak, rheumy eyes seemed almost ready to fall through the flesh which had withered away to the bones of his face. He was a living example of the black-mailer's victim as he labored along, now and then catching at the stair-rail for help, and looking behind and around him as if fearing some sudden discovery. Arriving upon the hall floor, he peered anxiously at the numbers upon the doors, and after settling in his mind what direction to take, went on tremblingly with bowed head towards the woman who was as remorseless as death itself.

He found the room after a little trouble, and tapped at it apprehensively. It was at once opened and immediately closed after, when Bristol sprang from his hiding-place and was in the adjoining room almost as soon as the next door had closed.

During the afternoon, when Mrs. Winslow had absented herself from her room, he had dragged the bureau against the door opening into her apartment, placed a quilt from his bed upon it in order that his jumping upon it might occasion no noise, and with his knife cut a diamond shaped piece out of the green paper covering the glass transom, darkening his own room so that his eyes could not by any possibility be seen through the aperture in the piece of paper, which had a dead black appearance from Mrs. Winslow's room ; and by the time the poor old man had confronted the woman in a scared kind of a way, and had seated himself upon the sofa obedient to her imperious gesture, the "retired banker's" eyes and eye-glasses looked calmly down upon a scene the whole terrible import of which, could it have been presented to the world in all its terrible hideousness, and in some form become eternally typical of the curse it illustrated, would have stood for all time a savage Cerberus frightening men from this kind of infamy and self-destruction.

In all my startling experience with criminals and the sad incidents which have in the peculiar nature of my business forced themselves upon my observation, there has been no one thing so reprehensible as the trade of the blackmailer, and there is a no more terrible torture than that inflicted by that class of criminals ; and I am satisfied that could heads of families realize their terrible danger when heedlessly forming some unholy alliance, which is sure to eventually whip and scourge them until life is a burden, there would be less of the moral laxity and lechery than now burdens the world from palace and pulpit to poverty-stricken hovel.

What more pitiable picture than that of a man just ready to pass from all that should be worth having and

loving to the unknown country, with fear behind and aw·
ful uncertainty beyond—with the work of a whole life,
which should now bring a reward of tenderness, gratitude,
and reverential esteem, embittered and blasted by the
relentless curse that ever trails after weakness and passion—fear, distrust, and apprehension between himself
and family, and the Damoclean sword ever above him,
ready to fall at the instant he endeavors to throw the
horrible shadow from him to regain honesty and upright
ness !

There the old man sat, a cowardly puppet before a
brazen adventuress—sat there a weak, drivelling, idiotic
wreck before one so vile that she was no longer capable
of regret—sat there ruined in everything worth the preser-
vation of, suffering what he had for years suffered—the
regret, the remorse, the shame, and the abject fear that
were worse than a thousand deaths ; while the utterly
heartless woman, with her hands folded across her waist in
a masculine sort of a way, looked at him smilingly, seemingly enjoying his efforts to recover the breath lost in the,
to him, severe labor of getting to her room ; as it appeared to be the custom for him to see her there rather
than in the parlor.

The interview was business-like, and, as it was not overwhelmed with sentiment, was not protracted.

Mrs. Winslow asked Devereaux if he had brought the
money, and he stammered that he had. Well, she wanted
it, and didn't want any nonsense with it, either, she said,
with a vast amount of meaning thrown into the words ; he

knew whether he *owed* her that amount or not, and, if he did, she didn't propose having any bickering about it.

Then the old man slowly rose, and cursing her, himself, and all the world, flung her the money and said he would go, as he knew that was all she wanted.

She told him frankly that it was pretty nearly all she wanted, but added jocosely that he was still "a charmer," and that that fact, too, had its influence in periodically drawing her to him; and then bade him an affectionate good-by as he feebly glared at her, and passed, whining, cursing, and tottering away.

Mrs. Winslow was very happy and gay now, and during the evening and on their return to Rochester was all smiles and winsomeness. Her detective companion could scarcely enter into her unusual joyousness, but did the best he could, and that was well enough, as she was so pleased with the success of her Toronto trip that her mind was altogether employed with it until nearing home, when her eminent business ability again asserted itself, and she became more affectionate than ever to the retired banker, repeating the proposition concerning the rooms, which Bristol had of course reported, and which he would be prepared to act upon when he could secure his mail at Rochester.

He told her he had thought favorably of it, and after he had ascertained whether he should remain in the city a stated period or not, would inform her of his decision, which he presumed would be favorable and permit of their continued pleasant intimacy; while Mrs. Winslow confided to him that she had thought seriously of the course for some time. She knew Lyon was having her watched, she said, and she had decided that it would be best to change her business to one which could not be so easily misinterpreted, or at least add to her present business something that in the eyes of those who scoffed at spiritualism would have a measure of respectability about it, and from which she could not only secure a livelihood, but such a pleasant companion as Mr. Bristol; and they parted upon the train before arriving at the depot with a thorough understanding about the future, and an appointment for another meeting at the first opportunity.

Unknown to Bristol I had sent another operative to keep him and Mrs. Winslow company, and on receiving the reports of each I decided to put my men in her rooms, where one of them could constantly observe her actions, and never under any circumstances give her an opportunity to make any new move without my knowledge. I therefore sent another man to Rochester for outside work, and directed Bristol to accept the woman's proposition and become her lodger, and, as soon after as possible without exciting her suspicions, appear to become acquainted with Fox, recommend him as a lodger, and secure his introduction to the place as M. D. Lyford, a book-keeper in some establishment of the city which they might settle upon, so that he might relieve Bristol, and *vice versa*, as occasion required.

So the furnished rooms sign went up over the clairvoyant sign, and Mrs. Winslow added to the charms of handsome medium those of an attractive landlady, while the three old maids under Washington Hall lost their prize, who became a sort of an aged page to the castaway woman who had such luxurious rooms for rent in the autumn of 186–, on South St. Paul street, near Meech's Opera-house, in the beautiful city of Rochester.

CHAPTER XVIII.

Harcout again.—" Things going slow."—A Bit of personal History.—
A new Tenant.—Detective Generalship.—Mrs. Winslow fears she
is watched.—Mr. Pinkerton cogitates.

IT is pleasant to realize that the world moves along
just the same, whether the many mild lunatics it carries attempt to interfere with it or not. There are countless men, precisely like Harcout, incapable of holding in
their little brains but one idea at a time, and that idea
invariably pushes to the surface their own supreme ego-
tism and self-consciousness, and just as invariably displays
their utter ignorance of what they are continually interfer-
ing with ; and it is both a grateful and charitable thought
that such small minds, burdened with such vast assurance,
are merely provided by Omniscience to make us patient,
to warn us from allowing such knowledge as we may fortunately gain from developing into similar self-assertion,
and to serve to illustrate true worth by contrast.

Here was this fellow sweeping into my office every
day, demanding every detail of my operations on Mrs.
Winslow, even intimating that I should consult with him
as to every move to be made, and submit to his consideration even the character of the men employed, the color
of their clothing and the quality, and every item or act

concerning or included in the work. He had, in some unexplainable way that is common to brazen assurance or unmitigated ignorance, fastened himself upon the weak old man as a sort of confidential agent, or what-not, worked upon his fears, his superstitions, and his foolish half-faith in a system of religion that has never yet made other than male and female prostitutes, adventurers, or lunatics, until the old man, standing alone and almost friendless, had learned to cling to him, and almost rely upon his consummate bravado to extricate him from the meshes of the web his own vileness and a vile woman had woven about him ; so that in one sense he stood in the relation of principal to me, and I found it impossible to shake him off, or relieve myself to any great extent of his impudent presence and foolish suggestions.

I knew that he was utterly without principle, and was only making a show of this extraordinary energy in order to appear to more than earn whatever he got from Lyon, and continue in the latter's mind the feeling that he was utterly indispensable to him. I also knew him to be as mean an adventurer as Mrs. Winslow was an adventuress ; that he was the villain who had first unloosed this vast flood of vileness and lechery upon society, and who, as the shameless Christian minister of Detroit, had put the fire-brand from hell in this woman's hand, to ever after continue her moral incendiarism wherever she might go, until thrust from life and infamous memory, and it annoyed me that this sort of a man should dictate to me.

I could have disposed of him at one stroke, and I am

satisfied that had I on only one occasion addressed him as the Rev. Mr. Bland, and casually inquired concerning his old Detroit friends, including Mother Blake, he would have slunk away without a word or a protest of any kind whatever; and had I gone farther, and showed him what he himself did not know, that this woman, whom he was so anxious to have brought down with some startling development, was none other than the one whom he had led into a life of sin from the pleasant Nettleton farm-nouse by the winding river, and that he was now playing guardian to a man that would have probably been free from the curse that was hanging over him, had it not been for Harcout's earlier and more rascally villainy, he would have disappeared altogether, but I realized that this would not do. It would have had the effect of putting Lyon at the mercy of a horde of new ghouls, while the existing one frightened all others away and was in a measure a protection to Lyon, for he was now only bled by one, where he would otherwise have been bled by twenty.

Aside from this, it would have probably resulted in Mrs. Winslow's being put on her guard, giving her time, not only to cover her tracks in many criminal instances we had already discovered against her, but also cause her to prevent witnesses from giving depositions, or, where depositions had already been taken, give her an opportunity to secure affidavits from the parties who gave them that they were mistaken as to the identity of the person named in those instruments, and in other particulars greatly destroy the effect of the work already done and that which I had planned; and I was consequently obliged to bear the fellow's dictatorial manner and suggestions, as he insisted on doing the work this way or that way, and urged that I was not "pushing things" fast enough.

"Why, Mr. Pinkerton," said he one day, his eyebrows elevated and the corners of his mouth drawn down, his whole face expressive of lofty condescension and gentle, though firm reproof, "things are going rather slow—rather slow. Hem! When we brought this case to you, we depended upon expedition—depended on expedition, Mr. Pinkerton."

"And have you any cause to complain?" I asked pleasantly.

"Well, I don't know as we should exactly call it 'complain.' No, I don't know as we exactly complain; but, if we might be allowed the privilege—hem!—we would beg to suggest, without giving offence—beg to suggest, mind you, without giving offence," he repeated, in the most offensive way possible, "that, if I might be allowed the expression, things are not pushed quite enough!"

"On the contrary," I continued good-naturedly, "we have secured what any good lawyer would consider an overwhelming amount of evidence, and are letting the woman take her own course, in order to allow her to completely unwind herself."

"But you see, Pinkerton, we supposed when we brought the case to you that you would, so to speak, smash things

—break her all up and scatter her, as it were—hem !— disperse her, you know."

He said this as though he had taken a contract with Lyon to compel me to avenge them both on the woman, and it heated my blood to be considered in the light of any person's hired assassin ; but I controlled myself, and explained the matter to him.

"Harcout," said I, "do you know anything about my history ? "

" Well, nothing save what I've seen in the newspapers. Merely by reputation," he added lightly.

"Well, sir, whatever that reputation may be, Harcout," I said, "this is the truth.   I never, that I know of, did a dishonorable deed.   I worked from a poor boy to whatever position or business standing I now have—worked hard for everything I got or gained, and I never yet found it necessary to do dirty work for any person."

" Quite noble of you—quite noble," said Harcout patronizingly.

"The detection of criminals," I continued, paying no attention to his moralizing, " *should* be as honorable—and so far as I have been able to do, has been made as honorable—while it is certainly as necessary. as that of any other calling.   No element of revenge can enter into my work.   You came to me with a case which I at first objected to take, on account of its nature.   I would not have taken it for all the money Mr. Lyon possesses, had I not been assured that this Mrs. Winslow was a dangerous woman.   Nor, knowing that she is one, as I now do, would I have any connection with the case if I found that Mr. Lyon insisted on my using the peculiar power which I always have at command for any other purpose than the, in this case, legitimate one of securing evidence against her which actually exists. I am satisfied that a no more relentless and terrible woman ever lived, but shall leave her punishment to her disappointment in not securing what her whole soul is bent on getting, and that is Lyon's money. I have nothing whatever to do with punishment, sir, and no person ever did or ever can use my force for that nefarious purpose!"

"Oh, exactly—exactly," replied the oily Harcout; "but, you see, we rather—hem!—expected something startling, you know. Now, for instance," here he raised his eyebrows and pursed his lips in a wise way; "supposing you had just ascertained all about her early history, you would probably have found that Mrs. Winslow had played these games all her life. Undoubtedly you could point to the very first man whom she blackmailed——"

"Undoubtedly," I interrupted, "I'm sure 1 could do it at this moment!"

Harcout looked at me quickly, but as I was gazing at the ceiling as if in deep thought, he went on quite enthusiastically :

"Exactly. They learn it early. They will swindle at sixteen, rob at eighteen ; blackmail at twenty ; and kill a man any time after that !"

"Why, Harcout are *you* a woman-hater ?" I laughingly asked, notwithstanding my annoyance.

"Oh, no," he suddenly replied; "but I had a friend who once suffered from very much the same sort of a woman as this Mrs. Winslow, and she was not eighteen years old either. But to resume: Get this point in her life, and the rest—hem!—the rest reads right on like the chapters of a book!"

"And then what?" I ventured to ask.

"Then what?" he asked indignantly; "go for her through the newspapers. Drive her out of the country. Make it impossible for her to ever return;" and then, as if reflecting, "ruin her altogether. Any reporter will listen to you if you have anybody to ruin! In fact, get up an excitement about it and show her up."

"And try your case in the newspapers instead of in the courts?" I added, "which would have the effect of leaving the matter at the end just where it was at the beginning, with nothing proven, and Mr. Lyon still at the mercy of any future surprise the woman might conceive a fancy of springing upon him."

But there was no means of changing this lofty gentleman's opinions, and these interviews were always necessarily closed by the threat on my part that I would have nothing further to do with the matter if I was not allowed to conduct my operations according to my own judgment in the light of my own large experience upon such matters, and Mr. Harcout would depart in a most dignified and frigid manner, as though it were a "positively last appearance," only to return the next day with more objections and a new batch of suggestions, which were given me for "what they were worth," as he would remark, and we would fight our battles all over again, with the stereotyped result.

I saw Mr. Lyon very seldom, and he always approached me in the timid, reluctant way in which he had come into my office when the case was first begun; but, contrary to what I had anticipated through Harcout's injunctions to "push things" and crush the woman out, he approved of my course throughout, and seemed wonderfully pleased that everything had been conducted so quietly and yet so effectively. Of course he shrank from the trial and the miserable sort of publicity all such trials compel; but he was *more* fearful of the woman's future unexpected and sudden sallies upon him, which both he and myself were satisfied would be made at her convenience or whim, and was only too glad to agree to any course which would compel silence and peace.

At Rochester everything was working smoothly. After Bristol had become located, his first work was to secure the admission to Mrs. Winslow's rooms of Fox, as Lyford, which was done by representing that, the same day he had himself gone there, he had suddenly come upon a sort of relative of his who was a book-keeper in a wholesale house on Mill street, and who was boarding at the Osborn House, and would be glad to make some arrangement whereby he might live comfortably, be near his business, and take his meals when and where he pleased. Thinking he would be more pleasantly situated, and, at the same time, be able to economize somewhat, Bristol said

9

he had recommended Mrs. Winslow's rooms very highly
and that Lyford had agreed to call and take a look at the
place, which he did, making a good impression, and arranging to have his baggage sent the next day.

The rooms were situated so that the two detectives in
a measure had their quarry surrounded, or, at least, completely flanked. The halls of the floor intersected each
other at right angles at the top of the stairs, and Mrs.
Winslow's reception-room was at the right, as the hall was
entered from the stairway, while her sleeping-room could
only be reached from this sitting-room, although being
situated next the hall running parallel with the front of the
building, while Bristol had shrewdly secured another sleeping-room fronting on St. Paul street, similar in size to
Mrs. Winslow's, adjoining hers, and also, like hers, opening into the reception-room, which they had agreed to use
in common, as it seemed that the fair landlady was all of
a sudden, for some reason, becoming close and penurious.
Fox's room was across the hall immediately opposite Mrs.
Winslow's, as he had expressed a strong desire to be as
near his cousin, Mr. Bristol, as possible, so that by chance
and a little careful work the parties were located with as
much appropriateness as I could possibly have wished for.
The operatives each paid a month's rent in advance, taking
receipts for the same, and immediately began paying particular attention to all parties who came in and out of the
building, circulated freely among the Spiritualists of the
city, and got on as good terms as possible with the charming landlady, who seemed at times to be a little suspicious

of her surroundings, as it introduced altogether too many strange faces to suit a person who had a no clearer conscience than she had.

From the gay, dashing woman she had been, she became unpleasantly suspicious. , She explained this to Bristol and Fox as arising from unfavorable visions and revelations from the spirits through the different mediums she had employed to give her the truth about her case with Lyon. The rooms had filled up rapidly with people whom the operatives had taken pains to ascertain all about, and who, as a rule, were honest folks; but Mrs. Winslow could not get it out of her mind that some of them were spies from Lyon, and were watching her in everything that she did.

There had been nothing whatever done to alarm her on the part of my men; but the fact alone that here were a dozen people all about her, any one of whom might at any time spring some sudden harm upon her, began to affect her as the fear she had all her life inspired in others had affected them; and she began to form a habit of talking pleasantly on ordinary subjects, and then turning abruptly and almost fiercely upon Bristol and Fox, who were now the only persons left whom she would at all trust —even distrusting them—with a series of questions so vital, and given with such wonderful rapidity, that it required the best efforts of the operatives to parry her homethrusts and quiet her regarding them.

It was a question in my mind whether she had laid by a large sum of money or not. Years before she had sev eral thousand dollars; up to the time she came to Rochester she had had the reputation of never paying a bill, and, however hedged in she might be by justice, jury, constables, or sheriff, she not only escaped incarceration, but **beat** them all without paying any manner of tribute. She **had** done a fair business in duping Spiritualists and other weak-minded people while in Rochester; she had evidently levied upon Devereaux often and largely, and to my certain knowledge had taken some thousands of dollars from Lyon, and I was at a loss to know why she was growing so grasping and exacting as the reports showed was true of her; for she soon complained of being poor, levied additional assessment for care of the rooms, insisted upon her tenants receiving sittings at a good round price from her, and in general dropped the veneer which had formerly made her extremely fascinating, and became, save in exceptional moments of good nature, a masculine, repulsive shrew, who, with a slight touch of hideousness, might have passed for a stage witch or a neighborhood **plague.**

CHAPTER XIX.

AFTER a time Bristol and Fox became Mrs. Winslow's only confidants. Their business was to become so, and they successfully accomplished their object. As Bristol said in one of his reports : " Only set her tongue wagging, and she spouts away as irresistibly as an artesian well."

Had she been possessed of womanly instinct in the slightest degree, this would have been impossible. But being a male in everything save her physical structure, it was quite natural that she should hobnob with those most congenial ; and as she had antagonized all her lodgers save my operatives, and they made a particular effort to keep up a good-natured familiarity, the three were certainly on as easy terms as possible, and passed the autumn evenings, which were growing long now, in conversation of an exceedingly varied nature, with an occasional sitting or seance, and not infrequently a visitation of spirits of more material character ; and the following are a few of the many facts in this way brought out, and by Bristol and Fox transmitted to me at New York in their daily mail reports.

In one of Mrs. Winslow's peregrinations, probably for blackmail purposes, she secured the indictment in Craw-ford County, Pennsylvania, of one George Hodges, for swindling. He was not at that time arrested, but a year or so after, finding that he was in Cincinnati, and claim-ing that he was a non-resident, had him arrested as a fugi-tive from justice. When the case was called before an obscure justice, no prosecuting witness appeared, where-upon Hodges was discharged and at once secured a war-rant against her for perjury, but afterwards withdrew it. Meantime the woman shook the dust of Cincinnati from her feet and repaired to St. Louis, where she began several suits against parties there, notably one against a leading daily newspaper of that city, from which she afterwards secured one thousand dollars damages for libel. She afterwards swung around the circle to Harrisburg, Penn-sylvania, where she obtained from the Governor of that State a requisition on the Governor of Ohio, at Columbus, upon whom she waited and requested him to designate her as the person to whom should be delegated the power un-der the law to convey the fugitive, Hodges, to the Key-stone State ; but the private secretary of the Governor of Ohio suspecting that the person who had presented the papers, and for whose benefit they had been issued, would make improper use of them, they were returned to the Governor of Pennsylvania, whereupon she had made

Columbus ring with denunciations of gubernatorial corruption, and threatened to cause the impeachment of Pennsylvania's Executive, although those two commonwealths were never completely shattered by her.

Again in conversation regarding her case, which now seemed never out of her mind or off her tongue, she informed Bristol confidentially that she intended keeping Lyon in the dark altogether, giving him and his counsel no inkling as to what course she intended to pursue, which would so worry him that he would be glad to settle for at least twenty-five thousand dollars, rather than have the case come to trial and be exposed as she would expose him ; and if he did not settle at the last moment, she would have subpœnas issued for Lyon's mother-in-law, all his children, several other women who, the spirits had revealed, had been similarly betrayed, and even Lyon himself, and then she *would* make a sensation.

At this stage she was positive he would settle, as she knew he was half worried to death about the matter; and besides this, he knew that she knew he had told a certain lawyer of the city that he had once loved her better than any other woman on earth, and the only reason he had discarded her was that he was sure her love had taken hold on his pocket and forsaken himself.

She had signed a release of all claims, but she would stoutly maintain that it was fraudulently secured, which would only further establish the fact that she had had a valid claim upon him. Nor did she fear the opposing counsel. She was lawyer enough to attend to her own case, she said.   Her legal knowledge helped her through many a difficulty, and as she had been lawyer enough to file a declaration, she could get a rejoinder in shape whenever the answer should appear upon the court records.   Oh, she knew how to handle a jury; she had done it before!   In *this* case she would say: "Gentlemen of the jury: — There are many who believe that I merely seek for money.   This is not true.   I ask for a verdict that I may gain a husband.   For all of the injury that I have received—lost time, lost money, lost reputation, years of suspense and hope deferred—I only ask for a verdict in consonance with what a man in Lyon's position should be compelled to give to one so grossly wronged.   Gentlemen, if you give me a heavy verdict, you give me Mr. Lyon.   I say this in all sincerity—yes, as a proof of my sincerity.   I want the man, not his money; and a heavy verdict gives me the man, for Mr. Lyon is so penurious that he will marry me rather than pay the amount I claim. With him, he has so won my whole being, even in poverty I would feel richer than to live without him the possessor of millions!"

In delivering this eloquent peroration, Mrs. Winslow in reality rose upon a chair, and, figuratively, upon the giddy altitude of her dignity, and tossing back her head, elevating her eyebrows, looking peculiarly fierce with her great gray eyes, and flinging the back of her right hand into the palm of her left with quick, ringing strokes, delighted her audience of operatives, and male and female Spiritualists, who on this occasion crowded the reception-room and

cheered their hostess as she descended from her impro-
vised rostrum to order something to refill the glasses
which had been enthusiastically emptied to her overwhelming success.

When business was dull with the woman, she would be
certain to retain the company of the detectives, as :
seemed that she was beginning to avoid being left alone
as much as possible, and would, under no circumstances,
allow them both to be absent at the same time. Though
ordinarily careful of, and close with, her money, to keep
my men at home on these, to her, dreary evenings, she
would send for cigars, liquor, and choice fruits, and after
considerable urging they would remain, when the conversation would invariably turn upon the Winslow-Lyon case,
or some incident in the fair plaintiff's eventful life, which
the gentlemen as invariably listened to with the closest
interest and attention.

On one occasion Spiritualism was being discussed, when
Mrs. Winslow touched on her early history, and the revelation then made to her which in after-life convinced her
of the possession of supernatural powers. Her father had
had several boxes of honey stolen from his bee-hives,
when she was but a little girl. Search was made for them
in every possible direction, but no trace of them could be
found, whereupon she conveniently went into a trance,
the first she had ever experienced, continuing in that
state several hours, and finally awakening from it terribly
exhausted. But the trance brought the honey, for a
wonderful vision came upon her, wherein spirit-forms ap-

9*

peared clothed in overwhelming radiance, and, after ca-
ressing her spiritual form for some time, and making her
realize that she was an accepted child of Light, pointed
their dazzling celestial fingers towards an old hollow
stump standing at the side of the road leading towards
town. So powerful and penetrating was the light which
radiated from these spirits that it seemed to permeate the
stump, leaving its form perfect as ever, but making it
wholly translucent, so that she could see the boxes of
honey piled up within the stump as clearly as though she
had been standing beside it and it had been made of glass.
She gave this information to her father, who ridiculed the
revelation, but was both curious and desirous of getting
the honey, and went to the old stump, where he found the
boxes uninjured and piled in precisely the same manner
as described by his precocious child ; all of which was related as if thoroughly believed—as it doubtless was—in a
voice as hollow and mysterious as the stump itself, while
the operatives preserved the utmost gravity and decorum,
and impressed her in every way with their belief in her
varied and wonderful power.

Her affection for Bristol continued for a few weeks
unabated, and her most powerful arts were used in endeavoring to compel him to reciprocate it. These attempts went as far as a naturally lewd and naturally
shrewd woman dare go—so far, in fact, that in one and
the last instance they became absurdly ridiculous. There
was no bolt upon the door of either of their sleeping-
rooms, and, besides, it was necessary for Bristol to either

retire first or step into Fox's room for a little chat, or a sociable smoke, as Mrs. Winslow had an unpleasant and persistent habit of disrobing for the night in the reception-room.

One evening, after Mrs. Winslow had given a select seance to a few admiring friends, including my detectives, Bristol had hurried off to bed, being tired of the mummery, and after being obliged to listen for some time to her tumblings and tappings about the room, had finally fallen into a peaceful doze of a few minutes' duration, when he was awakened by that undefinable yet irresistibly increasing sense of some sort of a presence, which often takes from one the power of expression, or action, but intensifies the mind's faculties. The gas in the reception-room had been turned low, and his door had been softly opened. The rooms were quite dark, but the light from the street-lamps were sufficient to show him the plump outlines of a form which he felt sure that if it had had an orthodox amount of clothing upon it he could recognize. It certainly seemed to be the form of a woman, and her long, dishevelled black hair fell all about her shoulders and below her waist, while her *robe de nuit* trailed behind her with fear-inspiring, tremulous rustlings. On came the robust ghost, and in the weird gloaming which filled the apartment, he saw the mysterious thing moving towards him, and in a sort of frenzy of excitement yelled :

" Who's that ? "

No answer ; but the slow, firm pace of the apparition

came nearer to Bristol's bedside, and he partially rose upon his knees as if to defend himself.

"Say!—you!" shouted Bristol, "get—get out of here!"

But the ghostly figure came on as resistless as fate until it reached his bedside. By this time he had risen to his feet and was edging along the wall to escape, when to his horror he saw the spectre bound into the bed he had so expeditiously vacated and reach for him with a very business-like grasp which he nimbly eluded, and with a series of bounds and scrambles reached the floor. He stood where he had struck for a moment, addressing some very decided and italicized remarks to the lively ghost in his bed, and then, in one grand burst of virtuous indignation, made an impetuous dive at the figure, caught it by one of its very plump arms, brought the ghost from the bed with a mighty effort, and securing its left ear with his right hand, trotted the animated shadow out of his room and into the reception-room right up to the pier-glass, and then turning on one of the jets at its side, said to the magnificent ghost, in a voice husky from excitement and rage :

"Woman! if you ever do that thing again, I'll—I'll—aren't you ashamed of yourself, Mrs. Winslow?"

At the sound of her name, and after a few moments' apparently bewildered reflection, Mrs. Winslow opened her eyes, which had previously remained closed, and in an affectedly startled way gasped :

"Oh! where am I? what *have* you been trying to do with me, Mr. Bristol?"

To have seen the couple thus in the full gaslight before the pier-glass, which both reflected and intensified the odd situation—the woman, held to the mirror so that she might more startlingly view the result of her gauzy pretence at somnambulism, and the man, in his night-shirt, his limp night-cap dangling from his neck upon his shoulder, the ring of stubby gray hair around his head raised by excitement until it almost hid the glistening baldness above, his legs bare below the knees, but with a face so full of virtu-ous resentment at the scandalous and shallow scheme of the woman to implicate him in something disgraceful, that his uprightness clothed him as with fine raiment—would have been to have witnessed the apotheosis of sublimely triumphant virtue and the defeat of shame.

"What have *I* been trying to do with *you?*" shouted the now enraged Bristol; "that's all very fine; but what have *you* been trying to do with *me,* madam?"

"Why, didn't I ever tell you that I often walk in my sleep?" she asked with apparent innocence; and then, as if noticing for the first time how meagrely both herself and her companion were clad, gave vent to a half-smothered "Oh!—shame on you, Mr. Bristol!" and broke away from him, running into her own room, while Bristol, after walking back and forth in a state of high nervous excitement for some time, muttering, and shaking his fist towards her room, finally smoothed his rebellious locks so as to admit of the readjustment of his night-cap, and trotted fiercely to bed, never more to be disturbed by sleep-walk-ing female Spiritualists.

There was nothing in all this save a quite common and silly attempt on the part of the adventuress to get some of the hard-earned money of which she thought he was possessed, and it disgusted her that he was no more appreciative than to look upon her charms, that had set the heads of so many other men all awhirl, with such a cool and impressionless regard for them.

This latter fact bothered her probably fully as much as in not being able to get at his bank account, and she finally settled into a sort of suspicious dislike of him, and turned her attention to Fox, who, being a quiet sort of a fellow, with less brusqueness than Bristol, was not so well fitted to keep her at arm's length, and was consequently immediately the recipient of her torrent-like attentions, caresses, and confidence.

A book-keeper was the next thing to a retired banker— sometimes even better off, Mrs. Winslow thought; and, believing that Fox was the book-keeper he represented himself to be, she conceived the idea of travelling during the pendency of the suit, and gave Fox glowing accounts of the vast sums of money they could make if she only had so presentable a man as he for a sort of agent, manager, and protector.

One afternoon Fox came in early, and said that as he was suffering severely from headache he had been excused from his duties, and had come home for rest: He passed into his own room and laid down upon his bed, where he was immediately followed by the woman, who threw herself passionately into his arms, declaring that he was the only man whom she had ever really and truly loved, and terminated her expressions of ardor by a proposition that he should "get hold of a big pile down there to the store," as she expressed it, and fly to some quiet spot where they might revel in love and all that the term implies.

Had he been a book-keeper instead of what he was, and able to secure any large sum of money, she would have probably so bedevilled him that he would have become a criminal for life for the sake of gratifying his passion and her demands, and in a week after she would have had nine-tenths of the money, and Fox would have been a penniless fugitive from justice.

He had more trouble than Bristol in dispossessing the mind of the adventuress of the idea that he was not the man to allow her to become his Delilah ; but when this was done, and she disgustedly realized that not all men were ready to sell themselves body and soul for her embraces, while she was indignant and suspicious, yet a sort of easy confidence was established between the mysterious three, which brought out a good many strong points in her character, and at the same time led to the securing of a large amount of evidence against her.   In fact, it seemed that so soon as she thoroughly understood the, to her, novel situation of being in constant contact with two men who, though probably no better than average men, were still from the nature of their business compelled to be above reproach in all their association with her, her self-assertion and consciousness of power, which she had been able to assert over nearly every man with whom she came in contact, in a measure left her, and she became, at least to my operatives, an ordinary woman, whose inherent vileness, low cunning, and splendid physical perfection, were her only distinguishing characteristics. This was all natural enough, for I had compelled these men to be her almost constant companions, and as they had been with her long enough to drive away any superfluous constraint, and she had found both of them unassailable, though sociable and agreeable, her conversation, which chiefly concerned herself, became as utterly devoid of decency as her life had been, so that no incident or rehearsed romance of herself lost any of its piquancy by unnecessary assumption of modesty in its narration.

CHAPTER XX.

A Female Spiritualist's Ideas of Political and Social Economy.—The
Weaknesses of Judges.—Legal Acumen of the Adventuress.—An
unfriendly Move.—Harcout attacked.—Lilly Nettleton and the
Rev. Mr. Bland again together.—A Whirlwind.

ONE evening, after Mrs. Winslow had had a very
busy day with her spiritualistic customers, which
had become quite unusual, she showed herself to be more
than ordinarily communicative, undoubtedly on account
of the spirits which had kept her such close company,
and at once started in upon an edifying explanation of
her political views, and confided to Bristol and Fox, as
illustrative of her high political influence, that certain
officers of the Government only held their lease of office
through her leniency.

From this she verged into political and social economy,
stating her earnest belief to be that every man should
have a military education, and that if they were found to
be unfit physically to withstand the rigors of a military
life, they should be immediately condemned to death,
and thus be summarily disposed of. And so, too, with
women. There should be appointed a capable examining board, and wherever a woman was found wanting in
physical ability to meet every demand made upon her by

her affinities through life, she should also be instantly de
prived of existence. She maintained that there should be
a continuous and eternal natural selection of the best of
these mental and physical conditions, just the same as
the stock-raiser bred and inbred the finest animals to
secure a still finer type, and that all persons, male or
female, failing to reach a certain fit standard of perfection
in this regard, should be condemned to death. She
would have no marriage save that sanctioned by the
supreme love of one eternal moment; and shamelessly
claimed that passion was the real base of all love, and
that, consequently, it was but a farce on either justice or
purity that men and women should be by law condemned
to lives of miserable companionship. In this connection she held that not half the men and women were fit to
live, and were she the world's ruler she would preside at
the axe and the block half of her waking hours.

These sentiments were quite in keeping with her
expressions concerning the late war, her gratification at
Lincoln's assassination, and her threats that she had Presi-
dent Johnson in her power through her knowledge of
some transactions in Tennessee. This was, of course, all
silly talk, but it showed the woman's tendencies and disposition, and enabled Bristol and Fox to gradually lead
her into narrations of portions of her own career during
and after the war.

She boasted of her ability in fastening herself upon a
command, or military post, by getting some one of the
leading officers in her power so they dare not drive her

beyond the lines, and then, when the soldiers were paid off, getting them within her apartments, drugging them, robbing them, and finally securing their arrest for absence without leave. She claims that in this way she often made over five hundred dollars daily, and would then buy drafts on northern banks, not daring to keep the thou· sands of dollars about her which would frequently accrue.

Interspersed with these narratives were numberless tales of adventure wherein Mrs. Winslow, under her *aliases* of the different periods referred to, had been the heroine, and where her shrewdness and daring, she wished my operatives to understand, had brought utter dismay to each of her opponents, all of which had for its point and moral that she was not a person to be trifled with, as Mr. Lyon would eventually ascertain to his sorrow.

To more thoroughly impress this, in another instance the question of being watched and annoyed by Lyon or his agents arose, when she insisted to Bristol that Fox was a detective, and to Fox that Bristol was one, and then abruptly accused them both of the same offence, express· ing great indignity at the assumed outrage; and when they had succeeded in partially pacifying her, she turned on them savagely, saying that they had better bear in mind that she did not care whether they were detectives or not; that she was a pure woman—an innocent wo- man; but still, she wanted not only them, if they *were* detectives, but all the world, to understand that she was capable of taking care of herself, whoever might assail her. Evidently the good legal mind which the woman certainly possessed had reverted to her criminal acts in other portions of the country, for she asserted very violently that, should Lyon undertake to have her conveyed to any other State upon a requisition to answer to trumped-up charges for the purpose of weakening her case, she would shoot the first man that attempted her arrest; and that, if finally overpowered by brute force, she would still circumvent him by securing a continuance of the trial at Rochester, and make that sort of persecution itself tell against "the gray-headed old sinner," as she most truthfully called him.

She further remarked, with a meaning leer, that she never had any trouble with the judges. They were generally old men, she had noticed, and her theory was that old men, even if they were judges, had a quiet way of looking after the interests of as fine-appearing women as she was; and even if they did not have, her powers of divination were so wonderful that she could at any time go into the trance state and ascertain everything necessary to direct her to success, giving as an illustration a circumstance where a certain St. Louis daily newspaper had grossly libelled her, whereupon she had sued its proprietors for ten thousand dollars, retaining two lawyers to attend to her case. When it came to trial her counsel failed to appear. With the aid of the spirits she grasped the situation at once, and, showing Judge Moody a receipt for attorneys' fees amounting to two hundred dollars which she had paid them, pleaded personally for a continuance until the next day, which he granted, show

ing her conclusively that he was in sympathy with her,
She then went home, and, again calling on the spirits,
they revealed to her that she should win a victory.

So she read all the papers in the case, in order to acquaint herself with the leading points, and then subpœnaed her witnesses. Having everything well prepared,
she proceeded to the court-room the next day, and on the
case being called, the spirit of George Washington in
stantly appeared. It had a beautiful bright flame about
its head, and floated about promiscuously through the
upper part of the room. She was certain that it was a
good omen, but it was a long time before she could get
any definite materialization from the blessed ministering
angel from the other side of the river. After a time, however, George's kind eyes beamed upon her with unmistakable friendliness, and the nimbus, or flame, that shone
from his venerable head in all directions, finally shot in a
single incandescent jet towards the head of the judge ;
and immediately after, the gauzy Father of his Country
placed his hands upon the former's head, as if in benedic-
tion. This was a heavenly revelation to her that the judge
was with her, as afterwards proved true.

George stayed there until the trial was ended, which she
conducted in her own behalf, constantly feeling that she
herself was being upheld by strong, though invisible hands.
When the jury was being impanelled, the flame, with an
angry, red appearance, pointed to those men who were
prejudiced against her, to whom she objected, and they
were invariably thrown out of the panel ; while all through

the trial the judge insisted that there should be no advan
tage taken of her, if she had been forsaken by her coun
sel; and with the aid of Washington she won a splendid
victory, securing a judgment of one thousand dollars,
which was paid; and there are scores of lawyers and
newspaper men in St. Louis who will remember this case,
that know of the woman and her almost ceaseless litigation in that action, and who will also recollect that she did
get a thousand dollars from one of the leading newspapers
there.

Her cunning and shamelessness were largely com-
mented upon at the time; but it was reserved for Mrs.
Winslow to inform the world, through my operatives, that
George Washington ever descended to this grade of pet-
tifogging. It can only be accounted for through a knowledge of that peculiar system of religion which gives to the
very dregs of society a mysterious, and therefore terrible
power, whether assumed or otherwise, over its better ele-
ments for their annoyance, persecution, and downfall.

There was also a poetical and religious element in the
woman's composition which very well accorded with her
superstitiousness. This was quite strongly developed by
a liberal supply of liquor, which she never failed to use
whenever she became worried and excited over the coming trial, both of which begat in her impulses for certain
lines of conduct exactly the reverse of those counselled
by her more quiet, calculating reflections.

One pleasant October day, when suffering from a peculiarly severe attack of romantic fancies, she conceived the

idea of breaking through all her stern resolves relative to not seeing Lyon, and making one more effort to win him back to her altogether, or so affect him by her fascinating appearance that he would be glad to settle with her at any reasonable figure he might name—say twenty-five or fifty thousand dollars.

It was a pleasant fancy, and Bristol and Fox were exceedingly interested as they noticed her excited preparations for her expedition of conquest.   She sang like a bird, and the bright color came into her face as she tripped about, busied in the unusual employment.   All the forenoon she dressed and undressed, posing and balancing before the pier-glass like a *danseuse* at practice, studying the effect of different colors, shades, and shapes, until at last, having decided in what dress she should appear the most bewitching, she retired for a long sleep, so as to rest her features and give her eyes their old-time lustre.

At about two o'clock she awakened, and, after dressing in a most elaborate and elegant manner, at once started out upon her novel expedition to the Arcade.

The Arcade in Rochester is a distinct and somewhat noted place in that city.   It has nearly the width of the average street, and extends the distance of a short block —from Main Street to Exchange Place—being nearly in the geographical, as well as in the actual business centre of the city.   It is covered with a heavy glass roofing, filled on either side by numerous book and notion stalls, brokers' offices, and the offices of wealthy manufacturers whose business requires a down-town office, and is also, as it has been from almost time immemorial, the location of the post-office ; so that, as the thoroughfare leads directly from the Union Depot to the up-town hotels, it is constantly thronged with people, and is the spot in that city where the largest crowd may be collected at the slightest possible notice.

To Mrs. Winslow's credit it should be said that up to this time she had kept so remarkably quiet that public scandal had nearly died away, and as she had gone into the different newspaper offices with some of the wicked old light burning in her eyes, and "warned" them concerning libelling her, both she and her suit were no longer causing much remark ; but now, when she was seen majestically bearing down Main street, with considerable fire in her fine eyes, determination in her compressed lips, and the inspiration of resolve in every feature of her handsome though masculine face, there were many who, knowing the woman, felt sure there was to be a scene, and by the time she had turned from Main street into the Arcade quite a number were unconsciously following her. After she had got into the Arcade she attracted a great deal of attention in sweeping back and forth through that thoroughfare, as in passing Lyon's offices she gave her head that peculiarly ludicrous inclination that all women affect when they are particularly anxious to be noticed, but also particularly anxious to not have it noticed that they wish to be noticed ; and continued her promenade, each time brushing the windows of Lyon's offices with her ample skirts, and growing more and more indignant that nobody appeared to be interested in her exhibition, save the lookers-on within the Arcade, who were increasing rapidly in numbers.

This seemed to exasperate the woman beyond measure, and finally, after casting a hurried glance or two through the half-open door, she apparently nerved herself for the worst and made a plunge into the office, while the crowd closed about the door.

Bristol had of course felt it his duty to inform Mr. Lyon of the fair lady's intended demonstration, and the latter had judiciously found it convenient to transact some important business in another part of the city on that afternoon; but the elegant Harcout had bravely volunteered to throw himself into the breach and bear the brunt of the battle—in other words, sacrifice himself for his friend, and was consequently sitting at Lyon's desk behind the railing, which formed a sort of a private office at one side of the general office, as Mrs. Winslow, pale with rage and humiliated to exasperation, came sweeping into the room.

"Ah, how d'ye do, ma'am?" said Harcout blandly, but never looking up from his desk, at which he pretended to be very busily engaged. "Bless my soul, you seem to be very much excited!"

"Sir!" said Mrs. Winslow, interrupting him violently, "I want none of your 'madams' or 'bless my souls.' I want Lyon, you puppy!"

"Ah, exactly, exactly," replied Mr. Lyon's protector with the greatest apparent placidity, though with a shade
10

of nervousness in his voice; "but you see, my dear, you can't have him !"

It was not the first time this man had called this woman ' my dear," nor was it the first time he had attempted to beat back her overpowering passion. Had he known it as Mr. Harcout, or had she recognized him as Mrs. Winslow, it would have made the interview more dramatic than it was—perhaps a thread of tragedy might have crept in; as it was, however, she only savagely retorted that she wouldn't have him, but she would see him if he was in, whether or no.

"Well, my dear good woman," continued Harcout soothingly, but edging as far from the railing and his caller as possible, "he isn't in, and that settles that. Further, you can't have, or see, him *or* his money, and that settles that. So you had best quietly go home like a good woman and settle all this," concluded Harcout winningly and yet impressively, and with the tone of a Christian counsellor.

The crowd laughed and jeered at this grave and sarcastic advice, and it seemed to madden her. Raising her closed sunshade and hissing, "*I'll* settle this !" she rushed towards Harcout, struck at him fiercely, following up the attack with quick and terrific blows, which completely demolished the parasol and drove him nimbly from place to place in his efforts to avoid the effects of her wrath.

For the next few moments there was a small whirlwind in Lyon's offices. The railing was too high for Mrs.

Winslow to leap, or she certainly would have scaled it. Harcout could not retreat but a certain distance, or he certainly would have sought safety in flight. So the whirlwind was created by rapid and savage leaps of Mrs. Winslow, as if to jump the railing and fall bodily upon her victim, and at every bound the woman made, the shat tered parasol waved aloft and came down with keen cer- tainty and stinging swiftness, upon such portions of the gilt-edged gentleman as could be most conveniently reached.

It is difficult to realize what the woman would have done in her mad passion, had not a lucky circumstance occurred. She and Harcout had never met since the time when, in the face of her robbery of him, she had un- blushingly compelled him to wed her to the credulous Dick Hosford at the Michigan Exchange Hotel in Detroit; and had she now recognized him as the villain who had made her what she was, it is a question whether she would not have made a finish of him there and then. But some one in the crowd raised the cry of " Police ! " which sobered her at once, and, giving the tattered rem- nant of her sunshade a wicked pitch into Harcout's face, she turned quickly, shot into the Arcade as the crowd made way for her and quickened her speed by wild jibes and taunts, until she had reached the street, where, in a dazed, hunted sort of way, she hailed a passing cab, sprang into it, and was driven rapidly away.

CHAPTER XXI.

Mrs. Winslow, under the Influence of " Spirits " of an earthly Order,
becomes romantic, religious, and poetical.—A Trance.—Detective
Bristol also proves a Poet.—A Drama to be written.

WHEN the evening came and Mrs. Winslow came
with it, she was observed to be in a high state of
nervous and vinous excitement, and at such times she
contrived to inaugurate a series of actions which proved
not only interesting, but illustrative of her strange
character.

She declared to Bristol and Fox that the Lord was
hardening Lyon's heart as in the olden times the heart of
Pharaoh was hardened, so that he should rush upon his
fated disgrace as the Egyptian king rushed upon his fate
while forcing the children of Israel into deliverance, and
destruction upon himself; and like the unrelenting Mrs.
Clennam in " Little Dorrit," had at command any number of scriptural parallels to prove the righteousness of
her sin. This sort of blasphemy is the most pitiable imaginable, and to hear the woman in her semi-intoxicated,
semi-crazed condition, mingling her vile catch-words with
scraps of spiritualistic sayings, snatches of holy songs,
couplets of roystering ballads, and crowning the hideous-

ness of the whole with countless Bible quotations, was to be in the presence of supreme garrulousness, temperamen-tal religious frenzy, and superstitious vileness.

It appeared that after she had escaped from the excite-ment she had created in the Arcade, she had been driven to the apartments of every clairvoyant of note in the city and had a "sitting" with each. In her excited condition, and being noted for having plenty of money, it was both easy to rob her and secure what was uppermost in her mind. Consequently, it was revealed to her by every medium that Lyon would settle with her for a large sum of money.

One medium averred that in her vision Lyon was seen, as it were, bending a suppliant at her feet, and, at the last moment, admiring her character as much as fearing the nature of the testimony he knew she could bring against him, he declared his love for her and begged that they might be married in open court.

Another depicted the sorrows she would be obliged to endure before her affairs culminated. She would be watched, annoyed, harassed; but her way would be well watched by the spirit-forms which were evidently floating around promiscuously to protect the pests of society; and, whether she got the man or not, she should share his fortune. This much could be surely promised.

Another was wonderfully favored with divine "spirit light" upon the subject—so favored, indeed, that time without number her other-life had insensibly and uncon-sciously wandered away in search of correct information regarding the result of the Winslow-Lyon suit, and, without her volition or bidding. it had delved into the mysteries for her suffering sister. She could assure her suffering sister, the clairvoyant said, that Lyon was spiritually at her feet. All the trouble had arisen between them from Mrs. Winslow's standing upon a higher spiritual plane than Mr. Lyon. He, as was natural to man, had more of the sensual element beclouding his spirit-life. Now, pleaded the clairvoyant, couldn't she adjust an average between them? She was certain—yes, the spirits, who never lie, had positively revealed to her that all that was needed was some one to properly discover each of these affinities to the other. In any case, all would eventually be well, and there was peace, prosperity, and a large amount of money in waiting for her.

This sort of absurdity was related by Mrs. Winslow to an unlimited extent that evening, as the three sipped the liquor she had provided, and she insisted with great fervor that all these revelations strongly corroborated the light she herself had received on the same subject.

As a long pause ensued after one of these heated asseverations, Bristol ventured to ask how she had been enlightened concerning the matter.

Raising her flushed face towards the ceiling, then lifting her right arm above her head and holding it there for a moment, she allowed it to slowly descend with a coiling, serpentine motion, when she burst into a sudden ecstasy of speech, movement and feature, and partly as in answer to the inquiry, and partly as if struck with a swift and irresistible inspiration, she said in a low, unearthly voice, and with weird effect :

"Yes, yes, I hear your angel voices calling ; I see your beautiful forms ; I feel your tender fingers touching my aching head ; I am listening to your sweet, soft whispers. Ah ! what is it you say ?—yes, yes, yes ! You *are* with me. You will watch over and guard me. You will ward off the evil influences that surround me, and despite the darkness which envelops me, even as the glorious sun leaps from his couch of crimson and with his burnished lances drives the grim hosts of shadows before him with the speed of the light !—What ! are you now leaving ?"

Here Mrs. Winslow gasped and kicked with her pretty feet alarmingly.

"What—what is that ?—that rosy, effulgent light that fills all space ? Ah, yes ! I see they beckon for me to look up, to not be cast down or despair. I *will* look up. See ! in their hands are long, feathery wands with which they sweep the flaming sky, while across its burnished arc I see, yes, I see in letters of purple that oft-recurring legend—*Twenty-five thousand dollars !*"

Now, although I am not arguing this question of Spiritualism, and am only giving to the public the history so far as I dare of an extraordinary woman and practical Spiritualist, I cannot resist asking the question, or putting forward the theory, which, during the progress of this case particularly, and a thousand times before and since in a general way, has irresistibly forced itself into my mind. I give it in all fairness, I am sure, and only with a view that it may dispel certain feelings of squeamishness with which a good many people approach the subject to investigate it. I may be accused of presenting it with too little delicacy; but the public must recollect that the nature of my business compels me *to get at the truth* of things, and to do that, matters must in a majority of cases be handled without gloves. This is my only excuse, and perhaps it may be a good defence; but in any event this is the question: Has there ever been a so-called Spiritual " manifestation " that has not subsequently been explained as trickery by persons more credible of belief than its medium or originator ? After that has been answered in the affirmative, for it can be answered in no other way, all there is left of this Spiritualistic structure is, how account for such exhibitions as that given by Mrs. Winslow and those given by others of her craft, even granting their personal purity, which is undoubtedly exceptional ?

This is the question which has oftenest come into my mind in my necessarily almost constant study of these people, and the answers, though continually varying, have all eventually forced upon me the conviction that this religion, as it is sacrilegiously called, only takes hold of people of abnormal or diseased temperaments—people diseased in mind, in morals, in body, or in all ; and if that is true, as I sincerely believe it to be, the dignifying of a disease or infirmity as a religion is simply an absurdity too foolish for even ridicule.

She sat rigid as a church-spire for a few moments, as *if*

the sight of so much money, even if only in purple letters upon a burnished sky, had transfixed her, and then, after a little hysterical struggling, became as limp as a camp-meeting tent after a thunder-storm ; and after a few passes of her long, white and deft fingers over her eyes in a scared way, asked, " Oh, gentlemen, where—where am I ? "

" On the boundaries of the spirit-land," gravely replied Bristol, pushing the bottle of liquor to the side of the table.

The woman was certainly exhausted, for she had worked herself into such a state mentally—precisely the same as in all similar demonstrations, whether visions are claimed to be seen, or not—that she was completely en-ervated physically, and said in a really grateful tone, " Thank you, Mr. Bristol," and, pouring out a large por-tion of liquor, tossed it off at one gulp, like a well-prac-tised bar-room toper.

" Yes, yes," she continued languidly, " I have a certain promise of eventually being victorious. When the good spirits are with one, there's no cause for fear."

" Not the slightest," affirmed Fox sympathetically.

" But it seems," replied Mrs. Winslow in a discouraged, desolate tone, " as though everybody's hand is raised against me—as though the dreary days pass so slowly— and that I haven't a true friend in the world ! "

" My dear Mrs. Winslow," interrupted Bristol in a calm, fatherly, even affectionate tone, " that melancholy's all very fine ; but we are your friends, and we will stand
10*

by you through thick and thin to the end of the suit.   A few fast friends, you know, are better than a thousand sunny-weather friends."

" Oh, yes ; oh, yes," returned the woman in a tone of voice that said, " I can't argue this, but I somehow *know* you aie both betraying me," and then, closing her eyes, and clasping her hands tightly together, sang in a weird contralto voice, cracked and unsteady from her excitement and exhaustion, some stanza of an evidently religious nature, the burden of which was :

> " I am weary, weary waiting
> While the shadows deeper fall ;
> I am weary, weary waiting
> For some holy voice's call ! "

Undoubtedly the song, though desecrated by the singer, the place, and the occasion, was a wailing plaint from the depths of the woman's soul, for moments of utter desolation and absolute remorse come to even such as she.

"Now," said Bristol, becoming suddenly interested, " I'm something of a poet myself.   When the seat of government was moved from Quebec to Ottawa, I con-structed a lampoon on the government that set all Can-ada awhirl.   Really, Mrs. Winslow, I'm surprised at your poetical nature."

"Poetical nature ? " repeated the woman excitedly ' Why ! that is what Lyon loved in me most.   My trance-sittings are wonderful exhibitions of poetical power.   In that state I can compose poems of great length and power."

The gentlemen of course seemed incredulous at this statement, and challenged her to a test of her poetical tiance-power, which she instantly accepted, the wager being a quart of the best brandy that could be had in the city of Rochester.

Putting herself in position, she asked : "What subject ?" Bristol replied, "Lyon," when she struggled a little in her chair, kicked the floor a little with her heels, rubbed up her eyes, gasped, and after a moment of rest began to incant in a kind of monotone tenor :

> "Oh, Lyon, Lyon ! don't you run ;
> The suit's begun ; we'll have our fun
> Before we're done.   I'll tell your son
> That I have won, although you shun
>   Your darling one ! "

> "Oh, Lyon, pray, why speed away ?
> To fight a woman is but play.
> Although you're old, and bald, and gray,
> Do right by your Amanda J.—
>   You'll soon be clay ! "

Amanda J. Winslow, for this was the woman's assumed name in full, might have continued in this divine strain for an indefinite period, had not the operatives burst into loud and prolonged laughter at her ludicrous appearance, which so disgusted the woman that, though communicating with celestial spheres, as she assumed to be, and un-doubtedly was doing as much as any of her craft ever did.

she jumped up with a bound, savagely told the men they were a brace of fools, and with a lively remark or two, which had something very like an oath in it, went to bed, leaving the men to finish the bottle and the poetry as they saw fit.

Mrs. Winslow was a thorough church-goer, and distributed the favor of her attendance among the orthodox churches and the "meetings" of the members of her own faith, quite fairly—perhaps, as was natural, giving the Washington Hall Sunday evening Spiritualistic lectures a slight preference; and soon after the Arcade affair, which had launched her into poetry, she returned to the rooms one Sunday evening, declaring that all her evil spirits had left her, and that her former passionate love for Lyon had also departed, her only desire now being for his money.

To show how thoroughly she had been dispossessed of her evil spirits, she remarked that she now thoroughly hated Lyon, but it would not do to let this appear on trial, or she would lose the sympathy of the jury. Every effort should now be bent towards compelling him to divide his wealth with her, whom he had so deeply wronged. There should be no compromise; she would not even be led to the altar by him now. She would have from him what would most annoy him, and that was his money.

Having resolved on this, the darkness that surrounded her was dispelled and the spirits of light rallied as a sort of standing army; and in this beneficent condition she

wished to either go into the country to recuperate foi
a few weeks, or seek the retirement of Fox's room and
there expend her superfluous brain and spirit power upor
a play to be entitled "His Breach of Promise." To this
end she proposed removing the elegant furnishings of hei
apartments and storing them in a spare room, giving out
to callers that she was absent from the city, and then,
after having secured Fox's room, she would be able to
burn the midnight oil unmolested so long as her inspiration might continue.

She also favored Fox and Bristol with a sketch of the
play, which was to be a sort of spectacular comedy-drama,
which, according to the lady's description, would contain
certainly seven acts of five scenes each, and would be preceded by a prologue which would play at least an hour;
in fact, it seemed that the great play "His Breach of
Promise" was to be constructed on the Chinese plan, to
be continued indefinitely, and admission only to be
secured in the form of course tickets. Outside of these
great aids to the popularity of the play, it was to have the
additional startling and novel attractions of represen-
tations of her first meeting with Lyon, his regret because she was married, his copious tears whenever in her
presence, his securing her divorce, the death of Lyon's
wife, and every manner of pathetic and ludicrous incident
connected with the case; how they each wooed and won
the other, including a grand transformation scene typical
of Lyon's subsequent treachery, and her reward of virtue
in a fifty thousand dollar verdict for damages.

CHAPTER XXII.

THE reports which I had for some time received
daily regarding Mrs. Winslow's behavior satisfied
me that the delay in reaching the Winslow-Lyon case—
which was at the bottom of the docket of the fall term,
and on account of a press of court business had been put
over. to the winter term—the strict silence I had en-
joined upon Mr. Lyon, and the general suspicion which
possessed her of everybody and everything, were all
having the natural effect of unsettling her completely, and
I determined upon a series of surprises and annoyances
to the woman, without in any way apprising Bristol and
Fox of what was to be done; so that although they might
imagine from what source the unwelcome "materializations" came, they would still be sufficiently uninformed
to share in the general surprise and escape the charge of
complicity.

I accordingly sent three additional men to Rochester

with thorough instructions and full information as to the madam's residence and habits, with a description of her tenants, including Bristol and Fox, who were unknown to the operatives sent.

My object in doing this was a double one. I desired, first, to test the woman's so-called spirit power ; for, should these annoyances prove of the nature of a persecution, she and her friends, the Spiritualists, would be able to call celestial spirits to her aid, or, better still, divine from whence the persecution came, and compel its discontinuance by the means provided by ordinary mortals. In case she could not do this, which was of course rather doubtful, I knew from her superstitiousness and the guilty fear possessed by every criminal, which she largely shared, that she would be quite likely to either make some confessions which would implicate her in further blackmailing operations, or force her into a line of conduct agreeing perfectly with her true character, and which would compel her to show herself thoroughly to the public; and further, I think I must confess to a slight desire to assist a little in punishing her, after I had become so fully aware of her villainous character.

Accordingly, while Mrs. Winslow was still deep in the plot of her great drama, but before the changes suggested —which would have made her a sort of literary nun in Fox's room—had occurred, she was the recipient of a large package of railway time-tables, with the farthest terminus of each road underscored, and further called attention to by a hand and index finger pointing towards it.

from Rochester, intimating that it was either desired or demanded, on the part of somebody, that she should leave Rochester for one of the points indicated.

When Bristol and Fox returned "home," as they had come to call their lodgings, that evening, Mrs. Winslow was at her escritoire, completely immersed in time-tables and manuscript, and had all the air of an important author struggling for fitting expressions with which to clothe some suddenly inspired, though sublime idea.

She looked at them closely a moment, as if she would read their very thoughts.   Whether seeing anything suspicious or not, she remarked very pointedly :

"Good deal of railroad rivalry nowadays, isn't there ?"

"Yes, considerable," replied Bristol pleasantly, and then asking, "Are you going to introduce some rival railroads in your new play, Mrs. Winslow ?"

"Not much !" she answered tersely.

"I wouldn't," replied Bristol, taking a seat near the chandelier and pulling a paper from his pocket; "they're dangerous."

Mrs. Winslow paid no attention to this, but suddenly eyed Fox, and sharply asked :

"They like very much to sell through tickets, don't they ?"

"I believe they do—ought to pay better," he promptly rejoined, eyeing her in return.

"Well," said she, after a slight pause, and as if with something of a sigh, "it's all right, perhaps; but if either of you should meet any railroad agent who seems to be laboring under the delusion that I want to found a colony in some far country, just tell him to expend his energies in some other direction!"

Of course my operatives were surprised, and demanded an explanation; but the recipient of the circulars was quite dignified, and would only clear the matter up by occasional little passionate bursts of confidence, as if finding fault with them for not being able to unravel the mystery to her. They protested they knew nothing about the matter, and she undoubtedly believed them; but she ventured to inform them that if anybody—mind you, anybody—supposed they could scare her away from Rochester by any such hint as that, they were mightily mistaken, that's all there was about *that.*

My detectives allayed her fears as much as possible, but it was plainly observable that she was really annoyed by the occurrence. There is always a hundred times more terror in the fear of unknown evil than in that which we can boldly meet, and this particularly applies to those who know they *deserve* punishment, as in Mrs. Winslow's case.

The next evening they were all sitting discussing general topics and a pint of peach brandy, and had become exceedingly sociable, particularly over the railroad circulars, which Fox and Bristol had by this time induced her to regard in the light of a huge joke, or error, when the party were suddenly startled by some object which caused a peculiar ringing, yet deadened sound, as it struck the partly-opened door and then bounded upon the carpet where it glisteningly rolled out of sight under the sofa where the thoroughly-scared Mrs. Winslow sat.

"My God! what's that?" she screamed, rushing to the door and peering down the staircase, as rapidly retreating footsteps were distinctly heard ; but not being able to discover anybody, scrambled back into the room, shutting and bolting the door behind her.

The woman was deathly pale, the color brought to her face by the brandy having been driven from it as if by some terrible blow ; but it came back with her into the room, where Bristol and Fox *appeared* nearly as frightened as she.

She looked at them a moment in a dazed, stupefied way, and then demanded : "What does this mean?"

"That's what I'd like to know!" returned Bristol, hunting for his quizzers, which he had lost in his jump from his chair. "This is all very fine, but it's pretty plain somebody here's sent for!"

"And *I* don't want to go!" chimed in Fox, climbing down from a safe position upon the *escritoire.*

The three looked at each other in an extremely suspicious way, and the woman again demanded, this time threateningly, what it all meant.

"Something with a glitter, and it rolled under there," was all Bristol could tell her about it.

"Let's get it, whatever it is!" said Fox, with an apparent burst of bravery and spirit.

So Bristol at one end and Fox at the other end of the sofa, rolled it out with a great show of caution, while Mrs.

The three looked at each other in an extremely suspicious way.—

Winslow, though preserving a good position for observation, kept nimbly out of the way.

"What can it be?" she persisted excitedly.

"A vial sealed with red wax, with a string attached, and containing some clear liquid," said Fox, stooping to pick it up.

"Don't—don't, Fox!" shouted Bristol, pushing him back impetuously; "the devilish thing may burst and kill us all—nitro-glycerine, you know!"

Mrs. Winslow shuddered, drew her elegant wrappings about her fair shoulders, as if the thought chilled her like the sudden opening of some cold vault, and looked appealingly at the two men.

"Or might contain some deadly poison," said Fox, in a warning tone.

"And the fiend who threw it in here expected the bottle to break and the poison to murder us!" said Mrs. Winslow indignantly.

"Things have come to a pretty pass when attempts like this are made on people's lives!" said Bristol, adjusting his spectacles and edging towards the mysterious missile.

"I shall move at once," stoutly affirmed Mrs. Winslow.

"Don't do any such thing," said Fox earnestly. "That will only show whoever may be committing these indignities that we are alarmed by them."

"We?—*we?*" repeated the adventuress, with a peculiar accent upon the word "we." "It isn't you men that is meant. It's *me*. This is some of that Lyon's doings. Oh, I could cut his heart out!"

The detectives saw that she was getting greatly excited, and Bristol, with a view of quieting her as much as possible for the night, picked up the vial by a string tied to it and hung it upon a nail, remarking that he was something of a chemist himself and didn't believe it was explosive, and also expressed a conviction that Mrs. Winslow should have it analyzed.

To this she acceded, and expressed a determination to "get even" with the author of these outrages, in which laudable resolve the detectives promised to assist her; but the peach brandy seemed the only relief possible to Mrs. Winslow for the remainder of the evening, which was chiefly passed in wild speculations and theories concerning the new "manifestations, which she began to fear might be the result of jealous clairvoyants and vindictive spiritualists, who had endeavored to blackmail both herself and Mr. Lyon, and, failing in this, were now persecuting her.

The next day Mrs. Winslow went out quietly and secured the services of a chemist under the Osborne House, who pronounced the contents nothing but water, which proved a great relief to the agitated trio, but did not remove from Mrs. Winslow's mind the anxiety and unrest that these undesired and unlooked-for materializations were causing.

About noon, after Fox and Bristol had come in from a little stroll and they were all laughing over the scare of the previous evening, a step was heard on the stairs, and soon after a little man with a big box on his shoulder, and a slouched hat on his head which hid his face pretty thoroughly, came to the head of the stairs, knocked at the door, and without waiting for an invitation to come in, entered, and depositing the box with the remark, "For Mrs. Winslow, from the Misses Grim," spryly sprang back, shut the door, and clattered away down the stairs and into the street before Mrs. Winslow could get a second look at him, though she sprang after him, shouting, "Here! here! come back here or I'll have you arrested!" But he only clattered away the livelier, and she returned to the room raging and vowing that the box contained some infernal machine for the purpose of distributing minute portions of her anatomy all over the city of Rochester. .

This became more likely when Mrs. Winslow recollected that the Misses Grim—Tabitha, Amanda, and Hannah—were the three old maids from whom she had thought she had secured a wealthy old banker to pluck; and though he had proven to her a very ordinary man, somewhat infirm from rheumatism, and a trifle quarrelsome, though eminently virtuous and punctilious, she had never, of course, let them know how badly she had been swindled; and as they yet regarded their lost boarder, Bristol, as a priceless treasure, lost to them through her perfidy, it was no more than natural, Mrs. Winslow thought, that in their chagrin and disappointment they should concoct some diabolical plan to injure her.

But still it might not be from them. She had other enemies, many of them, and the Misses Grim's name might have been given to cover up some other person's misdeeds.   But whatever it might be, her curiosity soon overcame her fear, and she requested Fox to open it.

After securing a hammer from his room, the latter proceeded to open the mysterious box ; but after the cover had been partially drawn and it was evident that the box had not been delivered for the purpose of exterminating anybody, it occurred to its fair owner that there might be something within it not desirable for her to let the gentlemen see, whereupon she requested them to retire ; but after Bristol had grumblingly disappeared, and Fox had got to the door, she recalled the latter and asked him anxiously if he would not open it for her.   He gallantly agreed to, and got down on his knees upon the carpet and began taking off the cover.

"I do wonder what it can be !" said Mrs. Winslow anxiously.

"I can't find anything but bran," returned Fox, digging about the box carefully.

"Bran !" she exclaimed incredulously ; "that box is too heavy for bran."

Fox dug away for a little while longer and finally shouted, "I've got something !"

"And what is that something ?"

The question was answered by the thing itself, which now appeared from the bottom of the box, vigorously lifted by Fox's hand and plumped through the bran upon the carpet.

"Well, what is it ?" she demanded.

"Vegetable," said Fox tersely.

"Oh, pshaw ! is *that* all ? " asked the disgusted woman.

"Yes, that's all," he replied, after digging about in the bran for a moment.   Mrs. Winslow also satisfied herself that it was all by searching in the bran, and the two then proceeded to investigate the vegetable.

"It's a turnip, and somebody's been digging in it," said Mrs. Winslow.

"I think you are mistaken," mildly interposed Fox. " It's something else entirely."

"What's this ! " exclaimed the woman ; "sure as I live, a cross-bones and skull on one side, and on the other side, ' D-e-a-d '—dead ! "

"It isn't dead turnip ! " interrupted Fox.

"Dead beet ? " she asked musingly, a sudden crimson flooding into her face.

"Shouldn't wonder," he answered.

Biting her lips she glided to a window.   It was a cold autumn day, and the panes rattled drearily as she seemed to shrink and hide between them and the heavy curtains, while the color came and went hotly in her face.   It hurt her, wounded her, showed her to be the thing she was in a way that could never have been effected by ten thousand innuendoes or direct charges ; and she pressed her face against the cold panes as if to force and drive away the hideous picture that a momentarily honest glimpse of herself had revealed to her, and continued standing thus, buried in the memories which build remorse, until, noticing the thing in her hand which had caused this humiliation, she flung it violently across the room, and rush-

ing into her sleeping-room, hastily prepared for going out,
then dashing through the reception-room, she passed into
the hall, and meeting Bristol, said :

" Bristol, I want you to come with me ! "

Bristol immediately complied, but was given a lively
chase, for Mrs. Winslow was strong of limb, fleet of foot,
and, on this occasion, was impelled by a burst of spirit
which, if rightly directed, would have led a conquering
army.

She started directly for Main Street, and turned up that
thoroughfare at a pace which attracted considerable attention. After rapidly walking two blocks she swept
across the street, and after having waited for Bristol to
come up with her, plunged into the little restaurant under
Washington Hall, with my operative close at her heels.

The sudden entrance of the couple caused a great commotion in the quaint little eating-room, and the drowsy
customers smiled when they saw the unaccustomed form
of the woman whom the Misses Grim—Tabitha, Amanda
and Hannah—had taken no trouble to prevent being
known as her deadly enemy.

Tabitha, the most ancient, at once bristled up and took
a position behind her neat counter, her wrinkled head
trembling with so much excitement that her sparse curls
created a kind of quivering nimbus about it.

"Well, ma'am, and what can *I* do for *you?*" asked
Tabitha with a flaunt of her head and a sarcastic tinge in
her voice.

Mrs. Winslow got to the counter in two or three **quick**

jumps or starts, and asked, husky with rage, " I—-I just want to know which one of you old straws sent that box to me ? "

" Box to *you !* " jerked out Amanda, the next less ancient of the Misses Grim, who had just entered and at once stopped stock still to catch Mrs. Winslow's remark ; " box to you?   Tush !—box to nobody ! " and she too sidled in behind the counter to reinforce, and tremble with, her very old sister.

" Oh, you can't play your innocence on me ! " retorted Mrs. Winslow very violently.   " You wear very white collars, and very black caps and very straight dresses, and look very saintly, but you're just three old witches ; that's what you are ! "

" Pooh, pooh ! " snorted Tabitha and Amanda hysterically.

" Pooh, pooh ! if you like ; but if I find out which one of you sent that box, I'll—I'll shake every bone in her old body into a match ! " shouted Mrs. Winslow, dancing up and down against the counter and working her fingers savagely.

" Match ? " responded Hannah, the least ancient and most fiery of the three virgins, and who entered at this critical moment ; " match indeed ! you're a match for anything villainous ! " and then she too trotted behind the counter to throw the weight of her presence into the conflict.

By this time the interested customers had gathered around, and people from the street, noticing the unwonted enthusiasm awakened in the Washington Hall restaurant, were rapidly collecting upon the outside and flattening their curious noses against the intervening panes.

Mrs. Winslow could no more control herself than could the old maids, and quickened by the presence of the increasing crowd, burst into a screaming demand for the person who sent the "dead" beet to her.

"Dead beat!—ha, ha, ha!" laughed the three sisters convulsively, at once realizing the appropriateness of the joke and excitedly enjoying it; "dead beat, eh? we didn't do it!"   "But," added Hannah, maliciously, "if you do find the person as did send it, Mrs. Winslow, and will send 'em around, we'll board 'em for a month free!"

There was war, direful war, imminent; and no one could imagine what might have resulted had the conflict of tongues culminated in a conflict of hands.   But to have seen the three ancient, prim, and trembling women on the one side, and the ponderous, though handsome Mrs. Winslow on the other—the old maids either with arms akimbo or with hands firmly clenched upon the counter's edge as if to compel restraint, their bodies weaving back and forth, their heads bobbing up and down, and their stray frills and curls wildly dancing as if each particular hair was in a mad ecstasy of its own; and Mrs. Winslow, upon her side of the counter, in a perfect frenzy of excitement, stamping her feet, jumping backward and forward, bringing her clenched hand down upon the counter with terrible force for a woman, and shaking it furiously at the agitated row of old maids, would be to

"A marvelous improvement over any form of the Punch and Judy show ever exhibited."—

have witnessed a marvellous improvement upon any form of the Punch and Judy show ever exhibited.

Bristol saw that unless they were separated he would become implicated in a case of assault and battery, and after great effort pacified the women sufficiently to enable him to pilot his landlady out of the restaurant, through the streets and finally into her own apartments, where she passed the remainder of the dreary day in weeping, storms of baffled rage, or protracted applications to the spirits which can be controlled, whether one is a spiritualist or not, so long as money lasts and total prohibition is not enforced.

CHAPTER XXIII.

MRS. WINSLOW now began to show great perturbation of spirits. In conversation with my
detectives, who endeavored to cheer her up and lead her
to regard these surprises as mere jokes not worth any
person's notice, she constantly argued the opposite, and
thus arguing, conjured up countless possibilities of harm,
gradually working herself into that condition of mind
where every little unusual noise or movement of any person in the building or upon the street was a signal for
some querulous inquiry or complaint.

She was also very much worried concerning her suit,
and went about among the Spiritualists seeking their advice and encouragement, and giving and receiving a good
deal of scandal concerning the case. From one she
would hear that Lyon was employing certain other mediums in his behalf, and that she had better look out for
them. Another would inform her that Lyon had several
other mistresses, among them a Miss Susie Roberts, and

a Madame La Motte, both Spiritualists and mediums, from whom Lyon intended to prove her bad character, and whom she, in turn, vowed she would have subpœnaed in her own behalf, and impeach their testimony through what she could compel them to admit of both themselves and Lyon. At other places she learned that these persecutions were Lyon's work entirely, or rather, the work of nis agents, principal among whom were the two ladies mentioned. And, in fact, wherever she went she heard or found something to give her uneasiness or cause her unrest.

"Yes," she said sadly to my operatives, "I can't stand this sort of thing much longer."

"Oh, nonsense!" rejoined Bristol; "you haven't been hurt, have you?"

"No; but I can't tell when I shall be. That's what I can't bear."

"But I thought you were a woman of too great force of character to allow trifles to trouble you," exclaimed Fox tauntingly.

"Trifles!" said she hotly; "trifles! Is expecting every moment to be murdered, or blown up, a trifle? Is fearing that everything you taste will poison you, or everything you touch do you deadly harm, a trifle?"

"People will think you deserve to be annoyed if you show them you are annoyed," argued Fox.

"I have long since ceased to care what people think. Sometimes I am sure I hate every human being; and I do believe the more the world hates me, the more money

I make.   If these things are not stopped soon, I tell you," she continued in a tone of voice that seemed to say they could stay the annoyances if they would, " I'll go to St Louis and attend to my cases there !"

This opened the eyes of my operatives, and they simul-taneously conveyed the intimation to each other that care ful working might secure some information about any St. Louis cases the woman might have which would be desir-able; and in a short time, by gradually leading Mrs. Winslow on, they discovered that the brazen adventuress, according to her own story, had pending no less than seven cases in the Circuit Court at St. Louis, every one of them being suits on some trivial, trumped-up charge.

It seemed fated that Mrs. Winslow should leave Roch-ester, if her remaining depended upon these mysterious offerings ceasing, for while they were yet in conversation upon the subject, a colored porter called with a great basket-load of provisions, and without a word, after spreading a newspaper upon the carpet, began unloading his store.

" In heaven's name, who sent you here with those ? " she entreated of the colored gentleman.

" It's all right ; it's all right," he said soothingly, and winking hard at my operatives.

" But it isn't all right ; it's all wrong !" she retorted, warming.

" Guess not, missus ; lemme see : Quart split peas, quart beans, one punking, jug m'lasses, 'n a mackerel Done got 'em all, sure !"

"Where did they come from, you black imp?" the woman demanded, advancing threateningly.

He grabbed his basket quickly, and, slowly retreating towards the door, winked again very knowingly at Bristol and Fox, tapped his forehead and shook his head deploringly, and then nodded towards Mrs. Winslow, very plainly saying in pantomime, "Poor thing!—badly demented!" and, as Mrs. Winslow, in the excess of her anger, made a dive at him, he sprang back through the door, ejaculating, "Lo'd, *ain't* she crazy, though!" and made good his escape, laughing with that expression of complete enjoyment which only an Ethiopian can give.

Mrs. Winslow was now thoroughly convinced that the two men who had been her constant companions of late had had something to do with annoying her, and she cunningly followed the negro to the store where he was employed, where she at once sharply questioned the proprietor, who told her just as sharply that only a few minutes before, a ministerial-looking man, claiming to be city missionary for some church up-town, called and purchased the goods, remarking that they were for some crazy woman living in the block next to Meech's opera-house, whom he had just visited, and found to be possessed of the peculiar mania that she would receive no provisions save in full dress in the presence of her physicians, and that it was his desire to so humor her. So he had entrusted the errand to the colored man, who had carried cut the instructions given him; and that that was all there was about it.

When she returned crestfallen to the apartments, and Bristol and Fox had heard her story, they so derided it, claiming that the groceryman had fallen in love with her and invented the story upon the spur of the moment, fearing to disclose his languishing affection, she now believed that they were innocent of complicity in the matter and seemed to lapse into a bewildered sort of condition, where she would wander about the rooms, suspiciously pass and repass my operatives and searchingly scrutinize their faces, and for long periods stand at the dreary window peering into the street as if into a dead blank, never noticing the scurrying snow-flakes which were coming as a silent prelude to another winter, and only occasionally breaking the silence by murmuring, "Crazy? crazy? Yes, I *shall* become so if these terrible things are not stopped!"

But Mrs. Winslow had seen too much of life and was too hard a citizen generally to be terribly borne down by these manifestations for any great length of time, though they completely overpowered her at their occurrence, and she was allowed to become quite cheery before being favored with another materialization, which came in the following manner.

They were having a pleasant little seance in the rooms one evening soon after the colored grocery porter had accused Mrs. Winslow of being crazy, and the several ladies and gentlemen collected there were engaged in communing with the Spiritualistic heaven in the old and very common table-rapping method. They were, as a rule, lank, lean people, the ladies wearing short hair, and the gentlemen wearing long hair. This, with a few other affectations and irregularities, was nothing against them, had it not been equally as true that, according to my operatives' subsequent inquiries, every member of the company was either living in open adultery or practising all manner of lewdness without even the convenient cloak of an assumption or pretension that the marriage relations existed. But, good or bad as they were, they were at the threshold of heaven, and had very appropriately darkened the room to get as near to it as possible without being seen, and only the faintest possible jet flickered in the chandelier. They had all, save Mrs. Winslow, been served with a message, and she was now the inquirer, solemnly asking of another medium some information from the dear departed from over the river.

"Shall I soon receive word from an absent friend?"—(evidently meaning Le Compte, who had disappeared a month or two previous). Three affirmative raps followed.

"Shall I succeed in my case against Lyon?" The spirits were certain that she would.

"Shall I be rewarded for all my trouble?" she asked, waiting tremblingly for an answer.

To this inquiry three thundering raps were heard at the door.

What could it mean?

The members of the little circle were completely unnerved. And it was not strange either. Here were

11*

nearly a dozen people closely huddled in the centre of a room so dark that only the dim, indistinct outline of any person, or thing, could be seen in the ghostly gloaming. They believed, pretended they believed, or acquiesced in the belief or pretension, that they were in direct communication with the spirit-land.

In the most ridiculous condition of mind which any person might enter into such a performance, the secrecy and mysteriousness of the seance, the hushed silence, the darkness, and that tension of the mind caused by a constant expectation of some startling manifestation, will compel in the most sceptical mind a strange feeling of solemnity akin to awe ; so that when Mrs. Winslow's last inquiry was answered so pat, as well as with such an alarming loudness, the entire company sprang to their feet, and on this occasion there was genuine surprise in the faces of my detectives.

Bang, bang, bang ! came the second series of raps, which promised Mrs. Winslow she should be "rewarded for all her trouble."

But the answer, in the way it came, didn't seem to satisfy her. Somebody stepped to the chandelier and turned on the light, which showed all the company to have been considerably startled ; but the hostess was white from fear.

"Won't *somebody* see what new form of the devil has been sent here to annoy me ? " she asked passionately.

Fox, as "somebody," stepped briskly to the door and turned the key just as the first "Bang !" of another

series of raps was begun, and opening it quickly discovered a dapper young fellow with a big black bottle held
by the neck in his hand, which was raised for the purpose
of giving the door bang number two.

In response to Fox's loud and sharp inquiry as to what
on earth was wanted, he reversed the position of the
bottle with the dexterity of a bar-tender, took from the
floor a huger basket than that brought by the colored porter, and slipping into the room, nodded familiarly to Mrs.
Winslow, and then coolly to the company, after which he
quietly proceeded to unload his store.

"Great heavens!" said she despairingly, "I *don't* want
those things left here. I have no need for anything of
the kind. I take my meals at the Osborne House!"

"Gettin' 'toney' lately!" responded the intruder with
a shrug, piling the packages up neatly in one corner and
taking no heed of her expressed wish concerning them.

There was no response to this, and he resumed in a
light and airy tone: "Times has changed, Mrs. ——, eh?
What *was* it at Memphis and Helena, anyhow?"

This reference to the less aristocratic, though quite as
respectable, vocation of a female camp-follower, though
it caused the woman to change color rapidly, only brought
from her the remark, "I don't know what you mean, sir!
I'll get even with whoever is responsible for this outrage'—here she glared around upon the company as if to
ascertain whether any one present was guilty—"if it
costs me a thousand dollars!"

The new-comer only smiled sarcastically at this and

checked off his packages, concluding the operation by carefully counting two dozen red herrings, whose aroma was sufficient to announce their presence if he had not exhibited them at all ; while members of the company looked about them and at each other as if for some explanation of the strange proceeding.

Finally, Mrs. Winslow, with a mighty effort to restrain herself, advanced and asked the young man if he would not please give her the name of the person to whom she was indebted for the articles.

He arose, and smiling blandly, remarked, " You didn't used to be so particular about presents and such things ! " Then he added with a meaning leer : " At Helena and St. Louis, ye know, old girl ! "

" Old girl ! " the ladies all screamed. " Why what *does* this mean, Mrs. Winslow ? "

" Nothing, nothing ! " she replied hastily ; and then she hurried the too talkative young fellow away, and came back into the room with a show of gayety. But it broke up the little party, and soon after the ladies, with frigid excuses about not having very much time, and the gentlemen, with peculiar glances out of the corners of their eyes towards the woman who had been so familiarly termed an " old girl," took their departure, leaving Bristol, Fox, Mrs. Winslow and the melancholy pile of packages surmounted by aromatic red herrings in a state of solemn, moody silence.

Bristol was first to break the stillness, which he did by asking rather testily :

"You think Fox and I have had something to do with this, don't you?"

She looked at him a moment as if she would read his innermost thoughts, and replied : " No, I don't ! It comes from some of those strumpets of mediums, and I would give a good deal—a good deal, mind you, Bristol !—to know who it was. I'd—I'd—— "

" What would you do ?" asked Fox, putting her on her mettle for a savage answer.

" I would either burn them out, poison them, push them over the falls, or lie in wait for them and shoot them ! "

Mrs. Winslow said this with as much sincerity and coolness as if giving an estimate on any ordinary business transaction, and evidently meant it.

" Oh, you wouldn't kill anybody, Winslow," replied Fox airily.

" Wouldn't I, though, Mr. Fox ? " she rejoined with the old glitter in her eyes and paleness upon her upper lip that had at an earlier period worried the Rev. Mr. Bland; " wouldn't I ? If you had fifty thousand dollars in your trunk, I would kill you, appropriate the money, cut you up and pack you in the trunk and ship you to the South —or some other hot climate by the next express ! "

She was just as earnest about the remark as she would have been in carrying out the act ; and after Fox had con-gratulated himself, both aloud cheerfully and in his own mind very thankfully, that neither his trunk, or for that matter his imagination, contained any such gorgeous sum, he went to his own room for the night, leaving the very ex-

cited Mrs. Winslow and the very calm Mr. Bristol to contemplate the groceries and each other.

After a few minutes' brown study she suddenly turned
to her companion with : " Bristol, you and I are pretty
good friends, aren't we ? "

" Certainly," he replied.

" And haven't I always treated you pretty well ? "

" Yes ; with one exception."

" What is that ? "

" The sleep-walking you did in my room."

" Oh, that's nothing, Bristol. Never happened but
once, and won't occur again. Otherwise I have treated
you pretty well, haven't I ? "

Bristol felt compelled to confess that she had.

" Well, then," she continued wheedlingly, " will you do
me a favor ? "

" What is it ? "

" I want you to take a walk with me."

" Pretty late, Winslow, pretty late ; nearly ten o'clock, '
replied the detective, looking at his watch.

" The later the better," she replied earnestly. " I want
to use those herrings."

" Use those herrings ! Why, there are at least two
dozen. How on earth will you use them all ? "

" Some of these humbug mediums," replied Mrs. Winslow in a style of expression that showed her to be very
familiar with the Spiritualists, " or old Lyon himself,
have sent me these things. I'm going to adorn the door-
knob of every one of their places with a string of herrings

In that way I'll hit the right one sure. Come, won't you go ? "

Bristol saw that the woman would go anyhow, and fearing that she might get into some trouble that would cause her arrest and thus expose him and Bristol to public notice, which a capable detective will always avoid, consented to accompany the woman, which so pleased her that she immediately sent out for brandy, and not only imbibed an inordinate amount of it herself, but also pressed it upon Bristol unsparingly.

Her mind seemed filled with the idea that Lyon had become the " affinity " of nearly every female medium of prominence in the city in order to further his designs against her ; and to remind them that they were watched, she had Bristol write " Lyon-La Motte," " Lyon-Roberts," " Lyon-——,"etc., upon about a half-dozen couples of herrings, and upon all the rest, save those intended for the Misses Grim, which were labelled " Tabitha, Amanda, and Hannah," she had written the names of the different ladies who, in her imagination, had supplanted her, and tied all the herrings so labelled together with one very dilapidated herring marked " Lyon." It is needless to say that the latter bundle of sarcasm was intended for the ornamentation of Mr. Lyon's residence.

Bristol felt like a very bad thief, and Mrs. Winslow acted like a very foolish one. The moment they gained the street she began a series of absurd performances that well-nigh distracted Bristol and greatly increased the danger of police surveillance. She laughed hysterically, chuckled, and expressed her delight in a noisy effort to repress it, until the tears would roll down her face. Occasionally they would meet or pass parties who knew her, who would say to companions, in the tone and manner with which they would have probably spoken of other sensations, "There's the Winslow!" when she would shrink and shudder up to Bristol's side, begging for the shelter and protection of his capacious cloak. Again, imagining she saw somebody following them, or was sure that loungers lingering in deserted doorways or at the entrance to dark hallways or alleys were detectives on their trail, she would give the patient Bristol such nudges as nearly took his breath away, and, at his lively protest, would whimper and tremble like a querulous child.

Their first work was to be done on State Street, near Main, and when they had arrived at a certain hallway, Mrs. Winslow insisted that Bristol should accompany her to the rooms which she desired to decorate. This he flatly refused to do, when she began moaning something about want of spirit, and then, with a sudden gathering of the admirable quality for her own use, stole quietly up stairs and in a moment after came plunging down, as if the inmates of the entire block had turned out to give her chase. But this was not the case, and the expedition progressed without any developments of note, Mrs. La Motte, Miss Susie Roberts, and the Misses Grim being properly remembered, until they arrived at Mr. Lyon's residence, some little distance from the thickly settled portions of the city.

The house was one of the rambling, moss-covered buildings of ancient style and structure, and was set back from the road some distance among a score of trees quite as grand and ancient as the mansion itself; and the old pile did have a gloomy appearance to the adventurous couple that paused breathlessly before the gates.

"Bristol," said Mrs. Winslow shiveringly, "do you know that sometimes, when I see that great black pile up there, I'm glad he didn't marry me?"

"Why?" her companion impatiently asked. He was getting cold and tired, and was in no condition to appreciate maudlin melancholy.

"Because I'm sure I'd die in the old rack-o'-bones of a place; and besides that, I'm sure there are spooks there!"

"Pooh, pooh!" sneered Bristol angrily; "go along and attend to your business, or I'll go back and leave you!"

Thus admonished, the sentimental lady proceeded with her work.

For some reason the gate was very hard to open, and considerable time was consumed in getting into the grounds. Then it was a long walk to the house. Bristol anxiously watched the woman move slowly along the broad walk until she disappeared in the shadows which surrounded the house and the darkness of the night; and it seemed an age to him, as he stamped his feet as hard as he dare upon the stone pavement and whipped his hands about his shoulders to drive away the chilliness which he found creeping on.

He heard her footsteps first, then saw her emerge from the gloom, and finally saw her stop as if to listen. He also listened very intently, and thought he heard somebody moving about the house; and was immediately satisfied of the correctness of his hearing by noticing that Mrs. Winslow suddenly turned towards the road and made remarkably good time to the gate, which, feeling sure of trouble, he made strenuous efforts to open.

"For heaven's sake, Bristol," she gasped, "why *don't* you open this gate. I'll be eaten up with the dogs, and we'll both be caught!"

The last clause of Mrs. Winslow's remark roused Bristol to a vigorous exercise of his muscle. He tugged away at the gate, shook it, threw himself against it from one side, and his companion threw herself against it from the other side; but all in vain. Not a moment was to be lost. Lights were seen flashing to and fro in the great mansion, angry voices came to them, with the by nowise cheering short, gruff, savage responses of loosened bulldogs, and in a moment more the front door was passed by two men and as many dogs that came dashing out in full pursuit.

Matters at the gate were approaching a crisis. The gate could not be opened, and Mrs. Winslow must pass it or get captured.

"Climb or die!" urged Bristol, reaching through the

"And she did climb!"—

pickets of the gate, which was a high one, and lifting on the portly form of the excited woman.

"I will, Bristol!" she returned, with a gasp.

And she did climb!

It was best that she did so, as a good deal of trouble was coming down that brick walk like a small hurricane, and it would logically strike her in a position and from a direction that would not enable her to respond; and if either or both of those dogs had been able to have grasped the situation, partially impaled as she was upon the pickets, the fascinating Mrs. Winslow would have fallen an easy prey.

She was very clumsy about it, but in her desperation she in some way managed to scale the gate, leaving a good portion of her skirts and dress flying signals of distress upon the pickets, and finally fell into Bristol's arms. It was a moment when silk and fine raiment were as bagatelle in the estimate of chances for escape, and it was but the work of an instant for Bristol to tear her like a ship from her fastenings and make a grand rush towards home.

Those portions of Mrs. Winslow's garments which were left flaunting upon the gate not only set the dogs wild, but served to detain them. The men were also halted a minute by the natural curiosity they awakened, after which they made a furious onslaught upon the gate, that only yielded after sufficient time had elapsed to enable the culprits to get some distance ahead, when the men and dogs started pell-mell down the street after them.

Bristol fortunately remembered that when they were nearing Lyon's house, he had noticed that the door leading to an alley in the rear of a pretentious residence had been blown open and was then swaying back and forth in the wind. With the advantage in the chase given by the dog's criticism upon Mrs. Winslow's wearing apparel and the men's hinderance at the gate, they were able to seek shelter here, which they did with the utmost alacrity, fastening the gate behind them, where they tremblingly listened to the pursuers tearing by.

Mrs. Winslow insisted on immediately rushing out and taking the other direction, but Bristol, feeling sure that the party would go but a short distance, held on to her until the two men returned with the dogs, swearing at their luck, and telling each other wonderful tales of burglaries that never took place, while Bristol thoughtfully put in the time by making Mrs. Winslow's skirts as presentable as possible, by the aid of the pins which every prudent man carries under the right-hand collar of his coat, and hurriedly ascertaining from her that she had unfortunately tied the herrings upon the door-bell instead of the door-knob, thus involving pursuit.

After everything had become quiet, and Bristol had made several expeditions of observation to doubly assure himself of the coast being clear, the couple stole cautiously out of the alley into the deserted street, and after much precaution and many alarms, caused by the creaking of signs, the sudden flaring of gas-lamps, and the fierce gusts of wind dashing after and into them around the sharp corners of buildings, they at last arrived at home past midnight ; and, having ordered it as they neared the block, for a half-hour longer they sipped hot toddy by a rousing coal fire, recounting their exploits of the night, and eventually retiring with something of the spirit of conquerors upon them.

Down came the snow and the wind next morning, two things which will usually in early winter call a whole city-ful out of bed, and set the human tides in a rapid motion. Fox and Bristol had long before got into the streets and had heartily enjoyed some newspaper items, one recounting racily the outrage of labeled herrings being hung to the door-knobs of the houses of many respectable citizens, and another, under glaring head-lines, giving the minutest details of a desperate attempt at burglary of Mr. Lyon's house, and a double-leaded editorial which agonizedly asked in every variety of form, "Where are our police?" But Mrs. Winslow, from her adventures and toddy of the previous night, slept late and long, and when she did come creeping out into the sleeping-room, half dressed and altogether unlovely in disposition and appearance, she looked out upon the snow-flakes and the crowds of people without any emotion save that of anger at being aroused.

The only thing to be seen of anything like an unusual object was a very large load of hay standing at the en-trance of the building ; but of course this had no particu-lar interest to a Spiritualist. She had had a half-formed impression that she had heard knocking at the door, and

she turned from the window to ascertain whether that impression had been correct. Throwing a shawl about her
head and shoulders, she unlocked the door and peered out
cautiously. There was nobody there, and the wind whistled up the stairs so drearily that she closed the door with
a slam, and after starting up the fire, which was slumbering
on the hearth, she crept into bed again.

She had no more than got at the drowsy threshold of
dreamland than she was startled by a loud knocking, this
time proceeding from something besides an impression of
the mind, each knock being accompanied by some lively
expression of German impatience. The demonstration
was intelligible, if the words were not, and Mrs. Winslow
bounded out of her bed and into the reception-room in
no pleasant frame of mind.

On protecting her form as much as her indelicate disposition required—and that was not much—she flung the
door open and savagely asked:

"What's wanted?"

"Ef you keep a man skivering and frozing to died mit
der vind und schnow-vlakes, I guess mebby I charge more
as ten dollars a don for 'em!"

He was all smiles at first, but he resented her brusque
manner as swiftly and severely as he could with his broken
brogue. He was an honest, broad-shouldered, big-headed
German farmer, and though wrapped and wound from
head to foot in woollens, the only thing that seemed warm
about him was his glowing pipe and his disturbed temper.
He shook his head at the woman, and again began a

stammering recital of his wrongs, when she cut him short with :

"You're crazy !"

"Grazy ? Of I make a foolishness of a fellar like as you do—well, dot's all right !" and he stood up very straight and puffed great clouds of smoke past her into her elegant room.

She had got a stolid customer on hand, and she saw it. So she asked him civilly what he wanted at *her* door.

"Yust told me vere ish der parn, und I don't trouble you no more."

"Whose barn ?"

"Vere der hay goes."

"Hay ? What hay ? I don't know anything about any hay," she replied, laughing at his perplexity.

"I shtand here an hour already, und ven I got you up no satisfagtion comes. Py Shupiter, dot goes like a schwindle !"

He was very mad by this time, and walked back and forth in front of her door, shaking his fists and gesticulating wildly; and to prevent a scene, which might cause a collection of the inmates of the building, she quieted him as much as possible, and ascertained that some obliging person, more enthusiastic about the amount than the character of some token of esteem, had taken the trouble to order a load of hay to be delivered at her number, describing the place, room, and woman so minutely that there could be no possibility of mistake, where the owner was to collect all additional charges above two dollars, which had been paid.

It took Mrs. Winslow a long time to persuade the farmer that she owned no barn, kept no animals, had no use for hay, and that there had been some mistake, or that some person had deliberately played a joke upon *him* but finally, after a shivering argument of fully fifteen minutes, and the expenditure of a dollar bill, with the seductive offer that she would give him ten dollars if he would find and bring to her the man who ordered the load, her obstinate visitor departed, roundly swearing in good German that he would have the *Gottferdamter schwindler* brought up by der city gourts and hung, to which Mrs. Winslow groaned a hearty approval as she shut the door of the—to her—desolate room.

If there had previously been any doubts in her mind as to there being a preconcerted plan to annoy and exasperate her beyond endurance, they were now entirely removed, and the woman broke down completely, wringing her hands in mute expression of bitter anguish. The storm without was not half so violent as the storm within, and the blinding flakes which swept from the bitter sky raged upon a no more barren, frozen, desolate soil than her own selfish heart.

There may be a kind of pity for such a woman ; there should be pity for every form of human suffering, or even depravity ; but in my mind there should be none to verge from pity into palliation and excuse for this woman. Great as was her mental suffering, there was in it not a sing a touch of remorse. Terribly as her mind was racked and tortured with doubt, uncertainty, fear, and despair, there was in it no trace of the womanhood which, however low it may descend, is still capable of regret. She was not heart-sick for the life she was leading, but dreaded the punishment she knew it deserved. Her nature had never shrunk from the countless miseries she had entailed on others, and her heart never misgave her only in the absence of her kind of happiness or in the superstitious fear of the evils which she felt assured were constantly her due. She was, as far as I ever knew, or can conceive, a soulless woman whose troubles only produced vindictiveness, whose utter aim in life was social piracy, whose injuries only begat hate, and whose sufferings only concentrated her exhaustless hunger and thirst for revenge.

After the first burst of rage and passion, she settled down into a condition of deep study and planning, and about the middle of the afternoon began passing in and out and visiting various places, in a way which, though it might not particularly attract attention, yet betokened some business project being resolutely and quietly carried out.

During one of the periods when she was within her apartments, quite a commotion was raised in the lower story, the stores of which were occupied by a tobacconist and milliner, by a call from a prominent undertaker of Main Street, who with a mysterious air exhibited the following note, at the same time asking whispered conundrums about it.

12

" Mr. Boxem :

" Dear Sir—Please quietly deliver a full-sized coffin at No. —South St. Paul Street, at the first room to the right of the stairway as it reaches the third floor. Enclosed please find five dollars, in part payment. Will make it an object to you to ask no questions below, and deliver the coffin as soon after dark as possible.

(Signed)   " Mrs. A. J. W——."

Mr. Boxem was by no means a solemn man ; but he had a heavy bass voice, which he used to such great effect in asking questions below stairs, that he succeeded in creating a fine horror there, so that by the time he had proceeded to Mrs. Winslow's rooms, it was settled in the minds of the tobacconist and the milliner, their employees, and any customers of either who had happened in during Mr. Boxem's preliminary investigation, that each and every one's previous solemn prediction as to " *something* being wrong upstairs " had now come true, as they each and every one reminded the other that " Oh, I told you so ! "

Mr. Boxem, finding Mrs. Winslow's door ajar, quietly stepped in and reverently removed his sombre crape hat.

" Evening, ma'am," he said politely, but with a professional shade of sympathy in the greeting.

" And what do *you* want ? " she asked in a kind of desperation, noticing an open letter in his hand.

" Your order, you know, " he replied tenderly ; " these

things are sad and have to be borne. Can't possibly be helped, more 'n one can help coming into the world."

Mrs. Winslow could not reply from rage and anger, and hiding her face in her hands, walked to the window.

"No, it's the *way* of the world," continued Boxem, with a sigh; "ah—hem!—might I ask if *it* is in there?' he concluded, producing a tape-line case.

"It?—in God's name, what *it*!" sobbed the woman.

"Why—the—the"—stammered her visitor somewhat abashed, "the body—the corpse, you know! Have come to measure it. Painful, I know; but business is business, if it's only coffin business; and I can't possibly do a neat job without I get a good measure. Something like the tailoring trade, you see!"

"Body?—corpse?—come to measure it? Oh, I shall go wild, I shall go wild," persisted the woman, half frantic at the intimation which came to her that a corpse was not only in her place, but in the very room where she slept, and that this fiend who was pursuing her—this Nemesis, who struck her pride, her ambition, her desires, her very life, at every move she made, had actually sent an undertaker there to measure the dead body.

It is hard to tell what would have happened if the good sense of the undertaker had not come to the relief of the situation; and, hastily answering her that there had probably been some mistake, that the order was probab y meant for the next block, and offering other similar excuses while hastily apologizing for the intrusion, Mr. Boxem very sensibly went back to his business and his coffins, five dollars ahead until more promising inquiries should bring to light the friend of the alleged dead, and the owner of the money, who, fortunately for Mr. Boxem, has not appeared to this day.

CHAPTER XXIV

Breaking up.—Doubts and Queries.—Suspected Developments.—The
Detectives completely outwitted.—On the Trail again.—From
Rochester to St. Louis.—A prophetic Hotel Clerk.—More Detec-
tives and more Need for them.—Lightning Changes.

BRISTOL and Fox happened around in time to par-
ticipate in the general excitement which the undertaker's visit had awakened, and after getting as full particulars as possible from the people below, who refused to
believe that some dark deed had not been committed upstairs, they proceeded to the rooms, where they found the
door to Mrs. Winslow's private apartment closed, and the
two, finding no opportunity to converse with their landlady, shortly went out for supper.

On their return they found Mrs. Winslow in a remarkably pleasant frame of mind, and quite full of jokes about
the order for a coffin—so much so, in fact, that my operatives were quite surprised at the change from her previous
demeanor under similar circumstances. Altogether they
passed one of the pleasantest evenings since they became
the woman's tenants. Several ladies that lived in the same
building were invited in, refreshments of wines and some
rare fruits out of season were served, singing, card-playing,

and piano-playing with some waltzing were indulged in, and it was noticed by the two men that Mrs. Winslow was almost hysterically happy, as if she had decided upon some exceedingly brilliant and satisfactory plan, the execution of which was being preluded in this way.

At the close of the evening she casually announced that the next time she had any company she hoped to show them a better place.

Somebody at once inquired if she was going away, whereupon she gayly replied that instead of going away she was going to make better arrangements for staying. She had intended all along, she said, tidying up the place, but had been so lazy that she had kept neglecting it until it was really too bad, and now she had decided to begin tearing up things to-morrow.

In answer to Bristol and Fox's inquiries as to what was to be done with them in the meantime, she said that she had already arranged that, and had secured a pleasant room at the Osborn House, where they were to remain without additional expense to themselves until she had concluded her changes. This rather dashed the operatives, but they made no further remark upon the subject until the company had dispersed, when they urged the propriety, both on the grounds of economy and convenience of " doubling up," as Bristol termed it, in one room until another was finished, and then removing to that, until their respective apartments had been renovated. But Mrs. Winslow was obdurate, alleging that on account of these annoyances she had become weak and nervous of late,

and did not desire to be annoyed with either the argu
ment or arrangement.

So that early on the next morning, when Mrs. Winslow
announced to the detectives that an express wagon was in
waiting to convey their baggage to the Osborn House,
there was no alternative but to go, as the persons engaged
to do the renovating were on hand and had already begun
their work of turning the rooms into chaos. Mrs. Winslow assured them that but a few days would elapse before they would all be together again in their old quarters; and as they grumblingly went away complaining of
short notice and the like, she bade them a merry good-
by, adding that she should stay about with some of her
Spiritualistic friends in the city, and perhaps take a little
trip down to Batavia; but in any event would let them
know the first moment that the rooms were ready for
occupancy.

While Bristol and Fox were settling themselves in their
new quarters they indulged in a very heated argument as
to Mrs. Winslow's object in this all but forcibly ejecting
them from their rooms, which they had occupied so long
that they had come to consider them something of a
home; as to whether Mrs. Winslow meant to do without
their presence hereafter or not, Bristol feeling sure that
the woman meditated some future action which was to relieve herself of their society, if indeed it did not mean
more than that, while Fox felt equally as certain that the
whole affair was only one of the whimful woman's whims,
that, being satisfied, would result in their early recall.

In any event in this way the combination of mediumistic and detective talent was broken up.

I was at once informed about the turn things had taken, and ordered that extra diligence should be used in keeping the woman under notice, as I felt apprehensive that making her rooms tidy was not her object at all. I had no right to detain her, go wherever she might ; but Lyon's counsel had been for some time absent from Rochester, and some things in connection with the defence had not yet received proper attention. The depositions as to the woman's character and adventures throughout Wisconsin, Iowa and Missouri had not yet been taken, nor indeed had the very necessary formula of serving notice upon Mrs. Winslow of the proposed taking of such evidence been gone through ; so that, as it would require some time to take this evidence after notice had been served, it was very desirable that she should be kept in sight.

The next development, showing her to be a very shrewd woman, was in her sending word over to the hotel, the same day that my operatives left her rooms, that she had been taken suddenly and severely ill, and had been obliged to turn over the work to a lady friend of hers, and might not be able to resume the supervision of it for several days.

Bristol called, ostensibly to tender his condolence, out was unable to find Mrs. Winslow, being met by a very smart little lady, who informed him that it would be impossible to see his former landlady, as she was extremely ill and could not be at present disturbed; but that should any change in her condition occur, both he and Fox should be promptly informed. I had instructed them to do their best in watching the premises, which I am satisfied they had done, and I had also put the two other men, Grey and Watson, on the lookout, but none of them had observed her either pass out of or into the place, and they began to be convinced that she really was lying ill within the building.

During this condition of things, and being somewhat anxious about the matter, I went to Rochester myself, and held a consultation with my men, having the block further examined under various guises and pretexts, which proved beyond doubt that the woman was gone, and had probably left the building a very few minutes after the operatives had departed; and, for some reason best known to herself, but probably on account of the mysterious annoyances which had been following each other very rapidly, had either left the city entirely or was hiding very closely within it, with a view to discover whether, with the two men out of her society, and herself in peaceful retiracy, she could not ascertain from what source her troubles came, or avoid them altogether.

To my further annoyance, the magnificent Harcout appeared and kindly offered me countless suggestions and theories, which were each one considered by Mr. Harcout to be worthy of immediate adoption; and in order to get rid of him, I was obliged to appear to acquiesce in an imaginative theory of Mrs. Winslow's flight to New York

12*

and represent myself as so interested in his idea of how she could be traced to her hiding-place, that I desired of him as a personal favor that he would follow the trail, giving him a man, and the man a wink—and there never was a finer picture of pomposity and assumption than when Harcout and his man started for New York. Rid of him, I again turned to my work of getting upon the right trail.

I was sure the woman had left the city, and further inquiry at the rooms convinced me that I was correct. The little woman finally acknowledged flatly that she had gone, but would under no circumstances tell whether she had left the city or not. She also exhibited a bill of sale of the goods and a transfer of the lease, and wanted to know if *that* did not look as though she had gone? But she persisted in her refusal to give further information, and that was the end of it.

No one had seen any trunks or packages leave the place, nor could my detectives get any trace of her having left the city over any of the different roads. Inquiries made at all the leading livery stables, express and hack-stands, of the city, failed to discover that Mrs. Winslow had been conveyed to any near railroad station where she might have taken a train; nor could it be by any means ascertained that such a person had purchased a ticket at any of the adjacent towns for any point to the east, west, or south.

In fact, all trace of Mrs. Winslow was lost, and I was satisfied that she had for some time been sure of the danger of her surroundings ; and, while not able to fasten any particular suspicious act upon Bristol or Fox, undoubtedly intuitively felt that they were either directly responsible for her troubles, or were in some unexplainable way connected with their cause ; and being enough of a professional litigant to be aware of the necessity of service of notice upon her as to the taking of evidence before such evidence could be taken, and that it would be possible by a sudden disappearance and remaining secreted until the case might be called, to defeat Lyon's attorneys from using this mountain of evidence which she knew existed against her, whether she knew we had collected it or not, the double motive for her mysterious absence was plainly apparent.

Remembering Bristol and Fox's reports as to her threat to go to St. Louis and "attend to her cases" there unless the annoyances ceased, and knowing from previous evidence already secured that she had figured extensively in various capacities, but principally as Spiritualist, blackmailer and courtesan in that city, I finally concluded that she had gone there, though her mode of leaving Rochester, if she had left the city, had certainly been such as to demonstrate ability worthy of a better cause.

I accordingly directed Bristol and Fox to return to New York, and detailed the two men who had made it lively for Mrs. Winslow, and who, of course, knew her, but whom she had not seen face to face, the "materializations" having all been done for them by other parties, to proceed to St. Louis in search of her, stopping at any point where

railroad divergences were made from the trunk lines be·
tween the east and the west, and make extremely diligent
inquiries for her, while I left another man in Rochester
for the purpose of watching for her reappearance there,
which would undoubtedly occur as soon as her former
tenants were gone, in the event that she was secreted in
Rochester, instead of being at the west, and to make this
plan more certain, caused Bristol to write a letter to Mrs.
Winslow, stating that both he and Fox had made number·
less efforts to see her, but, failing to ascertain either
where she was, or the cause of her sudden disappearance,
and both being out of active business, they had concluded
to go on to New York, but would return to Rochester
should she resume charge of the rooms and desire them
for tenants.   I made arrangements also at the post-office
to ascertain whether any letters were reforwarded to her
at any point, and also at the express office regarding
packages, so it could be hardly possible for her to keep
up any correspondence or relation of any kind with parties
in Rochester without disclosing her place of retreat.

Having completed these arrangements, I returned to
New York and anxiously waited for some news from the
West.

No trace was found of the woman until Operatives
Grey and Watson had arrived at Chicago, where they im·
mediately circulated among the Spiritualists of that city,
who are both numerous and of rather doubtful moral
standing.   They ascertained that a woman answering her
description had been there, and advertised largely under

another *alias* than Mrs. Winslow, but nothing definitely could be learned until in their reports I discovered that the little Frenchman, Le Compte, was figuring as the unknown lady's companion and business manager, when I telegraphed to follow Le Compte and his woman, being morally certain that these two were Monsieur the Mineral Locater and the celebrated plaintiff in the Winslow-Lyon breach of promise suit.

It was discovered after some trouble, and with the assistance of my Chicago Agency, that Le Compte had suddenly left that city for some southern or south-western point, possibly St. Louis, but no information could be gained as to what direction Mrs. Winslow had taken, it being evidently her plan to avoid pursuit, should there be any made. My conviction still being strong that her objective point was St. Louis, I ordered the men on there, without positively knowing that either of the parties were there; but was gratified to learn that Le Compte had been in the city, whether he was there or not on the operatives' arrival. The operatives, Grey and Watson, at once searched the newspapers and found no advertisements which would cover the desired couple, or either of them; but, notwithstanding, visited all the mediums, clairvoyants, and prominent Spiritualists of the city, but could find no trace of the fugitives from that generally very prolific source, and began to have the impression that her trip there, if she were in the city at all, was one of pleasure or of blackmail business outside of her regular clairvoyant line.

The next move made by the men was to search about among the hotels and boarding-houses, and really ferret her out. This was a tedious process, and very little success was made in this endeavor for two or three days, when one noon, as Grey was wandering about the city in a seemingly useless endeavor to find the woman, he stepped into the Denver House, formerly the old City Hotel, and began to search over the register. He had not proceeded far when the clerk, eyeing him cautiously, said :

"See here, Mister, ain't you lookin' for somebody ?"

"Certainly I am," he replied pleasantly.

Grey looked at him a moment and saw that he would not drop the subject, and immediately endeavored to mislead him by answering, "Of course I am ; I came in from the country this morning, and I don't know what hotel she was going to."

"Ah, ha," mused the clerk, as if at loss how to proceed, "I guess you didn't know where to find her, and you havn't found her yet, have you ?"

"No," Grey replied quietly.

"Is she big or little ?"

"Well, she ain't little," answered Grey.

"Now, see here, my friend, that's all right ; but I'm pretty sure you didn't just come in from the country, and further, I think I can show you the woman you've been hunting."

Grey smiled and intimated that he was perfectly willing to be shown the woman.

" Well, you just let me have your hat; I'll put it on the hat-rack inside the dining-room door, then you go to the wash-room and pass into the dining-room as though you had forgotten your hat and had come back for it. Look at the head of the first table over by the windows, and if you don't find your woman with a little Frenchman, I'll treat ! "

Grey was surprised at the revelation, as there could be no possible means for him to know of his mission ; but the clerk's reference to the " little Frenchman " convinced him that there was something worth following up in the matter, and he followed his new friend's instructions implicitly, passed into the dining-room, took his hat from the rack, turned and got a good view of the fair Mrs. Winslow and the faultless Monsieur Le Compte, who were evidently enjoying life as thoroughly as perfect freedom from restraint, and spiritualistic free love, would enable them.

He expressed no surprise, however, at seeing the woman, and remarked to the clerk as he passed into the hall, " Why, that isn't any friend of mine ! "

" Nor anybody else's ! " said the clerk with a leer. " But really, now," he anxiously added, " *ain't* you after her ? "

" Certainly not," Grey stoutly replied ; but as the clerk took him into the bar-room to treat him according to agreement, which he submitted to unblushingly, he admit-ted that he had a curiosity to know something about her, as he had either seen her, or heard of her, previously.

Then the clerk told him a good deal about the woman unnecessary for me to recite to my readers, which only fnrther showed her vile character, and so worked upon my operative's curiosity and interest that he decided to come to the hotel for a few days ; but as he was informed that Mrs. Winslow's intentions were to remain there the remainder of the week, and the clerk promised to keep a good lookout for her, he concluded to hunt up his companion, inform him of his good fortune, and transfer their baggage to that hotel.

As it was now about two o'clock, Grey did not find Watson before six, and it was fully eight o'clock before they got settled at the Denver House. But their eyes were not gladdened by a sight of the fugitive on that evening, nor was she at breakfast next morning. The operatives began to be alarmed lest the bland clerk had taken them in, and were particularly so, when, at their request, for the purpose of ascertaining whether she was in her room, he knocked at her door, and after a few minutes returned with a blank, scared face, saying that the Jezebel had left, and more than that, that she owed the hotel over fifty dollars for board and wine furnished on the strength of her elegant and dashing appearance.

On further examination of the room it was evident that the woman had not occupied it at all during the previous night, but had left the hotel immediately after dinner whether from a previous decision to do so, or from one of those sudden impulses, quite contrary to the general rule of human action, which made her an extraordinarily diffi cult quarry to follow, or still, from some suspicion that she was being followed.

Grey felt quite crestfallen that he had lost Mrs. Wins‧ low by one of her characteristic manœuvres, and at once made inquiries concerning her baggage, ascertaining from the clerk that she only had a portmanteau with her at the hotel, but had had a trunk check which she had exhibited when asking some question about the arrival and depart‐ ure of trains.

Grey sent Watson to intersections of prominent streets to keep a lookout for parties, while he at once proceeded to the " Chicago Baggage Room," as it is called, under the Planters' House, where he ascertained, after considera‐ ble trouble and representing himself as an employee of the Chicago, Alton, and St. Louis road, looking for lost baggage, that Mrs. Winslow had come there personally about two o'clock the day previous and presented the check for her trunk, which had been taken away by an expressman with " a gray horse and a covered wagon."

The next step, of course, was to find the expressman with the gray horse and covered wagon, who had taken the woman's trunk, and this was no easy matter to do. There were plenty answering that description, but Grey labored hard and long to find the right one, and finally found it this way.

Being an Irishman himself, and a pretty jolly sort of a fellow, he was not long in finding a compatriot the owner of a gray horse and a covered wagon, of whom he asked :

" Did you move the big woman with the big trunk at two o'clock yesterday ? "

" An' if I did ? " said the expressman, on the defensive.

" Nothing if you did ; but *did* you ? " replied Grey.

" It's chilly weather," replied the expressman, winking hard at a saloon opposite.

" Yes, and I think a drop of something wouldn't hurt us," added Grey, following the direction of the expressman's wink and thought quickly.

They stepped over to the saloon and were soon calmly looking at each other through the bottom of some glasses where there had been whiskey and sugar. They looked at each other twice this way, and finally they were obliged to take the third telescopic view of each other before they could resume the subject.

Then the expressman looked very wise at Grey, remarking musingly, " A big 'oman with a big trunk, eh ? "

" Yes, a pretty fine-looking woman, too."

" Purty cranky ? "

" Yes."

" And steps purty high wid a long sthride ? "

" Exactly."

" 'N has clothes that stand up sthiff wid starch 'n silk r. the makin' ? "

" The very same," said Grey anxiously.

" I didn't move her," said the expressman, shaking his head solemnly.

Grey felt like " giving him one,' as he said in his reports, but repressed himself and said pleasantly that he was sorry he had troubled him, and turned to go away, knowing this would unloosen his companion's tongue, if anything would.

"Sthop a bit, sthop a bit; you didn't ax me did I know ef any other party moved her?"

"That's so," said Grey, smiling and waiting patiently for developments.

"Av coorse it's so." Then looking very knowingly, he said mysteriously, "The man's just ferninst the Planters', —not a sthone's throw away. He's a big Dutchman, 'n got a dollar fur the job."

They were both around the corner in a moment, and Grey at once made inquiries of the German owner of a "grey horse and a covered wagon" as to what part of the city he had removed the trunk.

He was very secretive about the matter, and refused any information whatever.

"Come, come, me duck," said the Irishman, "me frind here is an officer, 'n ef ye don't unbosom yerself in a howly minit, ye'll be altogether shnaked before the coort!"

He said this with such an air of pompous sincerity, as if he had the whole power of the government at his back, that the German at once began relating the circumstances in such a detailed manner that he would have certainly been engaged an entire hour in the narrative, if Grey had not, as he himself expressed it, "out of the tail of his eye" seen Mrs. Winslow, not twenty feet away, sailing down Fourth street, towards the Planters'. In another moment she would pass the corner of the court-house square, where she could not help but see the little crowd of expressmen, hackmen and runners, his inquiries, and the statement by his companion that he was an officer, had attracted.

CHAPTER XXV.

GREY took in the situation at once, and was equal to the emergency. He knew if the German saw Mrs. Winslow, and thinking him an officer who might arrest him for complicity in something wrong, he would probably shout right out, "There she is, now!" He was also just as sure that his new-found Irish acquaintance, in the excess of his friendliness, would rush right over to Fourth street and stop the woman. So in an instant he created a counter-attraction by calling the German a liar, collaring him, and backing him through the line of wagons out of sight, and as Mrs. Winslow passed farther down Fourth street, backed him through the line of teams in the opposite direction, while the German protested volubly that he was telling only the truth; and just the moment Mrs. Winslow's form was hid by the

Planters' House, he released the now angry expressman, flung him a dollar for " treats," and running nimbly around the block, fell into a graceful walk behind Mrs. Winslow. keeping at a judicious distance, and following her for several hours through the dry-goods stores, to the Butchers and Drovers' Bank, where she drew a portion of the amount which she had secured from the prominent St. Louis daily as damages, and which had remained undisturbed in that bank until this time ; into several saloons, where she boldly went, and, in defence of the theory of women's rights, stood up to the counter like a man, ordering and drinking liquor like one too ; to the Four Courts, where she at least *seemed* to have considerable business ; to numberless Spiritualist brothers and sisters, including, of course, the mediums ; and finally to a very elegant private boarding-house kept by a respectable lady named Gayno, whom the adventuress had so won with her oily words and dashing manners, accompanied by her large Saratoga trunk, that not only she, but a little French gentleman named Le Compte—whom Grey had hard work to avoid, as he had followed Mrs. Winslow at a respectful distance, and as if with a view of ascertaining whether any other person besides himself was following the madam —had managed to secure quarters in an aristocratic home and an aristocratic neighborhood, for all of which the experienced female swindler had no more idea of paying, unless compelled to, than she had of paying her fifty-dollar hotel bill at the Denver House.

On receipt of this information, I directed Superinten

dent Bangs to proceed to Rochester and hurry up Lyon's attorneys in securing the legal papers necessary to avail ourselves of the large amount of evidence already discov ered, and serve notice upon her while she was still in sight, and before her suspicions of being watched and followed, which it was evident was now growing upon her, had forced her into still more artful dodges to evade us.

It was certainly her determination to clothe all her acts with as much mysteriousness as possible, and in this manner work upon Lyon's feelings and fears until she would compel him, through actual disgust of and shame at the long-continued public surveillance of his affairs, to end the worrying tension upon his mind by a compromise that would yield her a large sum of money.

That she was able, and had the means to make these quick moves and sudden changes, was equally as certain, though it was a question in my mind then, and has been to this day, how much money she might have had at command. I know that at times she must have had almost fabulous sums in her possession. I was also often quite as sure that she was absolutely penniless, when, of a sudden, she would carry out some bold scheme that required a great deal of money, which invariably came into requisition from some mysterious source in the most mysterious manner possible. Whatever might have been the woman's pecuniary resources, I must confess that in nearly every instance I underrated her, and in fact that, in every respect, the more I endeavored to analyze her the more of an enigma she became.

Like nearly all women of disreputable character, she was terribly extravagant, reckless, and improvident; but as an offset to this she was supreme in the meanness ordinary courtesans are above—that petty but never-ceasing swindling so terribly annoying to the public.

With all these things in her favor, so far as being an ingenious pest is concerned, she was also possessed of the power of physical as well as financial recuperation to a wonderful degree; and to whatever depth of temperamental dejection or physical exhaustion and degradation she might descend, she would of a sudden reappear, fresh and blooming, with no perceptible trail of her vileness upon her, in which condition she would remain just so long as would conserve her interests.

While Superintendent Bangs was on his way to St. Louis, Grey and Watson were being led a lively chase about the city by Mrs. Winslow, and the bland clerk of the Denver House was devoting nearly all his time in tracking her from place to place to enforce the collection of his employer's bill.

Her first exploit was to borrow twenty dollars from Mrs. Gayno on her baggage, who was thus prevented from turning her out of doors when her true character was learned; and as a further illustration of her shrewdness, after she had remained at the house as long as she desired, she left between days, without refunding the borrowed money or paying her bill, and in some mysterious way also spirited away all her baggage.

This of course caused more trouble in finding her, and

she was finally discovered in furnished rooms. Even here she suddenly made her presence so unbearable to the landlord that he gladly paid her a bonus to depart, which she did equally as mysteriously as on the previous occasion, when she was lost again, and the third time found at a Spiritualistic gathering at the hall near the corner of Chestnut and Seventh streets, where she was one of the speakers of the evening and did herself and the cause justice.

In this way—following her while she was securing abstracts of her many cases against the people of St. Louis, the number and trivial character of which had become a matter of public scandal, newspaper comment, and universal condemnation among members of the bar, keeping track of her in numberless conditions and localities, and listening to endless tales of the woman's reckless conduct during her previous residence in the city—Mrs. Winslow gave the two men all they could possibly attend to.

One Wednesday morning about eleven o'clock, when Grey had just stepped out upon the street from a late breakfast at the Planters'—having been out until nearly morning the night previous on a fruitless attempt to keep the woman under surveillance for a few hours, that detective was looking up and down the street quite undecided as to what course to pursue—he saw Mrs. Winslow just leaving an expressman at the court-house square, who immediately jumped into his wagon and drove off.

Grey ran quickly down Fourth street, and after a few

13

minutes' chase succeeded in overtaking the vehicle. Halting it he asked the driver :

"Are you going to move that woman ?"

He checked his horse with an air that plainly said that kind of interruption was neither profitable nor desirable ; but driving on at a brisk pace, there was jolted out of him the remark : "My friend, I'm working for the public. Sometimes it pays better to keep one's mouth shut than to open it, especially to strangers."

Grey hurrying on at the side of the wagon, and holding to it with his left hand, with his right he found a green-back.　Handing this to the driver, he sprang into the seat beside him, saying, "Sometimes it pays better to open one's mouth !"

"That's so," replied the driver stuffing the bill into his pocket and elevating his eyebrows as if inquiring what Grey wanted him to open his mouth for.

"I want you to drive slowly enough for me to keep up with you.　Mind, you needn't *tell* me anything unless you have a mind to."

"Oh, I'd just as leave tell you as not," he replied. "She's going over to East St. Louis to try and get the 'Alton Accommodation,' if it hasn't gone yet.　The Chi-cago train's way behind, and the 'Alton' don't go until the 'Chicago' comes ; ye see?"

Grey knew this was partially true, for he had but a few moments before received a telegram from Mr. Bangs, stating that he was aboard the down train which had been belated ; so that the best thing to do was to take the expressman's number, so that he could find him again in case of a mistake, or any deception being practised, which he did. He then returned to the Planters', paid his bill, wrote notes to both Watson and Superintendent Bangs stating how matters stood, went to the levee, and in a few minutes had the pleasure of seeing the trunk put on board the ferry, where its owner shortly followed.

Grey went on board, taking a position near the engines, where he could have an unobstructed view of the stairs, so that if this should prove to be another ruse of the madam's to get him started across the river and then glide off the boat to take up still more retired quarters, he could beat her at her own game. But Mrs. Winslow remained on the boat, and just as it was pushing off for the Illinois shore the landlord of the Denver House, accompanied by a constable, came rushing on board.

Seeing Grey, he immediately applied to him for information as to whether the woman was on board. He replied by pointing her out where she was leaning over the guards immediately above them. The landlord and his man at once proceeded to interview the woman, threatening all sorts of things if that bill was not paid, to all of which she gave evasive answers until the Illinois shore was reached, when she reminded them that she was outside the jurisdiction of the State of Missouri, and that if either of them laid their hands upon herself or her property, she would feel compelled to cause a St. Louis funeral, as she was a good shot, and when in the right did not hesitate to shoot ; which so frightened the hotel man and the little minion of Missouri law," as Mrs. Winslow c lled the constable, that they retreated empty-handed and with a confirmed disgust at the active exponents of modern Spiritualism.

Grey was now in a quandary as to what to do. The Chicago train was reported as over two hours late, and he was informed by the conductor of the Alton Accommodation that though his train could not leave St. Louis until the Chicago train had arrived, yet that he dare not hold the train a moment after that time. This precluded Grey's informing Mr. Bangs of his whereabouts, as the train was now too near the place to admit of his being reached by a telegram; and should he risk losing the woman to apprise Mr. Bangs, it might be impossible to find her again at all. Fortunately he learned that the passenger train stopped at the Baltimore and Ohio railroad crossing, and, interesting a brakeman in his behalf, he arranged with him to go up to the crossing, board the train, rush through it and call out for Mr. Bangs as he went, directing the latter to pay the brakeman two dollars for his trouble, then jump off the train, walk rapidly back to the crossing and there board the Alton train as it was going out, if possible; which latter plan would have succeeded, no doubt, had not Mr. Bangs been chatting upon the rear platform of the rear car, and failed altogether to hear the extremely loud inquiries made for him.

Mrs. Winslow recognized Grey as a person in somebody's employ who was following her, and the moment he seated himself in the single passenger-car attached to the train, the woman began such a terrible tirade of abuse against him that he was made to feel that the detective's life is not altogether one of roseate hue, and so annoyed the other passengers that a large-sized brakeman was selected as a delegation of one to quiet her. It was evident she had been drinking heavily, and she kept this brakeman pretty well employed for some time in not only endeavoring to quiet her termagant tongue, but to keep her in her seat, as she would often rise in the ecstasy of her wrath and denounce poor Grey, who meekly bore it all with a patient smile, until the conductor again appeared, when Grey showed him his thousand-mile employee's ticket and claimed that he was an employee of that road looking up lost baggage ; that it was suspected that Mrs. Winslow had stolen the trunk she had with her, and that he had been ordered to follow her for a day or two until he got further instructions from headquarters. This put him all right with the trainmen, and caused the conductor to compel the woman into some sort of civility and silence.

At about two o'clock the train arrived in Monticello, where Mrs. Winslow left the train, and the detective followed. The agent informed Grey that it was at least a mile to a telegraph office uptown, but that no train save a "wild-train" would pass either way until after he would have time to send a dispatch and return. He immediately went uptown and sent a telegram to the agent at East St. Louis to please inquire for a Mr. Bangs about

the depot, and if there, to have him answer ; also one to
Mr. Bangs himself at the Planters'.

Returning to the depot, the agent informed Grey that
Mrs. Winslow had also been uptown, which was quite evident, as she had donned an entirely different suit of clothing, evidently with some inebriated sort of an idea that
this might change her appearance enough to enable her
to escape him.   She finally bought a ticket to Brighton,
and got her trunk checked to that point.

On their arrival at Brighton, Grey saw several ladies
get off the rear platform of the ladies' car, among whom
was his unwilling travelling companion, and watched
until they had passed into the depot.   In order to make
sure that she was to stop here, he ran rapidly to where
the baggage was being unloaded, where he found that
her trunk had been put off.   He waited there until he
saw the trunk wheeled into the little baggage-house, when
he leisurely walked back to the depot and stepped into
the ladies' waiting-room, to keep the company of the
adventuress.

What was his surprise to see it almost deserted, no
Mrs. Winslow there, and no surety of anything at all.
He rushed into the gentlemen's room, galloped around
the depot, looked in every direction, only to turn towards
the train. with the startling suspicion that he had again
been outwitted by the shrewd Spiritualist who made her
livelihood by villainy and shrewdness, which was quickly
confirmed as he made an ineffectual attempt to overtake
the departing train, only to see the face of Mrs. Winslow

pressed hard against the rear window of the ladies' car, and almost white with a look of fiendish enjoyment and hate at the useless attempts of her relentless pursuer whom she had so neatly foiled.

Mrs. Winslow had slipped a detective—and a good detective, too—again, was gone, and all Grey could do was to wait at Brighton until Superintendent Bangs could overtake and counsel with him.

By telegrams to and from conductors it was speedily ascertained by Superintendent Bangs, who had come on to Brighton and directed Watson to report at the Chicago Agency, that the woman had gone to Springfield, Ills., and, after arranging with the station-agent at Brighton to send information to Chicago regarding any call that might be made for her trunk, or as to any orders that might be received to have it forwarded, Mr. Bangs and Grey went at once to Springfield, where a trace of the woman was found at the St. Nicholas Hotel.

It was ascertained that she had remained at the hotel over night, and the clerks thought it probable that she was then at the house, her bill not having been paid ; but a thorough search for her only developed the fact that she was at least absent from the hotel, whether with an intention of returning or not.

Mr. Bangs directed Mr. Grey to remain at the St. Nicholas, keeping on the alert for her, while he visited the more elegant houses of ill-repute with which that capital abounds during legislative sessions and which were just at this time getting in readiness to receive lawmakers and lobbyists; and also the other and less respect able establishments for piracy, managed by professed mediums, astrologists, fortune-tellers, and all the other grades of female swindlers; and after a considerable time spent in investigation, found a certain Madam La Vant, astrologist—who professed to cast the horoscope of people's lives with all the certainty of the famous Dr. Roback—who was descended from the vikings and jarls of the Scandinavian coast, but in reality kept a house of assignation, that most dangerous threshold to prostitution.

Madam La Vant at once acknowledged that Mrs. Winslow *had* been there; even showed Superintendent Bangs a bundle she had left with her. She stated that she had called there early in the morning and left the package, with the promise to return about three o'clock in the afternoon, when she was to occupy a room she had engaged there, and had already paid in advance for its use. Mr. Bangs did not feel exactly at rest about the matter, but could not do otherwise than return to the hotel for his dinner, promising to call in the afternoon, and alleging that he had information to give the woman regarding certain persons who had been, and then were, following her; for if she were then in the house she would remain there, and he had no legal authority to molest her or search the place without Madam La Vant's consent, which he could not of course get if she was shielding her, which she undoubtedly was; and if Mrs. Winslow was really away from the house, the madam would take some means of preventing her return.

He went to the hotel as quickly as possible, found Grey, whom he immediately sent to watch for the ingress or egress of the adventuress, took a hasty dinner, and then relieved my operative so that he might dine, after which the two watched the house until dark.

But their closest vigils over the place failed to cause the discovery of Mrs. Winslow, who was doubtless by this time many miles away from Springfield, enjoying peace and quiet in some other city. Superintendent Bangs called on Madam La Vant as soon as the evening had come, and that lady expressed great surprise that he had not seen his " friend, Mrs. Winslow," as she expressed it ; following this remark by the explanation that she had returned to her house not over a half-hour after he had left it, and had stated that she had decided to go on to Chicago immediately, whereupon Madam La Vant had refunded her the money advanced for the room, and the woman had taken her bundle and departure simultaneously.

The detectives were satisfied that the astrologist was squarely lying to them, and that she had in some way aided the fugitive to escape, or had effectually secreted her—the former opinion being the most reasonable ; and when I had been apprised of the turn things had taken, I was satisfied that Mrs. Winslow was in Madam La Vant's house at the very time that Mr. Bangs was first there ; that her friend, the madam, was merely carrying out her instructions in stating that she had been there, was then out, but would return, and that at the very moment Mr

13*

Bangs had started for the St. Nicholas she had left La Vant's, and, as soon as possible thereafter, the city.

I immediately concluded that as I had no authority to arrest or in any way detain the woman—which put my men at a great disadvantage, preventing their telegraphing in advance for her detention, or securing and using official assistance of any kind for the same purpose—that I had better recall Mr. Bangs at once, which I did, and trust to Grey's doggedness in following her, instructing him particularly to if possible prevent being seen by her, or in any way alarming her, hoping either for her speedy return to Rochester, on the principle that the guilty mind constantly reverts and is drawn towards its chief topic of thought, and that strive to keep away from it as much as she might, she would be irresistibly drawn to it; or that through the former plan I might get her into some little village or secluded spot, or quiet town, where, upon Grey's announcement, Mr. Bangs or some other deputized person might cautiously reach her before she was aware of her danger, and serve the notice that would make the legal fight not only possible, but a stormy one on account of the vast amount of crushing evidence I had secured for Mr. Lyon against her.

It was more and more apparent that the woman's plan was to beat us in this way, and thus by long and unbearable suspense, mysteriousness of action, and constant annoyance in the shape of threatening letters, which now continually poured in upon Mr. Lyon, not only from Rochester, but from other portions of the country, compel him to settlement; and I saw that the whole supreme and devilish ingenuity of the Spiritualistic adventuress was being aimed at avoiding legal process, and to the accomplishment of this result.

So much time had now elapsed that it was necessary for Lyon's attorneys to go into court to explain the difficulties attendant upon reaching the woman, and secure an extension of time in serving the papers; and by the time this was accomplished, Grey had tracked her from town to town and city to city, all through Central Illinois, riding on the same train with her times without number, doubling routes and meeting her at unexpected points, travelling at all hours and in all manner of conveyances, never sleeping for days, eating from packages and parcels, with scarcely time for personal cleanliness or care, which often debarred him from admission to places where a woman, by that courtesy which is due to her for what she ought to be, was admitted and very properly protected from such hard-looking citizens as Grey had become; so that finally the two came into Terre Haute together, the adventuress as fresh as a daisy, and perfectly capable of another grand expedition of the same extent, and the detective completely worn out and entirely unfit for further duty.

Anticipating something of this kind and knowing that the woman might quite naturally gravitate to that point, I had ordered Operative Pinkham to proceed from Chicago to Terre Haute, and there assist Grey, or relieve him altogether, as occasion required, and continue the trail east towards Rochester, to which point the woman seemed gradually drifting, though evidently determined to prolong her journey so as to arrive in Rochester not more than a day or two before the time set for trial of the Winslow-Lyon breach of promise case.

Arriving at Terre Haute, Mrs. Winslow immediately went to Mrs. Deck's boarding-house, and upon telling that sympathetic old lady a harrowing tale about her persecutions, was received with open arms, and it was not long before her pitiful story had drawn a crowd of attenuated automatons to sympathize, suggest, and harangue against the entire orthodox world.

So impressed were these people with the woman's pitiable condition, that word was immediately passed among them that the persecuted lady should lecture to them at Pence's Hall, after which a sort of a general love-feast should be held, to be followed by seances and a collection for the benefit of the now notorious plaintiff.

That winter afternoon a quiet gentleman dropped into Mrs. Deck's and secured accommodations for a few days' stay, representing himself as a commercial traveller from Cincinnati. Mrs. Deck was absent working energetically in the interests of her spiritualistic guest, and the quiet man was obliged to transact his business with the handsome Belle Ruggles He was a pleasant, winning sort of a fellow, young, shapely, and adapted to immediately gaining confidence and esteem.

From a little conversation with her the quiet man, who was none other than Detective Pinkham from my Chicago

Agency, was sure that he could trust the girl, whom he at once saw had no sympathy with these people or their crazy antics. He saw that she was full of spirit, too, capable of carrying out any resolve she had made, and altogether the single oasis of good sense in this great desert of unbalanced minds.

So it was not long before he had her sentiments on Spiritualism, on Spiritualists, and on Mrs. Winslow, whom she denounced with tears of anger in her eyes as a disgrace to womanhood and to their place, and he had not been three hours in the house before the young lady and himself had entered into a conspiracy to give the woman such a scare as she had not recently had, and drive her from the pleasant though quaint old home her presence was contaminating.

The snow and the night came together, and the storm shook the old house until its weak, loose joints creaked, and every cranny and crevice wailed a dismal protest to the wind and the driving snow. It would take more than that though to keep people of one idea at home, and the entire household departed at an early hour for Pence's Hall, from which, whatever occurred there, Mrs. Deck's large family did not return until nearly midnight, by which time Operative Pinkham and Belle Ruggles had concluded their hasty preparations for a little dramatic entertainment of their own, and were properly stationed and accoutred to make it a brilliant success.

" Good-night, my poor dear ! " said the kind-hearted old body as she ushered Mrs. Winslow into her best

room, a long antiquated chamber, full of panels, wardrobes set in the wall, and ghostly, creaking furniture. " I
have to give you this room, we are so full. My first husband died there, but you don't care for anything like
that. I never sleep there, the place scares me; but I
know you will like it, you are so brave ! "

Whether brave or not, Mrs. Winslow seemed all of a
shiver when she had entered the room where Mrs. Deck's
first husband had died.

She closed the door carefully, and putting her candle
upon a grim old bureau, began a thorough and seemingly
frightened examination of the room. The storm had not
gone down, and as it beat upon the old place with exceptionally wild and powerful gusts, the feeble structure
seemed to shrink from them and tremble in every
portion.

On these occasions doors to the wardrobes and closets
of the strange room would open suddenly as if sprung
from their fastenings by unseen hands, while panels
would slide back and forth, cracks in the ceilings and
walls would open alarmingly, until, in fact, to the woman's vivid imaginations every portion of the lonely old
chamber or its weird furnishings seemed possessed of
supernatural life or motion. The fact is, Mrs. Winslow
was trembling like the house itself; but after a few
moments she snuffed the waning candle which the frugal
Mrs. Deck had given her, and in its flickering rays hastily
began preparing for bed.

Just as she bent over to blow out the candle, some

invisible assistant did the work for her, and at the same moment a hissed "*Beware !*" caused her to start with a scream and plunge for the bed, into which she scrambled after upsetting a chair or two, when she pulled the covering over her head and groaned with fright.

And now the blessed materializations began.

A sudden click and then a sliding sound above her head announced that the "control" had begun operations, and in a moment a few grains of plastering and some strange and weird combinations of musical sounds seemed to simultaneously fall into the room. The plaster, of course, came right down, some of it upon exposed parts of the trembling medium's person; but the music, which seemed to be badly out of harmony, appeared to have the power of circling in the air, which it did for some little time, and as suddenly ceased as it had begun, when from these mysterious upper regions came a long, low, tremulous, unearthly groan, that died away into a ghastly sigh as the storm clutched the decayed old mansion and shook it until it rattled and rattled again.

"My God!" quavered the half-smothered woman, "that's Mrs. Deck's first man's ghost; he'll kill me ! Mur——!"

She had begun to shout "Murder !" but a still more awful voice proceeding from the direction of the bureau bade her keep silence.

She was silent for a moment, but the storm wailed about the house so dismally that the "poor dear," who, according to Mrs. Deck, was brave enough to cheerily retire in what had been the bed-chamber of the dead, could bear the horror of her position no longer, and began a vocal lamentation which gave promise of attracting more than a spirit audience, when the materialized spirit of "Mrs. Deck's first man," or whatever owned the voice, laid a heavy hand upon the trembling woman, sepulchrally warned her to desist from her outcries, and then read her such a lecture from the Other World as she had never transmitted in her most effective "seances;" after which she was ordered, on pain of instant death, to leave Mrs. Deck's and Terre Haute as soon as morning should come, and a pledge being secured from her to the effect that she would, and that she would under no circumstances leave the room for the night, the spirit—which had very much the appearance of Detective Pinkham, the commercial traveller from Cincinnati—left the room by the door in a twinkling, very like a mortal, and still very like a mortal, quietly stole upstairs and helped extricate Miss Ruggles from her gloomy position, where she had done "utility" business as a groaning garret ghost.

All that dreary night the wicked woman moaned and wept for day. Her coward heart shrank from the evil she knew she deserved. The storm never ceased, but rose and fell as if keeping pace with her terrors, and the old place furnished her crazed imagination untold horrors.

At last the dawn came, but she had found no moment's sleep, and before the household was astir the wretched woman crept out upon the street, and plodding through the swollen drifts, followed by a very pleasant appearing commercial traveller from Chicago, she staggered to the station, and was rapidly borne away from her sympathizing friends towards the east.

Being apprised by telegraph of Pinkham's rather strange method of giving her an impulse in the direction of Rochester, I at once proceeded to that city with Superintendent Bangs, anticipating her arrival there shortly after our own; but was again disappointed, the adventuress having doubled on the detective, and so successfully avoided him, that the third day after leaving the Hoosier City he arrived in Rochester with a long face and in an extremely befogged condition.

After having directed Mr. Bangs and Pinkham to remain and watch every incoming train, one stormy evening, as I was about returning to New York, by the merest chance I espied the woman cautiously emerging from the Arcade, and following her I soon housed her in the apartments of an old mediumistic hag on State street. Calling a carriage I was rapidly driven to the Osborn House, where I found Mr. Bangs, and with him and the legal papers returned to the place in less than fifteen minutes from the time I had left it.

Cautiously approaching the room, we listened and heard low, earnest voices within. Through the transom we could see that the light inside was turned very low, and rightly judged that somebody was being given a "sitting," for, carefully trying the knob, I found that the place was secured against ordinary intrusion, and throwing my weight against the door it flew from its old and rusty fastenings, and in an instant we were within the medium's room.

"That is the woman!" said I, pointing to Mrs. Winslow, who had sprung from her chair white with fear, while the wretched-looking medium, though previously in the "trance state" stared at us with protruding eyes.

"And who are *you?*" she gasped, looking from one to the other in dismay.

"Persons whom you will give no more trouble after the service of these papers," gallantly replied Mr. Bangs, passing the legal documents into her hands, which closed upon them mechanically; and after I had politely handed the medium sufficient money to repair the damage I had caused her door, we bade the two spiritualists a cheery good-night and left them to a consideration of the contrast between mortal and immortal "manifestations."

CHAPTER XXVI.

MRS. WINSLOW was quite crushed by her failure
to evade service of the notice to take evidence
in just those sections of the country where she had been
too well known for her present good, and for a few days
seemed to be in that peculiar mental condition where one
may be easily led, or driven, into committing a desperate
act for mere relief from a too great conflict of emotions.

She flitted about the city in a state of great unrest for
a little time, not being able to dispossess her mind of the
fear or feeling of being pursued; stealing into the houses
of those of like belief, and with an air of great secrecy
insisting that they should give her refuge and protection
from Lyon's minions, who, she claimed—and perhaps had
come to believe—would yet in some way do her bodily
harm; mysteriously gliding about the Arcade and in the
vicinity of his house, as if expecting by some occult power
to be able to divine what might be the rich man's plans
concerning her; and like the very evil thing that she was,

hiding in uncanny places, scared at her own voice or footsteps, until the spell had left her.

About this time New York city dailies, and many of the newspapers of large circulation throughout the interior of the State, were publishing the following advertisement :

"Immense Success !—Miss Evalena Gray, the cele-brated Spiritual Physical Medium, lately from the Queen's Drawing-room, Hanover Square, London, also Crystal Palace, Sydenham, and assisted by Mlle. Willie Leve-raux, from Paris, will give one of her marvellous seances this evening at her elegant parlors, No. 19 West Twenty-first street, opposite the Fifth Avenue Hotel, at 7:30 P.M."

New York city knew Miss Evalena Gray as a new aspirant to the honors and emoluments derived from her ability to do mysterious things very gracefully. She was as beautiful a woman as had ever come into New York on this kind of business, and those who considered her a true medium were in ecstasies over the magnificent con-tortions and superb evolutions which her "great spiritual power" enabled her to execute with bewildering rapidity, while disbelievers in the source of these phenomena originating in celestial spheres could not resist her fasci-nating powers ; and the consequence was that her adroit-ness and beauty had created a great sensation, so much so in fact that respectable people had begun arguing about her, which answered just the purpose sought.

New York also knew her as a woman so full of soul—

that latter-day substitute for brains and personal purity—as to have readily confused and silenced great throngs in Europe wherever she had appeared ; and she had invariably challenged investigation, and that, too, with as much audacity as success, which had in every instance been wonderfully marked and complete.

Mrs. Winslow knew her as a little sprite she had met three years before at Chardon, Ohio, a pleasant little village of about 3,000 inhabitants, twelve miles south of Painesville, where Mrs. Winslow had been giving seances. Miss Gray was then just starting in her Spiritualistic career, and Mrs. Winslow, seeing her aptitude and general fascinating qualities, endeavored to persuade her to accompany her.

Miss Gray evidently believed in her own powers, at least had considered the proposition unfavorably ; but the two had become warm friends, and Mrs. Winslow had cheerfully imparted to the demure novitiate all her supply of manifestations, which she had rapidly acquired, and the two had parted with the promise to meet again at the very first opportunity, each drifting away to fulfil her traitorous course against society and blasphemous satire upon respectability.

So, Mrs. Winslow, being in that condition of mind wherein its possessor *must* have some person's confidence, saw this advertisement, and feeling sure that Miss Evalena Gray had been in clover, concluded that she could go to her for rest and consolation ; accordingly, she threw off the clouds which had seemed to settle upon her, gathered her baggage together from various secret places where it had been deposited, took rooms at the National Hotel for a few days in quite a rational manner, and after a week of perfect rest and physical care, which told wonderfully in her favor, in connection with her great recuperative powers, and having provided a wardrobe of no mean character, left Rochester for New York as handsome and attractive a woman as one would meet in a day's journey.

I was apprised of her departure by telegraph, and had a spry little operative at the Hudson River depot at Thirty-first street, ready to play the lackey to her. She at once proceeded in a carriage to the Fifth Avenue Hotel, where she secured fine apartments overlooking the entrance to Miss Evalena Gray's elegant parlors at No. 19 West Twenty-first street; and although I had no previous information as to what called Mrs. Winslow to New York, I was for several reasons satisfied that it was for the purpose of communicating with Miss Gray, and at once took measures for securing the substance of the interview.

As Mrs. Winslow had arrived late in the afternoon, I thought probably she would make no move until the following day, but took the precaution to secure a room adjoining hers for the use of an operative, sending another detective to Miss Gray's seance at half-past seven, to ascertain whether Mrs. Winslow was at any time present, and also, if necessary, to devise some means to remain in the house until the two women had met, should they do so.

The detective sent to Miss Gray's place was barely able to secure admission, on account of having come on foot, that fact alone laying him liable to suspicion. For an hour's time, splendid equipages, at short intervals, rolled up to the mansion, and their occupants were turned over to a negro butler of such gigantic proportions and gorgeous livery as to give the ordinarily aristocratic place an air of oriental splendor, the interior appointments being fully in keeping with the promise of sumptuousness which the reception always gave. Once entered, my operative had an opportunity to study these appointments.

The carpets were of such rich and heavy texture that they gave back no sound to the foot-fall, and by an ingenious arrangement, beneath the lambrequins adorning the windows, two noiseless fan-like blinds opened or closed instantly, lighting or darkening the room as suddenly, and evidently for use during day seances, which were sometimes given ; while opposite, two broad parlors led away, *en suite*, to a raised dais at the rear, upon which Miss Evalina Gray, assisted by Mlle. Leveraux, from Paris, gave her wonderful spiritual manifestations.

At either side of the centre of the first room, and on a level with the floor, was a fountain cut in marble, back into the basin of which the water fell with a dreamy, tinkling sound which suggested poetical luxuriousness. Rare statuary filled every accessible niche. Heroic paintings of the olden times, and the softer, more sensual paintings of the late French schools, blended together until they gave the walls a rosy glow. Flowers loading

the air with fragrance, warmed the room with the color
and life which flowers only can give. Hidden music-
boxes gave forth the rare and blended melodies of sunny,
southern climes ; while rich divans, arranged with that
pleasant kind of taste that bespeaks no arrangement at
all, were scattered negligently about the room, now rapidly being filled with the aristocratic people who had arrived
and were constantly arriving.

My operative, having gained a good point for observation, now turned his attention to the rapidly-increasing
assemblage. Almost without exception, they were men
and women of evident wealth and leisure, but with
scarcely a face denoting culture and refinement. They
were representatives of that numerous class who, after the
rapid acquirement of money, have found no good thing
with which to occupy their minds, or, what is more probable, have no minds to be thus occupied ; and, while not
giving Spiritualism any public endorsement, secretly follow its, to them, fascinating superstitions and mysteries,
and practice, in an easy way that prevents scandal or infamous notoriety, the sensualities which inevitably result
from its teachings or association with those hangers-on of
society professing its belief, all the time building a hope
that a lazy, sensuous heaven may be reached without effort or struggle by merely cherishing a secret faith in what
most satisfies their animal nature, and yearning to live
hereafter as they most desire to live here—were it not for
the voice of society—in a brutal freedom from restraint,
utterly devoid of moral and social purity, and without the

slightest semblance of that law, written and unwritten, which, from the creation of man and woman, has built about the domestic relations a protection and defence of sacred oneness and sanctified exclusiveness which no vandal dare attack without eventually receiving some just and certain punishment.

A conscientious detective will allow but little to escape his attention, and my operative, who had already had considerable experience with these illusionists, noticed a few arrangements which the spirits had evidently insisted on being made to insure the success of Miss Gray's seances, which were varied in their character, and "never comprised her entire repertory," as the actors would say, so that she was able to continue an attraction for some time to those persons who came to see her and witness her manifestations out of mere curiosity.

The frescoing of the walls of the back parlor had been done in lines and angles, which admitted of any number of apertures being cut and filled with noiseless pantomime doors, so neatly as to almost defy detection. The semi-circular platform was raised fully three feet, sloping considerably to the front, and—whether it did or not—might have contained a half-dozen "traps" such as are used for stage effects ; while, as is contrary to all rules for lighting places for public entertainment, the front parlor was lighted very brilliantly, the back parlor scarcely at all, while but a few glimmering rays fell from the chandeliers over the platform, where the spirits, like certain "star" actors, could not appear unless under certain conditions.

14

Shortly Mlle. Leveraux conducted Miss Gray through a side door to the platform, and as the latter smiled recognition to the large number present, exclamations of "Isn't she sweet?" "How beautiful!" "Almost an angel as she is!" and other expressions of extreme admiration, filled the room.

A deft little woman was Evalena Gray ; a sprite of a thing, light, airy, graceful, and with such ,a gliding, serpentine motion when walking, glistening with jewels as she always did, that one instinctively thought of some lithe and splendid leopard trailing along the edge of a jungle with an occasional angry flash of sunlight upon it. From her feet, both of which could have rested within your hand, and given room for just such another pair, to her shoulders, which were sloping and narrow though beautifully symmetrical, she was as straight as an arrow. Then her slender, faultless neck carried her head a little forward, with a slight bend to the side, which gave her face a half-daring or wholly appealing expression, as people of different temperaments might look at it, though it always attracted and held an observer, for it was as strange a face as its owner was a strange woman. The chin stood there by itself, though shapely, and at the point was prettily depressed by a little dimple, just needed to save the lower part of the face from a shrewish look. Above this the lower lip curved gradually to the edge of the carmine point, but was stopped there by a sort of drawn look, which with her dazzling white, though slightly irregular teeth, thin upper lip quickly parting from the lower, at either pleasure or anger, rather large, thin nostrils, which noticeably expanded and contracted with the rise and fall of her not over large bosom, and her languid blue eyes, one a trifle more closed than the other. but both looking demurely from under lashes of wonderful depth of sweep and length—all gave the face, which was witchingly attractive notwithstanding these marked features, either a plaintively spiritual appearance, or a wickedly fascinating expression beyond the power of description; while her hair, of that nameless color which might be formed of gold and silver, mingled and fell from her fine head, half hiding her delicate ears—pretty and faultless ears they were—in wonderful richness and profusion.

Never were seen more beautiful hands and fingers than those belonging to Miss Gray, and they had a way of assuming all manner of positions in harmony with the changes of her expressive face and the motions of her supple form, while her little body was a mere bundle of pliable bones and elastic sinews, which could compel all manner of contortions without change of posture, by mere will-power. She was not a beauty; but altogether, with her real or assumed languor, her strange eyes that might mean lasciviousness or might arouse your pity, her parted lips which would seem to protest of weariness or be ready to whisper a naughty secret to you, with her elf-like form that made her appear at once a dainty innocent thing and a pretty witch—she was a woman possessing a terribly fascinating power and capable of any devilish human accomplishment.

When the murmurs of admiration had died away, she arose, and in her languid manner especially prepared for the public, told her audience a long, though interesting fabrication, of how she first discovered she was possessed of this blessed spirit-power ; how she had at first doubted it, and endeavored to free herself from its possession; but finally saw that it could not be forced from her. On thorough conviction that she was a medium she had begun a laborious scientific investigation into the subject, and finally resolved to fathom the remotest secret of Spiritualism.

But even to her the blessed gates had been barred when she came with this spirit of unclean scepticism. Still, being assured that it had been given to her to walk with celestials, her future course was only a natural sequence. What had most sorely tried her in this life, she remarked, was to be herself morally sure of these wonderful medi·umistic powers, and then realize how cruelly the world scoffed at her as well as at all others who were anchored upon the same beautiful faith. To prevent this and find use for her powers in the highest spheres, she had travelled in Europe from Rome to St. Petersburg, and from Vienna to London.

In every instance the impossibility of any deception being practised in her manifestations was admitted ; but until she had arrived in London, she had failed to find anybody of repute honest enough to speak the truth. But there she had met a high-minded man who had broken through the barriers of prejudice, and, in an open, manly way, fearless of the sneers of the common herd, or of his business peers, had thoroughly investigated her exhibitions, found that they had proceeded from supernatural power, and had publicly stated his belief in their genuineness.

With such irrefutable evidence of the possession of this spirit-power, she was now fulfilling her mission of convincing the public of the existence of these heaven-inspired phenomena, explainable upon no other possible theory than that of the inter-communication between this and the other world of ministering angels, self-determining their actual existence by more or less perfect materializations.

With this and much more of the same sort, Evalena Gray began her revelations, all of which had previously been performed and exposed as ordinary tricks of an illusionary character, but which were given by the languid, *spirituelle* lady with such a show of her being on the threshold of the celestial spheres, that the very atmosphere, already charged with everything to provoke mystification and solemn curiosity, now seemed filled with some weird, supernatural influence and presence.

First the little lady, who was dressed in white muslin, with long flowing sleeves exposing very pretty arms, came down from the platform and seated herself in the centre of the back parlor, inviting the forming around her of a circle of from twelve to fifteen persons, who should sit so closely together that there could be no possibility of her passing out of the circle, and, if the rest of the audience chose, they might form a circle around the inner circle so that no confederates might reach her. This was done, when she requested some gentleman to place his feet upon her tiny feet to assure the audience that she did not leave her chair.

Members of the mystic circle then clasped hands, and the lights were turned off completely. The stillness of death followed, broken only by a low, shuddering sigh announcing the control of the medium by the spirits, and immediately after came raps so loud and distinct as to almost give the impression that an echo followed them. Then the medium began patting her hands together *as an absolute proof that none of the succeeding manifestations could by any possible means be produced by her.* While this continued without interruption, in the face of some came a whispered " God bless you !" others were patted caressingly upon the face and head ; whiskers and mus-taches were delicately tweaked ; watches were taken from one pocket and put into another ; a gent's quizzers would be placed upon a lady's nose, and *vice versa ;* music floated about in the air over the heads of those compos-ing the circle ; lights were seen to glitter like fire-flies above the medium's head, and a score of other equally startling phenomena occurred. When silence, with the ex-ception of the soft and delicate, but never-varying hand-patting, again fell upon the assemblage, a few raps an-·nounced the departure of the spirits ; and when the gas was turned on, the dainty little medium sat in precisely the same position as when the circle was formed, and the geutleman had taken good care to hold her neat little feel between his own. A sceptical lady now held Miss Gray's feet—held them as securely as only a sceptical lady could —when precisely the same manifestations occurred. Again her feet were secured as before, with the addi- tional precaution of their being tied. She was then tied to her chair securely, her hands tied firmly with a large handkerchief, and a delicate wine-glass filled with water placed upon the floor several feet from the chair. The lights were again turned off, the raps were heard as be- fore, and were in turn immediately followed by the hand- patting, and when the room was again lighted the wine-glass of water was found delicately poised upon Miss Evalena Gray's head.

Many startling variations of the same general character were introduced, and when this portion of the seance was concluded, the astounded company gathered about the pale and interesting medium with expressions of un- bounded wonder almost amounting to awe, mingled with terms of endearment; for she sweetly conversed with them for a little time, and, with rare insight into char- acter, gave each a pleasant word of recognition espe- cially fitted to every case, in a manner winning beyond expression.

She now retired for a short time, while Mlle. Leveraux entertained the assemblage with selections from her com- panion's exceptionally interesting European experiences as put in form probably by some enterprising, though im pecunious, New York Bohemian.

When Miss Gray returned she was attired quite differently. Instead of wearing the white, soft muslin which had given her a peculiarly graceful appearance, she had donned a closely-fitting basque of black rep silk, heavily trimmed with the costliest of lace, while the skirts to her dress were drawn very tightly around her form into a neat panier.

It *might* have been noticed by any other person in the room, as it *was* noticed by my operative, *that her bust and shoulders seemed to have undergone considerable change during her absence.* She seemed much more full across the breast, and her waist was certainly not so narrow and graceful as when she was operating in muslin within the circle. But then, the spirits might have caused this sudden growth, and she was still physically handsome and shapely.

A committee of gentlemen was then called for, and Miss Gray announced that she would submit to being tied to a chair as securely as it was in the power of the gentlemen selected by the audience to tie her; whereupon Mlle. Leveraux walked about the room and exhibited the rope to be used, which, though slender, seemed strong as a Mexican lasso.

There could have been no deception or fraud about this rope.

The three who had been selected to do the work then expressed their determination to tie Miss Gray "so the devil himself would have to help her," as one said, proceeding with the interesting operation in the bright gaslight, while all the people gathered about as if anxious to see that it was done properly, or curious to notice how the little woman would bear the ordeal. They certainly did their work well, and as the rope was wound around and about her, being drawn taut in every instance, it seemed to sink into her delicate flesh in a cruel way that made her wince and tremble, the operation calling forth numberless sympathetic remarks from those present, which she acknowledged by a painful martyr-like smile as she patiently bore the infliction until thoroughly tied. At her special request, as she said, to prevent a stoppage of circulation, her hands were tied at the wrist over a fold of silk to prevent abrasion of the flesh; and after all the knots had been sealed with wax, she was pronounced tied so securely that, without connivance of confederates, it would require superhuman aid to release her.

With a pleasant smile she looked around upon the wondering spectators and said:

"Good friends, I will absolutely and incontestably prove to you that I am possessed of that kind of aid. I want you all to form a circle around me. Every one in the room should join.it. Stand so closely together, clasping hands, that no living person can pass the circle either way."

The circle was then formed as she had requested, half upon the platform and half upon the floor, Miss Gray being at least ten feet from any of the persons composing it. She then asked anxiously:

"Are you all really satisfied—yes, convinced, that there can be no shadow or form of deception about this?"

14*

Some hesitated about giving a decided affirmation to that belief, when she swiftly singled out the doubters and pressed upon them not only the privilege, but the desirability and necessity, if they sought the truth, of personally examining the manner in which she had been tied. After this had been done and all scepticism had been silenced, she bade them a cheerful " Good-by !" and closing her eyes in a weary manner, seemed to pass into a peaceful slumber, as the lights were gradually turned off, finally leaving the room in total darkness, and with no sound to relieve the painful stillness save the orthodox rappings announcing the arrival of the spirits, the hidden music stealing softly to the hushed circle or the still softer water-wimplings from the fountains making *their* music in the carved marble basins.

It seemed a long time to the breathless people composing the circle, but probably not more than ten minutes had elapsed when the raps again startled the listeners, and in an instant the full light of the chandeliers flooded the room.

There sat the marvellous Physical Spiritual Medium utterly free, but as if just recovering from a swoon—the ropes, their seals unbroken, lying a few feet from the chair.

There was a simultaneous rush to where she was sitting apparently limp and exhausted from the great struggle which the spirits had had through her human personality, to release her from bondage, during which Mlle. Leveraux took occasion to remark that the strain upon Miss Gray's

There sat the marvelous Physical–Spiritual medium, utterly free, but as if just recovering from a swoon.—

powers had been too great, and begged that the ladies and gentlemen would excuse her at once, as the medium's condition would unfortunately necessitate the immediate termination of the seance for that evening; whereupon she left the room supporting the delicate Miss Gray in a manner that would have done credit to any theatre in the world.

There was no illusion and could have been no collusion.

Every one in the parlors had seen the woman tied so firmly that the ropes had sunk into her very flesh. The circle had been formed so securely as to admit of the passage out or in of no person whatever. They had all seen her sitting in the chair in a secure condition, and could have heard any movement on the part of any person within the circle who might have attempted to steal to her assistance. But there were the ropes with unbroken seals, lying there, silent but absolute evidence that no human agency had uncoiled them.

In the face of all this, what were reasoning people to believe?

They could not but believe the one thing that they generally did believe after having visited Evalena Gray's seances, and that was that there *does* exist an intercommunication between this and the " Land of the Leal ;" that all persons at times feel these spirit forces working upon or within them in different forms and with different degrees of intensity; and that there are these fine organisms, so free from earthly conditions or hinderances, as to almost permit the rehabilitation of spirit-lives which, as truly friendly aids and assistants, often perform what seem to the comprehension of ordinary mortals as past belief, giving in their materializations many blessed glimpses of the spirit-land.

All of which would be thrillingly pleasant to believe and ruminate over if it was not true that there are proba·bly hundreds in this country alone who can do this sort of thing without looking pale and interesting over it; without necessitating the indorsement of a millionaire brewer or anybody else; and who would consider it hardly fair to charge two dollars admission, as Miss Gray did, for the utter humbug of sitting within a circle as a woman dexterous enough to have her feet held and then be able with the left hand to pat the right palm for a moment, then the right arm—made bare from the wrist to the shoulder by the sudden unloosening of a delicate elastic, clasped into the bracelet—or her cheek, forehead, or neck, as necessity compelled, but making this patting incessant and so like that of the two hands, that detec-tion (in the dark) would be a matter of impossibility; and with this same bared right arm and hand producing all of these manifestations, ordinarily so marvellous, even to taking a little music-box out of the pocket, springing a catch to start the melody, "floating" it all about the heads of those composing the circle, shutting off the music, and putting the box in the pocket; or even neatly balancing a wine-glass of water upon the head.

And when this was all done, without claiming any par

ticular nearness to heaven regarding it either, I am satisfied that I have lady operatives in my employ who can step into a room adjoining a seance-parlor, adjust a rubber jacket, inflate it, hiding the tube of the same under a closely-fitting collar, allow themselves to be tied so that the ropes would seem to cruelly sink into the flesh; and that, after a room had been darkened ten minutes they would be able to have allowed the air to so escape from the rubber jacket, that, with the contraction of the form possible to many, the ropes, with unbroken seals, would almost fall from their forms of their own weight.

This is precisely how Miss Evelena Gray performed her tricks.

They did not reach to the dignity of respectable sleight-of-hand ; and I could go on endlessly multiplying these farces, which are so continuously and disgustingly played upon the public for just what money they will bring and nothing more ; for who ever saw a Spiritualist that went about the world bringing ministering spirits from heaven to earth for the good such materializations might do? And further, who ever saw a Spiritualistic medium, preacher or lecturer that did not make his religious faith, assumed or otherwise, yield him his living and provide him his luxuries besides?

CHAPTER XXVII.

IT appeared that Miss Evalena Gray and Mlle. Leveraux, and their male companions, or affinities, did not
reside at No. 19 West Twenty-first street, but in more
modest quarters farther down-town ; and after the assemblage had dispersed, the two Misses, an attendant or two,
a tall, gaunt, meek-looking fellow, whom the no longer
angelical Evalena called " Daddy," and a very fascinating
young man called in the advertisements W. Sterling Bischoff, manager, were gathered in the front parlor previous
to being driven home, when W. Sterling said quickly, and
as if suddenly recollecting something which it would not
be profitable for him to forget :

"See here, Gray ; 'most forgot. Here's a note sent
over from the Fifth Avenue. None of your larks now !"

The person addressed so familiarly as Gray was none
other than the interesting Evalena, who, putting her languor aside, and snatching the note from the " manager,"
said :

"Oh daddy don't mind:—do you daddy?."—

"Give it here, now !   I'll lark if I like, and *you* won't hinder."

"But there's Mr. Gray," persisted the manager, nodding towards the meek, gaunt man, whose lips seemed to move, though he ventured no remark.

"Oh, Daddy don't mind, do you, Daddy ? "

"Daddy" was Miss Evalena Gray's husband, but was under such peculiarly good spiritual "control" that he merely smiled a sickly smile and murmured that he be-lieved not.

Miss Gray proceeded to examine the note without wait-ing for the timid Mr. Gray's opinion, and suddenly exclaimed :

"Gracious ! I'm going right over there ! "

"What for ? " inquired Bischoff anxiously, while Mr. Gray's lips pursed into the form of an unspoken inquiry ; "man or woman, eh ? "

"None of your business !" she answered promptly. 'Here, Leveraux, help me on with my wrappings. You drive home. A friend of mine that I haven't seen for all the last three years is stopping over there, and wants to see me. I may stay all night. If I shouldn't want to, I'll order a carriage and come down in an hour or two."

The three, who were elegantly supported by this woman's juggleries, seemed to realize that there was no use of opposing her; and without knowing whether it was a man or woman she intended visiting at that hour of the night, went gloomily home, while a few minutes later Miss Gray, unannounced, and at the unseasonable

hour of eleven o'clock, was knocking at the door of Mrs
Winslow's room.

In a moment more, though Mrs. Winslow was on the
point of retiring, and was in that easy *déshabillé* in which
women love to wander about, doing a hundred unmen-
tionable and unimportant things before getting into bed
for good, Miss Gray was pushing her lithe form through
the cautiously opened door, and at once unlimbered her
tongue and her reserve ; the result of which, as noted by
my operative, showed the eminent vulgarity of the two
female frauds, and illustrated the fact that whatever pre-
tensions they might make, their conversation alone would
serve to discover the inherent and low vileness of their
character.

"Oh, you dear old fraud!" said Evalena, entering,
after Mrs. Winslow had virtuously given herself sufficient
time to ascertain that there was no evil-minded man at
the door, and had gladly admitted her visitor ; " if you've
got any other company, of course I won't come ! "

Mrs. Winslow laughed knowingly, and then told her
visitor how really glad she was to see her. She was
sincere in this, and sincerity, even in a bad cause, is a
redeeming feature.

"Well, well, you rascal," continued Miss Gray in a
jolly, rollicking sort of a way, "couldn't wait until
to-morrow. Where *have* you been, what *have* you been
doing, and how *are* you, anyhow? Come, now, tell me
all about yourself ! "

Saying this in a kind of a rush of excitement, Miss

Gray settled herself in a corner of the luxurious sofa, pulled her feet under her to get a more comfortable position, and like an interested philosopher, waited for and listened to the narrative which comprised many of the facts I have given; but instead of telling the whole truth, only gave that part of it which made her appear to have been eminently successful in her swindling operations, and showed life with her to have been floating calmly upon one continuous, peaceful stream.

"And now, Evalena," said Mrs. Winslow, rounding off her story with a great flourish over what she was to make out of Lyon, whom she described as still madly in love with her, "where have *you* been, and what have *you* been doing since I saw you at Chardon?"

The glib tongue of the marvellous Physical Spiritual Medium began at once, and she rattled away at a terrible rate.

"Well, I've got the same husband——"

"Oh, pshaw!" interrupted Mrs. Winslow half con temptuously.

"But he's such a dear, good old fool that I can't throw him over. Why, I can make him shrink from six feet two to two feet six by just looking at him! Money couldn't hire such a devoted servant anywhere. He'll do just anything I tell him; and if I want him out of the way for a few days," she continued with a comical wink, "I just give him a fifty-dollar bill and say: 'Daddy, you don't look well; take a run into the country, and I'll write for you when I want you!' He goes away then with his face about a yard long. But he goes ; and he never made a rumpus in his life !"

"Oh, that's quite another thing," said Mrs. Winslow, evidently relieved to know that Miss Gray had had so good a reason for living so long a time as three years with the same man.

"Yes, he's what I call an 'accommodation husband.' He accommodates me, and I—" here Miss Gray sighed piously—"accommodate myself!"

"Exactly," remarked Mrs. Winslow, beginning to appreciate the pleasant nature of such an arrangement.

"Well," resumed the marvellous medium, "we went all through the Ohio towns giving *exposés;* went out through Chicago, and then down to St. Louis. But the *exposé* business didn't pay. We found that people would pay more money to be humbugged than to learn how some other person might be deluded !"

"Every time !" tersely observed Mrs. Winslow.

"So at St. Louis we resolved to become Spiritualists.

"The very best thing you could have done !" said Mrs. Winslow approvingly.

"And at Quincy," resumed Evalena, "we blossomed out. Oh, but didn't the papers go for us, though !—called us everything."

"D——n the newspapers, anyhow !" exclaimed Mrs. Winslow in a burst of indignation over her own wrongs.

"Oh, no, no, no ! *that* won't do. Make huge advertising bills. That's better—much better. That's what *we* did, and we made big money too. By and by we came on here to New York, made a huge show, took in a vast pile, and then went to Europe.   Oh, that's the only way to do it ! "

" Yes," said Mrs. Winslow with a deep sigh.   " I have often felt the want of that peculiar tone which going to Europe gives one."

" Well, we did have a gay time, though," said Miss Gray in a dreamy way, as if ruminating over her conquests ;   " and at Venice—oh, that delicious, ravishing, dreamful Venice !—I bilked a swarthy nobleman from the mountains out of five thousand dollars.   At Rome I did a swell American out of everything he had.   At Vienna, a Hungarian wine-grower fell, and I trampled upon him as his brutes of peasants beat out the grapes in vintage-time.   At Berlin a German student killed himself for me ; and at St. Petersburg I fooled the Czar himself.   But when I got back to London I got better game than him."

" Bigger game than the Czar ?   Oh, my ! " exclaimed Mrs. Winslow, thinking how she had wasted her sweetness on two detectives like Bristol and Fox.

" Well, bigger game this way," pursued little Miss Gray, reasoning it out slowly.   " This Spiritualistic business can only be played on low, ignorant people ordinarily.   Get the recognition of so big a man as one of the wealthiest brewers in Great Britain, and then, if Miss Gray has money and can open sumptuous parlors in so fashionable a vicinity as Madison Square, and can own a quarter of a column of the New York papers every day, Miss Evalena Gray's fortune is made.   Do you see ? "

Mrs. Winslow did see, but wanted to know how she had secured such approval.

Her companion looked at her a moment in blank astonishment ; then drawing down the corners of her mouth as if protesting against such verdancy on the part of so old a Spiritualistic soldier as Mrs. Winslow, gave a very expressive series of winks, broke into loud laughter, and then suggested that if she wanted anything like *that* explained it would be no more than fair to order either Krug or Monopolé to help her through so dreary a recital ; whereupon the latter did as requested, and after the two had washed down a ribald toast with wine, the angelic Miss Gray continued:

" Well, you see, we came directly from St. Petersburg to London, and got up a big excitement there right off. The *Times* denounced us, and we replied savagely through the *Telegraph* at a half-crown a line. We kept this up until all London was engaged in the controversy, and our rooms were constantly thronged."

"What luck !" sighed Mrs. Winslow, sipping her wine.

" By and by the 'nobbies' got discussing the matter at the clubs. We challenged examination by committees everywhere, of course, and one day a batch of M.P.s, clergymen, merchants, and all that, came down upon us. I picked out one man named Perkins—a brewer from the Surrey side, and one of the wealthiest men in all England, and a man of education and standing, too—for game right off."

" Must be lots of fools over in London, ' remarked Mrs. Winslow, as if she would like to help pluck them.

" Yes," answered Miss Gray, " and millions in this country. We're going to take a run over to Washington this winter."

" I would if I had your talent," replied her companion.

" Well," resumed the medium, " I saw Perkins was an easy-going fellow, and I wrote him, saying it was something unusual for me to do, but as the ' spirits ' "—here Miss Gray winked very hard at Mrs. Winslow, who snickered—" had revealed to me that he was an arrant unbeliever, but at the same time a fair, honorable man, magnanimous enough to be just—I wished him to make a private investigation."

" ' Private investigation's ' good !" said Mrs. Winslow, laughing heartily.

" Certainly good for me," continued the little medium in a self-satisfied way. " He came, though, and I gave him my tricks in my best possible style. I pretty nearly scared him to death. Then I let him tie me, and the old man's hands trembled as he put the ropes around my waist and over my bosom. ' Miss Gray,' said he tenderly, ' I shall injure you ! ' ' Mr. Perkins,' I replied, also tenderly, ' the good spirits will protect me. Pull the ropes tighter ! '

" He pulled the ropes tighter and tighter, and finally got me tied. Then he darkened the room and in a few minutes I was entirely free of the ropes of course, and I told him to raise the curtain. As soon as he did so I left, telling him I was ill ; and as soon as I could change my dress, came back and sat down with him. I got close to him—as close as I am to you now, Mrs. Winslow—and then, putting my right hand on his knee, and my left hand on his shoulder——"

"Splendid !" interrupted Mrs. Winslow, pouring more wine for the ingenuous Miss Gray, and taking some herself.

"Then," continued Miss Gray, laughing in a peculiarly wicked manner, "I got my face pretty close to his and asked : 'Mr. Perkins, I want you to give me an answer that you are willing to have made public. On your honor as a man, do you not now believe in the genuineness of these spiritual manifestations produced through me?' 'I do,' he said passionately, throwing his arms around me, and—and I don't know what he would have done had not Leveraux entered the room at that supreme moment !"

"Oh, *I* see !" murmured the other blackmailer.

"Think of it, Mrs. Winslow !" added Miss Gray tauntingly ; "think of it ! In the arms of a man who can draw his check for a million sterling—and poor little me from Chardon, Ohio ! "

"My ! but you are a little rascal, though !" said Mrs. Winslow admiringly. "I always knew you'd make an impression somewhere."

"' Leveraux !' said I indignantly, and springing from Perkins's embrace after I had kissed him in a way that set him shaking again, ' if you ever breathe a word of this, or annoy Mr. Perkins in any manner under heaven, I'll kill you ! Go !'

"Levereaux entered the room at that supreme moment."—

"Poor Leveraux knew her cue and replied hotly, ' I'd kill myself before I'd do so disgraceful an act !' and then flounced out of the room."

" *What* a pair !" exclaimed Mrs. Winslow.

"He thought I was just perfectly splendid after that ; kept coming and coming, indorsed me publicly, got wild over me ; but I held him at arm's length for months, until I thought the man would really go crazy ; and final- ly—well, you know I told you Daddy was an ' accommo- dation husband,' and if he hadn't been one after I had tripped up one of the richest men in all England, I would have just hired somebody to have dumped him into the Thames, sure !"

The sparkling flow of Miss Gray's experience was here interrupted by Mrs. Winslow's ordering another bottle of wine, and after the couple had partaken of the same, the spicy narrative was continued :

"But now comes the fun, Winslow. I can't tell you *how* my rope trick is done. I've got a little addition to it that makes it a regular sensation. It don't hurt me a particle, and allows the strongest men to pull away with all their might."

"I'd give a thousand dollars for it, Evalena," said her friend warmly.

"No good ; no good for you," replied Miss Gray, critically looking over Mrs Winslow's splendid physical completeness. "Fact is, Winslow, you aren't built exactly right for that kind of work. There's too much of you to do the rope trick with eminent success. I

played Daddy as my brother, and myself for an innocent,
so neatly that Perkins honestly thought he had made a
wonderful conquest. He believed it all, for he was one of
those honest fools—in fact, came near being too honest
for me."

"Why, how?"

"Well, he installed me as his mistress in grand style;
but, of course, I insisted in giving seances and compelled
public recognition through *his* public recognition of my
'wonderful spirit-power.' The man was so infatuated
that he bored me terribly with his visits. Why, I could
hardly get time to attend to business. You know we
always have a stock of ropes on hand in the seance-rooms,
so that when any one objects to the one I ordinarily use,
there are always other ropes at hand that I *can* use. One
night some fellow broke my best rope, and the next day I
was carelessly practising with another with my door un-
secured. Perkins had been down to Brighton for a week
or two, and of course had to rush over to see me the
minute he got in London—to give me a 'happy surprise,'
I suppose. There I sat when he suddenly bolted into
the room and saw the thinness of the whole thing in an
instant."

"What did he see?" asked Mrs. Winslow abruptly.

"You *are* shrewd, Winslow, but you can't catch me
that way; no, no, no! But he did see the whole trick as
clear as a June day. Do you think I fainted?"

"Not much," said her companion tersely.

"No; but *he* nearly did. He reeled and staggered as

though he had been struck by a sledge-hammer, and I saw in his face a determination to rush from the room and denounce me to all London. It was make or break with me then, Winslow, and with a bound I got to the door, turned the key, and sent it crashing through a five-pound pane of glass into the street below. Then I just whipped out this little derringer," she continued, producing a beautifully mounted, though diminutive weapon, "just run it right up under his eyes, and backed him into a seat."

" ' Great God ! ' he whimpered, ' I'm undone ! I'm undone !—what a very devil you are ! '

"My heart did go thumping to see the man used up so ; but I had to be rough, and said : ' Yes, I *am* a devil, Perkins, and you must pledge me your word—yes, you must take a solemn oath before that God you have called upon, that you will never expose me, or I will blow your brains out ! ' "

"Splendid ! splendid !" ejaculated Mrs. Winslow. "Did he do it ? "

" I should say he did do it ! He got down on his knees and begged like a baby. And do you know, my blood was up so then, and I so despised him for his **want of** manliness, that I came within an ace of killing the infernal booby !"

"He deserved it !" said Mrs. Winslow sympathetically.

"After I had him nearly scared to death," resumed the marvellous medium, "I began reasoning with him, and, by being excruciatingly tender, convinced him that by exposing me he would gain nothing, but would lose in

15

.verything that a man of spirit prided in—honor, social
.eputation, and business standing, and drew a lively picture
of his disgrace at the clubs and in social circles, and of the
cartoons which would certainly appear in *Punch* and the
other comic papers ; and the result was that I held on to
his affection and his purse-strings by compelling him to
feel that my detaining him in the room and threatening to
shoot him was the only thing which prevented him from
rashly ruining both.   Altogether, Winslow, I got over two
thousand pounds out of him. He wasn't deprived of a first-
class mistress while I remained in London, and—and we
are so good friends now that every little while I get a splendid remittance from him ; and if I ever should want to go
back, I could have the very best in all England ! "

" Well, well, well ! " murmured Mrs. Winslow for the
want of something better with which to express her
admiration.

" I *do* think I played it pretty well," resumed Miss
Gray ; " and I made him swallow it all, too.   He really
believed everything from the moment I fell into his arms
until he caught me with the ropes. I was his spirit-wife—"
another hard wink—" and he my only affinity. Leveraux
helped me in the whole thing splendidly.

"Who is Mlle. Willie Levereaux ? " inquired Mrs.
Winslow.

" She is a sister of Ed. Johnson, the ' bank-burster,'
and a keen girl, too," answered the medium.

" How did you happen to get hold of her ? "

" Well, you see, Ed. Johnson, Mose Wogle, Frank

Dean— 'Dago Frank'—and Dave Cummings, with Chief of Police McGillan and Detective Royal, of Jersey City, put up a job on the First National Bank there. McGillan was to keep everybody away from them; and he, or Royal, was to always remain at headquarters to let the boys off if they got nabbed. They played it as plaster-workers—Italians, you know—and began working from a room over the bank down through the ceiling into the vault; but an old scrub-woman about the place got suspicious, and had them arrested one day when both McGillan and Royal happened to be in Philadelphia. They had promised the boys help to break jail, but they failed everywhere; and Willie, thinking to get Johnson off, went to the bank officers and told them the whole story. They promised to help her brother, but said her evidence would have to be corroborated. So she sent for McGillan and Royal, got them into her rooms, then over on Thirty-seventh street, and had a Hoboken official in a closet, with a stenographer, who took all the conversation, which amounted to a complete confession of their complicity. It never did any good, though. McGillan and Royal got the most swearing done, and got clear; while Johnson and the rest of the boys got fifteen years' solitary confinement in the New Jersey penitentiary. It almost broke Willie down; but she is splendid help now."

Mrs. Winslow drew a long sigh, and the two drank again to drown the doleful feelings raised by this recital; for even high-toned and uncaught criminals do not find the contemplation of stone walls and iron bars by any means pleasant and refreshing; and with this lively history of herself and her companions, the "Marvellous Physical Spiritual Medium" called a servant, ordered a conveyance, and was driven home, after having promised to call with her own carriage on the next day; while Mrs. Winslow, after surveying her own magnificent physique as reflected in the pier-glass, muttered :

'*I'll* make an effort, go to Europe, and, like so many others, win fame too !"

Then with a resolute toss of her head the adventuress plumped into her bed, where, for aught we know, she carried on her vile conquests and miserable villainies in her dreams the whole night long.

CHAPTER XXVIII.

MRS. WINSLOW'S stay in New York was rather an interruption to Miss Evalena Gray's business, as those two champions of the theory that earth and heaven are connected by a spiritual hyphen only adjustable, or to be made serviceable, by the brainless imbeciles or the remorseless sharks of society, to the exclusion of people of purity and worth, indulged in several lapses from sobriety, and in spiritual love-feasts of such remarkable length and enthusiasm that W. Sterling Bischoff, Mlle. Levereaux, and the mournful accommodation husband, "Daddy," became quite alarmed for the result, were obliged to discontinue the marvellous seances at No. Nineteen West Twenty-first Street—on account of the "alarming illness of the fascinating little medium," as the manager was careful to see that the truthful newspapers announced—and at the close of a term of spirituous rapture of remarkable intensity and duration, the three who were vitally interested in Miss Gray's recovery from her peculiarly alarming illness, managed to part the loving couple, induce the languid Evalena to return to her fascinations and fools, and sent Mrs. Winslow to Rochester and her roguery.

Although her trip to New York had been one of pro·longed dissipation, Mrs. Winslow had evidently gained courage from it from the assurance of Miss Gray's friend·ship, and through that ingenious little woman's recitals of daring and conquest now applied herself with new vigor and dash to her infamous work.

During her absence in New York, Superintendent Bangs and a legal gentleman from Rochester had proceeded to the West and were rapidly gathering in the harvest of evidence I had reaped, and which subsequently became so serviceable.

Mrs. Winslow, seeing she had been outwitted, began diligently arranging matters for the coming trial, and having lost the main point of dependence which she had hoped to make in our inability to use the evidence which she was sure Lyon's counsel could get by a liberal expenditure of money, which she also knew must be at hand, she began the tactics of delay, and secured a change of venue from Rochester to Batavia, on the ground of prejudice ; and, without the assistance of counsel, boldly manœuvred her case nearly as carefully and judiciously as the most proficient of criminal lawyers.

Ascertaining that Lyon's counsel had secured damaging evidence against her in those sections of country where she had previously been the spiritualistic harlot that she was, she rapidly followed Mr. Bangs and his companion, and through her wonderful personal magnetism, physical force, consummate bravado, and skilful manipulations, succeeded in securing numberless affidavits—not that she was a pure woman, but that as far as the affiant knew, she was not a bad woman.

Some, who had given Lyon's counsel depositions comprehensive enough to have crushed her in court, were compelled by her to depose under oath that their previous depositions given Mr. Bangs were made under a misapprehension of facts. Others were induced to swear that they were mistaken in her identity, which would naturally have the effect of breaking the chain of evidence connecting her with her numberless different aliases, and therefore with her numberless offences against the laws and society ; so that unless our work had been, in this respect, anything but faultless, Mr. Lyon would have certainly suffered defeat.

As the date of trial at Batavia neared, however, although the woman had showed great skill in her management of her own case, and had got things into as good shape for herself as nearly any lawyer in the country could have done, she suddenly changed her decision regarding conducting the case personally, and engaged the services of a Rochester lawyer of good repute, who certainly would not have pleaded her cause had he at first been aware of her character in the slightest degree.

At last the case came to trial at Batavia, Judge Williams presiding, and was considered of sufficient importance to command the quite general attention of newspapers, and a large number of reporters were in attendance, while the little city had never before attracted such a crowd of curious people, brought there and kept there by the great interest which the trial had awakened.

Mr. Lyon seldom appeared in court, being detained in Rochester by the faithful and still voluble Harcout, where the latter busied himself in predicting Mrs. Winslow's downfall on account of the thorough manner in which he had conducted matters, and in constant trips to the newspaper and telegraph offices for the latest news concerning the progress of the case.

At Batavia Mrs. Winslow had in some unexplainable manner worked up quite a feeling in her behalf, and had busily engaged herself, laboring day and night, in all the little things that form public opinion as well as cause the application of law to individual preferences, whether justice enters into such decisions or not.

Especially was her business ability shown in securing a jury a portion of whom she brazenly boasted *dare* not find for the defendant. She had evidently given up all expectation of a verdict in her favor; but, in perfect accord with her line of policy to annoy her victim into a settlement, had arranged matters in every respect so that there would be delay, that as much as possible nauseating scandal should reach the public to react upon Lyon, and that in every way the outcome of the case would be to belittle, bemean and disgrace him, for having had to do in any way with so bad a woman as she knew herself to be.

The latter was a point most people's pride would prevent them from making. She had lost that, but her active mind saw how revolting it all would be to him, and her cupidity, greed and vindictiveness made the prosecution a persecution that had a measure of fiendish pleasure in it for her.

Here her mental and her pecuniary resources were again demonstrated in a way that surprised everybody at all cognizant of her habits and history. The cost of carrying on a case of this importance was very large. Money had unquestionably been largely used in bribery. Many of the affidavits she had so expeditiously secured had been purchased outright. The court costs were no inconsiderable sum. Her lawyer, feeling somewhat doubtful of her character, and wholly satisfied of her irresponsibility, demanded his fee—and it was a large one—in advance. But every demand, save those that would not injure her case by refusing, was promptly met, and the mysterious source of supply seemed as exhaustless at the end as at the beginning; though at all times she was a female combination of the Artful Dodger and Job Trotter, capable of compelling confidence and sympathy. During the progress of the trial she also had time for the practice of her spiritualistic mummeries, and so worked upon the ignorance, passions, and pockets of a few wealthy farmers, who were in attendance at court, that she drove a thriving trade in revelations and prophecies that, whatever other effect they might have, certainly brought her large sums of money.

Although the larger amount of evidence on both sides
15*

was of a documentary character, the case occupied near
ly a week, and public interest was wrought up to the high
est possible pitch of excitement as day after day some
startling episode or dramatic incident was developed;
and finally, when Judge Williams charged the jury and
that body retired for consultation, both sides of the case
had been so ably conducted, such a terrible flood of vileness had been launched upon the community, and so intense was the feeling against the woman on the part of
the public—who condemn with a terrible intensity when
once made aware of the danger in the heart and life of a
social assassin, that the pretty city of Batavia was all
awhirl from agitation and excitement.

All this had been greatly increased by the following
dispatches from St. Louis to the Rochester papers, which
had, of course, been received and widely read in that section, and were all preceded by an item clipped from the
Detroit *Tribune*, to the effect that the notorious female,
Mrs. Winslow, had been indicted in St. Louis as a common scold, and several public speakers therein named had
better take warning.   The first dispatch read:

"The trial of Mrs. Winslow, charged with common
barratry, has been proceeding in the Four Courts all day.
Scores of lawyers are here from all parts of the West, as
witnesses for the prosecution. The case excites great interest, a similar one never having occurred in St. Louis
before."

The second and final dispatch from St. Louis on the
subject was:

" The case of the notorious Mrs. Winslow, indicted for common barratry, terminated to-day. The jury assessed her punishment to be six months' imprisonment in the county jail."

These dispatches, with the editorial comments they evoked, had been received during the progress of the case, and though it was too late to offer the facts in evidence as to the woman's character, they had intensified the feeling against her until Mrs. Winslow was given an opportunity of realizing something of the depth of human scorn.

A day passed, but no agreement. What could it mean? the public asked. The second day, being Sunday, passed slowly over the town, for no news of the jury could be obtained ; and though it was a raw winter's day, the streets were full of people anxious to learn the result. Monday came and went, and still the jury were out. Whispers of bribery now began to fly about the city, and when the fourth day had passed with no agreement and with repeated requests from the jury that they might be discharged, the whole city was filled with indignation, while public resentment ran so high that it was with some personal risk that this exponent of Spiritualism passed to and fro between the court-room and her hotel.

Finally, it being ascertained that the jury disagreed irreconcilably, they were called into court for their discharge, and filed solemnly into their box. After a silence that could be felt had settled upon the vast audience, Judge Williams wheeled around, and, facing the jury—many of whom shrank from his severe and penetrating glance—in a

voice of quiet power, his whole bearing being one of dignified scorn, he delivered with great solemnity the following
well-deserved rebuke and protest against the corruption
of the power of the jury, and its contempt of justice and
the sacred dignity of the Court :

"GENTLEMEN OF THE JURY—I had hoped you would
agree upon a verdict. The cause is a plain one, and there
is no need of a disagreement. Another trial would be
expensive to the county, and would occupy much time.
A second trial would again crowd this court-room with a
throng of auditors, who would listen day after day to the
disgusting depositions which are on file in this cause.
One trial such as this is too much for the decency and
morality of any community, and another jury should
never be called to pass upon this case. It is the policy
of all courts to secure agreements from juries, and in
such a case as this, more than in almost any other, a disagreement should not be allowed.

"You are, after being out four days, irreconcilably divided. Some of you, I know, are determined to be only
guided by the evidence and the law, as given to you by
this Court. For your long and persistent resistance of
all attempts on the part of some of your number to prevent justice, you are entitled to my sincere thanks and
those of all right-minded men in this community. Others
there are upon this jury who, I am bound to believe, have
consulted only their passions and prejudices ; have deliberately ignored the evidence and the instruction of the
Court, and are anxious to perpetrate what they know

or might have known, was gross injustice. If there are such men upon this jury, their conduct merits severest condemnation. I have great respect for the honest convictions of jurors, even when I think they are wrong. I could not censure jurors for honest prejudices ; but I can have no respect for men who, from base and unworthy motives, seek to secure unworthy ends.

" If any one was to look leniently upon the plaintiff, it would, of course, be her counsel. But to make twelve honest men ever see that she was entitled to a verdict of even one cent, is a work that transcends human ability.

" One of the plainest principles of law applicable to all civil cases, is that the plaintiff can only recover where there is a fair preponderance of evidence in his favor. Upon the principal question in this case—that is, whether or not there was an agreement of marriage between plaintiff and defendant—they were the only witnesses. Supposing both to be equally credible, how can the plaintiff recover when every act affirmed by her is denied by the defendant ? But are they equally credible ? The defendant is proved by the evidence to be a man of character, reputation, and social position. Who is the plaintiff ? By her own evidence she is one who years ago deserted her husband and three children in Wisconsin, and commenced the life of an itinerant fortune-teller. Since then, as a clairvoyant, a mesmerist, a medium, she has perambulated the country, professing in her handbills to predict future events and to cure all manner of diseases by her occult arts.

She has assumed in her travels those invariable proofs

of guilt, *aliases.* She has been proven, by her own writing, daily conversation, and every-day conduct, to be grossly profane and indecent. By the testimony of several unimpeached witnesses, produced by defendant, she is shown to have been an inmate of a house, or houses, of ill-fame, and to have committed acts of the most shocking indecency and lewdness. And yet this is the woman whose testimony some of you have received with absolute verity, while rejecting the testimony of the defendant as of no value in comparison with it. The question before you was, whether between this woman and the defendant there had been a binding contract of marriage. There is no one of you so low that you would have entered into such an obligation with this woman. You would have started back in horror at such a proposition; and yet you have been so lost to decency that you have seemed determined, by your verdict, to thrust such a disgrace and outrage upon the defendant !

" You were told by the Court that if the plaintiff was married at the time when she said the defendant agreed to marry her, such a promise was absolutely void. The plaintiff had herself sworn that the promise was made in 186-, and that she was then, and had remained for nearly two years thereafter, a married woman. Did not the Court tell you that such a promise was void ? The Court told you that no subsequent ratification of such a promise could make it binding. The Court further instructed you that if the plaintiff was unchaste at the time of the promise of marriage, and her unchastity was not known to defendant, that the marriage contract, if entered into, was not binding. The entire record in this case teems with the history of her licentiousness. No witness has been so reckless as to swear that within the last ten years she has had either virtuous habits or virtuous associations. That she was virtuous in 1860, or rather, that if then vicious, her character in this regard was then unknown to her neighbors in Indiana and Wisconsin, is rendered highly probable from the evidence. But there was a period preceding this by many years, when the maiden merged into the woman, that the almost exhaustless evidence produced by the defendant shows to have been a time without shame, and when her keen shrewdness and wicked nature had already been developed to a degree of depravity beyond human belief; and there has since been a period when the vilest inmate of the lowest den of prostitution was happy in her virgin purity in comparison with this woman!

"Previous to the first-mentioned time the plaintiff had followed the army of the Southwest in its weary marches —not, however, as the evidence discloses, for any honest purpose. She had wandered infinitely further from purity than from her Northern home. And yet you have attempted to render a verdict that after all these wanderings, and after this incomparably vile career, she is fit to become the wife of a respectable citizen of Rochester, the mistress of his mansion, and the sharer of his large fortune.

'You were further instructed that if a promise of marriage had been made, and if the plaintiff had at that time been virtuous, and had subsequently become unchaste the defendant was released from the obligation of such a promise ; what regard, in view of the evidence in this case, have you paid to that instruction ?

Am I too severe, then, when I say that when, through four long days and nights in your jury-room, some of this jury have attempted to force a verdict in favor of the plaintiff, notwithstanding she was not entitled to it, and the defendant's witnesses had proven that she was utterly unworthy of it, you have been actuated by passion and prejudice, and have attempted to pervert justice? Had you been able to infect all your comrades with your pestilential breath, and had a verdict in her favor been rendered, I should certainly have set it aside immediately.

" I cannot but express my severest censure at the result of this cause at your hands, knowing, as I cannot but know, that the same vile machinations which have left a hideous trail of this female monster over every portion of the land, have brought about this disagreement which is a shame and a disgrace to yourselves, to Genesee County, and this Court !"

The suit necessarily went over to the next term of court, over which Judge Williams also presided, when no developments worthy of note occurred, the same evidence being introduced, the same tactics on the part of Mrs. Winslow—who, however, had been obliged to secure new counsel—being attempted, and the same crowd of morbid curiosity-seekers being in attendance.

But the woman had by this time become too well known for the slightest hope of success, or even to enable her to receive the ordinary consideration and protection of the Court.

Without leaving their seats the jury found for the defendant, and the woman, defeated yet insolent and daring, passed out into the summer-decked streets of the little city of Batavia a scorned, dreaded being, driven from everything but infamous memory.

I was never sufficiently interested in Le Compte to trace his future, but it is safe to say that he never visited "La belle France" and "Paris, the beautiful, the sublime, the magnificent," in company with the once fascinating Mrs. Winslow.

Harcout is still the pompous henchman of the harassed millionaire, Mr. Lyon, and quite covered himself with glory from having claimed the entire work of securing the evidence that caused the overthrow of the adventuress.

Were I a novelist, rather than a detective and obliged to relate facts, I could have made an effective climax by a tragic meeting between Harcout and Mrs. Winslow, where Lilly Nettleton would have recognized the Rev. Mr. Bland and wreaked summary vengeance upon him; but, so far as I am aware, they never met, and the much-named social scourge is now wearing out an inconceivably vile and wretched old age—the irrevocable result of her course of life—an outcast and a wanderer among the lowest classes that people portions of the Pacific Slope cities, with remorse and wretchedness behind, and utter hopelessness beyond ; while Mr. Lyon, now a feeble old man, who has atoned, through regrets and humiliations, for his part of the wrong launched through his as well as her sin upon society, has at least become thoroughly satisfied of the thousands of evils following in the trail of this so-called spirit-power, his fulness of knowledge of its workings having been gained through this particular experience with THE SPIRITUALISTS AND THE DETECTIVES.

THE END.

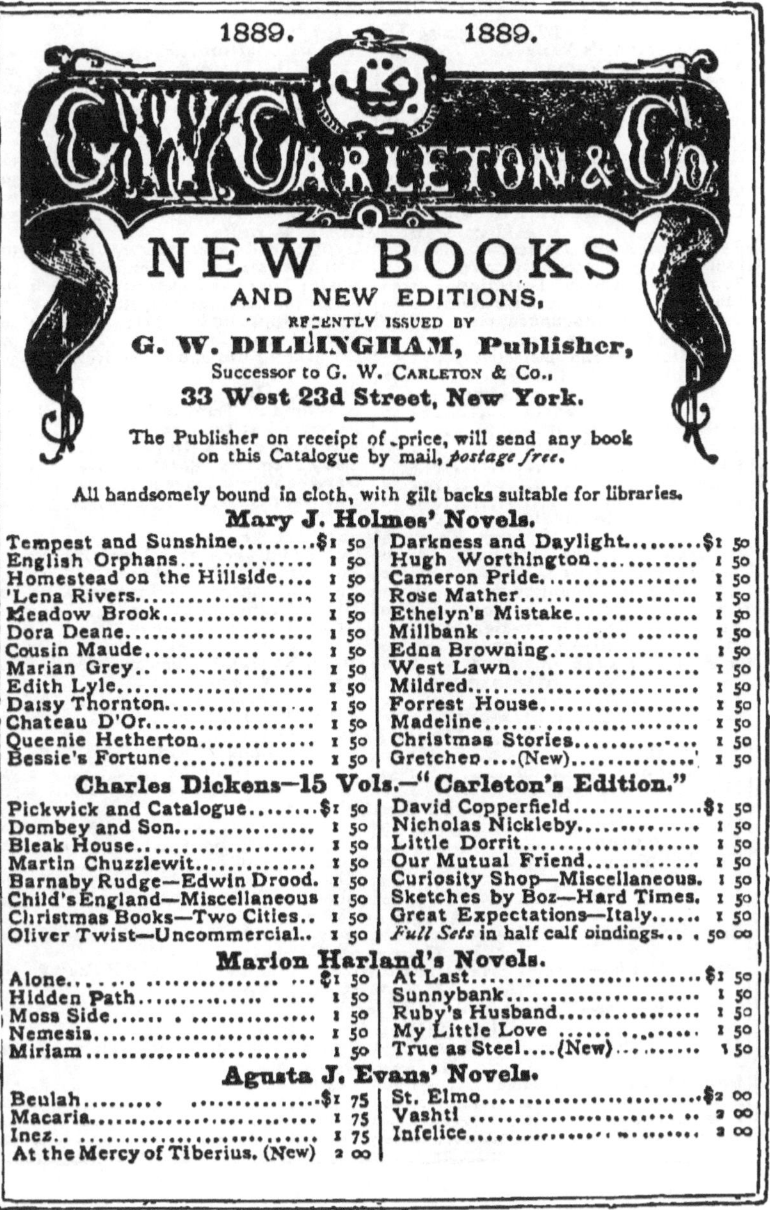

1889. 1889.

NEW BOOKS

AND NEW EDITIONS,

RECENTLY ISSUED BY

G. W. DILLINGHAM, Publisher,

Successor to G. W. CARLETON & Co.,

33 West 23d Street, New York.

The Publisher on receipt of price, will send any book
on this Catalogue by mail, *postage free.*

All handsomely bound in cloth, with gilt backs suitable for libraries.

Mary J. Holmes' Novels.

Tempest and Sunshine	$1 50	Darkness and Daylight	$1 50
English Orphans	1 50	Hugh Worthington	1 50
Homestead on the Hillside	1 50	Cameron Pride	1 50
'Lena Rivers	1 50	Rose Mather	1 50
Meadow Brook	1 50	Ethelyn's Mistake	1 50
Dora Deane	1 50	Millbank	1 50
Cousin Maude	1 50	Edna Browning	1 50
Marian Grey	1 50	West Lawn	1 50
Edith Lyle	1 50	Mildred	1 50
Daisy Thornton	1 50	Forrest House	1 50
Chateau D'Or	1 50	Madeline	1 50
Queenie Hetherton	1 50	Christmas Stories	1 50
Bessie's Fortune	1 50	Gretchen....(New)	1 50

Charles Dickens—15 Vols.—"Carleton's Edition."

Pickwick and Catalogue	$1 50	David Copperfield	$1 50
Dombey and Son	1 50	Nicholas Nickleby	1 50
Bleak House	1 50	Little Dorrit	1 50
Martin Chuzzlewit	1 50	Our Mutual Friend	1 50
Barnaby Rudge—Edwin Drood.	1 50	Curiosity Shop—Miscellaneous.	1 50
Child's England—Miscellaneous	1 50	Sketches by Boz—Hard Times.	1 50
Christmas Books—Two Cities	1 50	Great Expectations—Italy	1 50
Oliver Twist—Uncommercial	1 50	*Full Sets* in half calf bindings	50 00

Marion Harland's Novels.

Alone	$1 50	At Last	$1 50
Hidden Path	1 50	Sunnybank	1 50
Moss Side	1 50	Ruby's Husband	1 50
Nemesis	1 50	My Little Love	1 50
Miriam	1 50	True as Steel....(New)	1 50

Agusta J. Evans' Novels.

Beulah	$1 75	St. Elmo	$2 00
Macaria	1 75	Vashti	2 00
Inez	1 75	Infelice	2 00
At the Mercy of Tiberius. (New)	2 00		

May Agnes Fleming's Novels.

Guy Earlscourt's Wife	$1 50	Heir of Charlton	$1 50
A Wonderful Woman	1 50	Carried by Storm	1 50
A Terrible Secret	1 50	Lost for a Woman	1 50
A Mad Marriage	1 50	A Wife's Tragedy	1 50
Norine's Revenge	1 50	A Changed Heart	1 50
One Night's Mystery	1 50	Pride and Passion	1 50
Kate Danton	1 50	Sharing Her Crime	1 50
Silent and True	1 50	A Wronged Wife	1 50
Maude Percy's Secret	1 50	The Actress Daughter	1 50
The Midnight Queen...(New)	1 50	The Queen of the Isle	1 50

Allan Pinkerton's Works.

Expressmen and Detectives	$1 50	Gypsies and Detectives	$1 50
Mollie Maguires and Detectives	1 50	Spiritualists and Detectives	1 50
Somnambulists and Detectives	1 50	Model Town and Detectives	1 50
Claude Melnotte and Detectives	1 50	Strikers, Communists, etc	1 50
Criminal Reminiscences, etc	1 50	Mississippi Outlaws, etc	1 50
Rail-Road Forger, etc	1 50	Bucholz and Detectives	1 50
Bank Robbers and Detectives	1 50	Burglar's Fate and Detectives	1 50
A Double Life.....(New)	1 50		

Bertha Clay's Novels.

Thrown on the World	$1 50	A Woman's Temptation	$1 50
A Bitter Atonement	1 50	Repented at Leisure	1 50
Love Works Wonders	1 50	A Struggle for a Ring	1 50
Evelyn's Folly	1 50	Lady Damer's Secret	1 50
Under a Shadow	1 50	Between Two Loves	1 50
Beyond Pardon	1 50	Put Asunder........(New)	1 50
The Earl's Atonement	1 50		

"New York Weekly" Series.

Brownie's Triumph—Sheldon	$1 50	Curse of Everleigh—Pierce	$1 50
The Forsaken Bride. do	1 50	Peerless Cathleen—Agnew	1 50
Earl Wayne's Nobility. do	1 50	Faithful Margaret—Ashmore	1 50
Lost, a Pearle— do	1 50	Nick Whiffles—Robinson	1 50
Young Mrs. Charnleigh—Henshew	1 50	Grinder Papers—Dallas	1 50
His Other Wife—Ashleigh	1 50	Lady Lenora—Conklin	1 50
A Woman's Web—Maitland	1 50	Stella Rosevelt—Sheldon..(New)	1 50

Miriam Coles Harris' Novels.

Rutledge	$1 50	The Sutherlands	$1 50
Louie's Last Term, St. Mary's	1 50	Frank Warrington	1 50

A. S. Roe's Select Stories.

True to the Last	$1 50	A Long Look Ahead	$1 50
The Star and the Cloud	1 50	I've Been Thinking	1 50
How Could He Help it?	1 50	To Love and to be Loved	1 50

Julie P. Smith's Novels.

Widow Goldsmith's Daughter	$1 50	The Widower	$1 50
Chris and Otho	1 50	The Married Belle	1 50
Ten Old Maids	1 50	Courting and Farming	1 50
Lucy	1 50	Kiss and be Friends	1 50
His Young Wife	1 50	Blossom Bud.....(New)	1 50

Artemas Ward.

Complete Comic Writings—With Biography. Portrait and 50 illustrations..$1 50

The Game of Whist.

Pole on Whist—The English Standard Work. With the "Portland Rules" $ 75

Victor Hugo's Great Novel.

Les Miserables—Translated from the French. The only complete edition....$1 50

Mrs. Hill's Cook Book.

Mrs. A. P. Hill's New Southern Cookery Book, and domestic receipts...$2 00

Celia E. Gardner's Novels.

Stolen Waters. (In verse)	$1 50	Tested	$1 50
Broken Dreams. do.	1 50	Rich Medway	1 50
Compensation. do.	1 50	A Woman's Wiles	1 50
A Twisted Skein. do.	1 50	Terrace Roses	1 50

Captain Mayne Reid's Works.

The Scalp Hunters...............$1 50	The White Chief.................$1 50
The Rifle Rangers.... .... 1 50	The Tiger Hunter... . ... 1 50
The War Trail........ .... 1 50	The Hunter's Feast............ . 1 50
The Wood Rangers 1 50	Wild Life. 1 50
The Wild Huntress............ 1 50	Osceola, the Seminole..... .... 1 50

Popular Hand-Books.

The Habits of Good Society—The nice points of taste and good manners. .$1 00
The Art of Conversation—For those who wish to be agreeable talkers...... 1 00
The Arts of Writing, Reading and Speaking—For Self-Improvement ... 1 00
New Diamond Edition—The above three books in one volume—small type. 1 50
Carleton's Hand-Book of Popular Quotations.. .... 1 50
Carleton's Classical Dictionary................................... 75
1000 Legal Don'ts—By Ingersoll Lockwood............................. 75
600 Medical Don'ts—By Ferd. C. Valentine, M.D...................... 75
Address of the Dead—By Charles C. Marble........................... 75
The P. G. or Perfect Gentleman—By Ingersoll Lockwood................ 1 25

Josh Billings.

His Complete Writings—With Biography, Steel Portrait and 100 Illustrations.$2 00

Annie Edwardes' Novels.

Stephen Lawrence........... .. $1 50	A Woman of Fashion $1 50
Susan Fielding. 1 50	Archie Lovell..................... 1 50

Ernest Renan's French Works.

The Life of Jesus. Translated...$1 75	The Life of St. Paul. Translated.$1 75
Lives of the Apostles. Do. ... 1 75	The Bible in India—By Jacolliot. 2 00

Mrs. E. D. E. N. Southworth.

The Hidden Hand..... ....$1 75

M. M. Pomeroy (Brick).

Sense. A serious book. $1 50	Nonsense. (A comic book).......$1 50
Gold Dust. Do. 1 50	Brick-dust. Do. 1 50
Our Saturday Nights........... 1 50	Home Harmonies................ 1 50

Miscellaneous Works.

Philosophers and Actresses—By Houssaye. Steel Portraits, 2 vols.......$4 00
Men and Women of 18th Century—By Houssaye. Steel Portraits, 2 vols.. 4 00
Fifty Years among Authors, Books and Publishers—By J. C. Derby.... 2 00
Children's Fairy Geography—With hundreds of beautiful illustrations.... 1 00
An Exile's Romance—By Arthur Louis....................... .... 1 50
Laus Veneris, and other Poems—By Algernon Charles Swinburne......... 1 50
Sawed-off Sketches—Comic book by "Detroit Free Press Man." Illustrated 1 50
Hawk-eye Sketches—Comic book by "Burlington Hawk-eye Man." Do. 1 50
The Culprit Fay—Joseph Rodman Drake's Poem. With 100 illustrations... 2 00
Frankincense—By Mrs. Melinda Jennie Porter......................... 1 00
Love [L'Amour]—English Translation from Michelet's famous French work. 1 50
Woman [La Femme]—The Sequel to "L'Amour." Do. Do. 1 50
Verdant Green—A racy English college story. With 200 comic illustrations. 1 50
Clear Light from the Spirit World—By Kate Irving........................ 1 25
For the Sins of his Youth—By Mrs. Jane Kavanagh...................... 1 50
Mal Moulée—A splendid Novel, by Ella Wheeler Wilcox........... .... 1 00
A Northern Governess at the Sunny South—By Professor J. H. Ingraham. 1 50
Birds of a Feather Flock Together—By Edward A. Sothern, the actor ... 1 50
The Mystery of Bar Harbor—By Alsop Leffingwell...................... 1 00
Longfellow's Home Life—By Blanche Roosevelt Macbetta. Illustrated... 1 50
Every-Day Home Advice—For Household and Domestic Economy........ 1 50
Ladies' and Gentlemen's Etiquette Book of the best Fashionable Society. 1 00
Love and Marriage—A book for unmarried people. By Frederick Saunders. 1 00
Under the Rose—A Capital book, by the author of "East Lynne". 1 00
So Dear a Dream—A novel by Miss Grant, author of "The Sun Maid.".... 1 00
Give me thine Heart—A capital new domestic Love Story by Roe.......... 1 00
Meeting her Fate—A charming novel by the author of "Aurora Floyd."... 1 00
Faithful to the End—A delightful domestic novel by Roe.................. 1 00
So True a Love—A novel by Miss Grant, author of "The Sun Maid.".... 1 00
True as Gold—A charming domestic story by Roe...................... 1 00

Humorous Works and Novels in Paper Covers.

A Naughty Girl's Diary	$ 50	Miss Varian of New York .. .$	50
A Good Boy's Diary	50	The Comic Liar—By Alden	1 50
It's a Way Love Has	25	Store Drumming as a Fine Art.	50
Abijah Beanpole in New York.	50	Mrs. Spriggins—Widow Bedott....	1 50
Never—Companion to " Don't."	25	Phemie Frost—Ann S. Stephens.	1 50
Always—By author of " Never."	25	That Awful Boy—N. Y. Weekly.	50
Stop—By author of " Never."	25	That Bridget of Ours. Do.	50
Smart Sayings of Children—Paul	1 00	A Society Star—Chandos Fulton.	50
Crazy History of the U. S	50	Our Artist in Spain, etc.—Carleton	1 00
Cats, Cooks, etc.—By E. T. Ely..	50	Man Abroad	25

Miscellaneous Works.

Dawn to Noon—By Violet Fane..$1	50	Death Blow to Spiritualism..$	50
Constance's Fate. Do. ..	1 50	The Life of Victor Hugo	50
Nellie Harland—Vance	1 00	Don Quixote. Illustrated	1 00
Lion Jack—By P. T. Barnum....	1 50	Arabian Nights. Do.	1 00
Jack in the Jungle. Do.	1 50	Robinson Crusoe. Do.	1 00
Dick Broadhead. Do.	1 50	Swiss Family Robinson—Illus..	1 00
How to Win in Wall Street....	50	Debatable Land—R. Dale Owen.	2 00
The Life of Sarah Bernhardt...	25	Threading My Way. Do.	1 50
Arctic Travels—By Dr. Hayes..	1 50	Spiritualism—By D. D. Home...	2 00
Flashes from "Ouida."	1 25	Princess Nourmahal—Geo. Sand	1 50
The Story of a Day in London.	25	Northern Ballads-E. L. Anderson	1 00
Lone Ranch—By Mayne Reid...	1 50	Stories about Doctors—Jeffreson	1 50
The Train Boy—Horatio Alger..	1 25	Stories about Lawyers. Do.	1 50
Dan, The Detective. Do. ..	1 25		

Miscellaneous Novels.

Doctor Antonio—By Ruffini $1	50	Was He Successful ?—Kimball. $1	75
Beatrice Cenci· ·From the Italian.	1 50	Undercurrents of Wall St. Do.	1 75
The Story of Mary.	1 50	Romance of Student Life. Do.	1 75
Madame—By Frank Lee Benedict	1 50	To-day. Do.	1 75
A Late Remorse. Do.	1 50	Life in San Domingo. Do.	1 75
Hammer and Anvil. Do.	1 50	Henry Powers, Banker. Do.	1 75
Her Friend Laurence. Do.	1 50	Led Astray—By Octave Feuillet.	1 50
Mignonnette—By Sangrée	1 00	Lava Fires—Smith	1 50
Jessica—By Mrs. W. H. White....	1 50	The Darling of an Empire	1 50
Women of To-day. Do.	1 50	Confessions of Two.	1 50
The Baroness—Joaquin Miller...	1 50	Nina's Peril—By Mrs. Miller....	1 50
One Fair Woman. Do. ...	1 50	Marguerite's Journal—For Girls	1 50
The Burnhams—Mrs. G. E. Stewart	2 00	Orpheus C. Kerr—Four vols. in one.	2 00
Eugene Ridgewood—Paul James	1 50	Spell-Bound—Alexandre Dumas.	75
Braxton's Bar—R. M. Daggett..	1 50	Purple and Fine Linen—Fawcett	1 50
Miss Beck—By Tilbury Holt.. .	1 50	Pauline's Trial—L. D. Courtney.	1 50
A Wayward Life	1 00	Tancredi—Dr. E. A. Wood.... .	1 50
Winning Winds—Emerson.. ...	1 50	Measure for Measure—Stanley..	1 50
A College Widow—C. H. Seymour	1 50	Charette—An American novel ...	1 50
An Errand Girl—Johnson... ..	1 50	Fairfax—By John Esten Cooke...	1 50
Ask Her, Man! Ask Her!....	1 50	Hilt to Hilt. Do.	1 50
Hidden Power—T. H. Tibbles...	1 50	Out of the Foam. Do.	1 50
Two of Us—Calista Halsey	75	Hammer and Rapier. Do.	1 50
Cupid on Crutches—A. B. Wood.	75	Kenneth—By Sallie A. Brock....	1 75
Parson Thorne—E. M. Buckingham	1 50	Heart Hungry. Mrs. Westmoreland	1 50
Errors—By Ruth Carter.	1 50	Clifford Troupe. Do.	1 50
Unmistakable Flirtation—Garner	75	Price of a Life—R. F. Sturgis...	1 50
Wild Oats—Florence Marryatt...	1 50	Marston Hall—L. Ella Byrd.....	1 50
The Abbess of Jouarre—Renan..	1 00	Conquered—By a New Author...	1 50
The Mysterious Doctor—Stanley	1 50	Tales from the Popular Operas.	1 50
Doctor Mortimer—Fannie Bean.	1 50	Edith Murray—Joanna Mathews	1 50
Two Brides—Bernard O'Reilly..	1 50	San Miniato—Mrs. C. V. Hamilton.	1 00
Louise and I—By Chas. Dodge..	1 50	All for Her—A Tale of New York.	1 50
My Queen—By Sandette	1 50	L'Assommoir—Zola's great novel	1 00
Fallen among Thieves—Rayne.	1 50	Vesta Vane—By L. King, R. ...	1 50
Saint Leger—Richard B. Kimball	1 75	Walworth's Novels—Seven vols.	1 50

MRS. MARY J. HOLMES' WORKS.

TEMPEST AND SUNSHINE.	DARKNESS AND DAYLIGHT.
ENGLISH ORPHANS.	HUGH WORTHINGTON.
HOMESTEAD ON HILLSIDE.	CAMERON PRIDE.
'LENA RIVERS.	ROSE MATHER.
MEADOW BROOK.	ETHELYN'S MISTAKE.
DORA DEANE.	MILLBANK.
COUSIN MAUDE.	EDNA BROWNING.
MARIAN GREY.	WEST LAWN.
EDITH LYLE.	MILDRED.
DAISY THORNTON.	FOREST HOUSE.
CHATEAU D'OR.	MADELINE.
QUEENIE HETHERTON.	CHRISTMAS STORIES.
BESSIE'S FORTUNE.	GRETCHEN. (*New.*)

OPINIONS OF THE PRESS.

"Mrs. Holmes' stories are universally read. Her admirers are numberless. She is in many respects without a rival in the world of fiction. Her characters are always life-like, and she makes them talk and act like human beings, subject to the same emotions, swayed by the same passions, and actuated by the same motives which are common among men and women of every-day existence. Mrs. Holmes is very happy in portraying domestic life. Old and young peruse her stories with great delight, for she writes in a style that all can comprehend." —*New York Weekly.*

The North American Review, vol. 81, page 557, says of Mrs. Mary J. Holmes' novel "English Orphans":—"With this novel of Mrs. Holmes' we have been charmed, and so have a pretty numerous circle of discriminating readers to whom we have lent it. The characterization is exquisite, especially so far as concerns rural and village life, of which there are some pictures that deserve to be hung up in perpetual memory of types of humanity fast becoming extinct. The dialogues are generally brief, pointed, and appropriate. The plot seems simple, so easily and naturally is it developed and consummated. Moreover, the story thus gracefully constructed and written, inculcates without obtruding, not only pure Christian morality in general, but, with especial point and power, the dependence of true success on character, and of true respectability on merit."

"Mrs. Holmes' stories are all of a domestic character, and their interest, therefore, is not so intense as if they were more highly seasoned with sensationalism, but it is of a healthy and abiding character. The interest in her tales begins at once, and is maintained to the close. Her sentiments are so sound, her sympathies so warm and ready, and her knowledge of manners, character, and the varied incidents of ordinary life is so thorough, that she would find it difficult to write any other than an excellent tale if she were to try it."—*Boston Banner.*

The volumes are all handsomely printed and bound in cloth, sold everywhere, and sent by mail, *postage free*, on receipt of price [$1.50 each], by

G. W. DILLINGHAM, Publisher,

Successor to G. W. CARLETON & CO.,

33 W. 23d St., NEW YORK.

CHARLES DICKENS' WORKS.

A NEW  EDITION.

Among the many editions of the works of this greatest of English Novelists, there has not been until *now* one that entirely satisfies the public demand.—Without exception, they each have some strong distinctive objection,—either the form and dimensions of the volumes are unhandy— or, the type is small and indistinct—or, the illustrations are unsatisfactory—or, the binding is poor—or, the price is too high.

An entirely new edition is *now*, however, published by G. W. Carleton & Co., of New York, which, in every respect, completely satisfies the popular demand.—It is known as

"Carleton's New Illustrated Edition."

COMPLETE IN 15 VOLUMES.

The size and form is most convenient for holding,—the type is entirely new, and of a clear and open character that has received the approval of the reading community in other works.

The illustrations are by the original artists chosen by Charles Dickens himself—and the paper, printing, and binding are of an attractive and substantial character.

This beautiful new edition is complete in 15 volumes—at the extremely reasonable price of $1.50 per volume, as follows :—

1.—PICKWICK PAPERS AND CATALOGUE.
2.—OLIVER TWIST.—UNCOMMERCIAL TRAVELLER.
3.—DAVID COPPERFIELD.
4.—GREAT EXPECTATIONS --ITALY AND AMERICA
5.—DOMBEY AND SON.
6.—BARNABY RUDGE AND EDWIN DROOD.
7.—NICHOLAS NICKLEBY.
8.—CURIOSITY SHOP AND MISCELLANEOUS.
9.—BLEAK HOUSE.
10.—LITTLE DORRIT.
11.—MARTIN CHUZZLEWIT.
12.—OUR MUTUAL FRIEND.
13.—CHRISTMAS BOOKS.—TALE OF TWO CITIES.
14.—SKETCHES BY BOZ AND HARD TIMES.
15.—CHILD'S ENGLAND AND MISCELLANEOUS.

The first volume—Pickwick Papers—contains an alphabetical catalogue of all of Charles Dickens' writings, with their exact positions in the volumes.

This edition is sold by Booksellers, everywhere—and single specimen copies will be forwarded by mail, *postage free*, on receipt of price, $1.50 by

G. W. DILLINGHAM, Publisher,

Successor to G. W. CARLETON & CO.,

33 W. 23d St., NEW YORK.